HOME AGAIN: STARTING OVER

The Sisters, Texas Mystery Series, Book 4

Becki Willis

ISBN: 1947686011
ISBN 13: 9781947686014

BOOKS BY BECKI WILLIS

He Kills Me, He Kills Me Not
Forgotten Boxes
Tangible Spirits, May 2017
<u>Mirrors Don't Lie Series</u>
    The Girl from Her Mirror, Book 1
    Mirror, Mirror on Her Wall, Book 2
    Light from Her Mirror, Book 3

<u>The Sisters, Texas Mystery Series</u>
    Chicken Scratch, Book 1
    When the Stars Fall, Book 2
    Stipulations and Complications, Book 3
    Home Again: Starting Over, Book 4
    Spring 2017: Genny's Ballad, Book 5

TABLE OF CONTENTS

1

Curls of smoke swirled upward. A small gust of wind stirred the night air, breathing life into the tiny flame. It flickered with uncertainty, hovering somewhere between extinction and survival.

The dry grasses surrounding it—parched from another Texas summer with too little rain—begged the light to survive. Teased it to come forward and dance within their brittle blades. Coaxed it to leap from one dry stem to another.

The tiny flame grew braver. Stronger.

No longer wavering, the flickering light decided to live.

In no time at all, an entire dry field had burst into flame.

According to Granny Bert, August in Texas wasn't for wimps. "It's what separates the real Texans from the wannabes," she insisted. "I'm thinking of putting in a hot tub, just so I can cool off every morning. Folks who can't handle the humidity don't deserve the title of Texan."

On days like today, Madison Reynolds wondered if she secretly fell into that undeserving category. Her clothes clung to her like a second skin, stuck in places that would make a virgin blush. After spending good money on a fashionable new cut, her brown hair hung limp and lifeless on the ends, while frizzing around her face in tiny corkscrews. Moisture gathered on her upper lip to mimic a bad mustache.

Humidity was not her friend.

Madison stepped into the blast of dense morning air, immediately mourning the air-conditioned comfort of her car. She waited for the fog to clear from her sunglasses and the breath to return to her lungs.

"This has been a miserable summer," she grumbled aloud. With the twins in Dallas and Brash off in a dozen directions fulfilling his duties as All-American hero, she spent most of the summer alone.

"Okay, you can stop feeling sorry for yourself." Madison gave herself the pep talk as she entered the blessed cool air of *Lone Star Law Offices*. "The heat index is down to a hundred and ten, so there's hope that summer will eventually end. You decided what tile to use in the downstairs laundry room and the library is almost completed. You pick the kids up this weekend. And you have an actual client again. Things are looking up."

That new client was Attorney Shawn Bryant. After the unexpected death of his secretary last month, the lawyer hired Madison's small firm, *In a Pinch Professional Services,* to organize his office.

Buoyed by her own encouraging words, Madison tackled the scattered files atop the desk. It was her job to decipher and revamp the late Gloria Jeffers' unique filing system. After three days of filing, she still was not done.

Her cell phone rang, flashing a familiar number across the screen. Madison fanned herself as she greeted her caller, still wilted after the short walk from the car to the office. "Hey, Gen, what's up?"

Madison could hear bubbles of excitement in her best friend's voice. "You are never going to believe this!"

"Oh?" She kept her response low key, knowing the announcement could go either way. With Genny, it could mean anything from discovering a new recipe to hitting the Texas Lotto jackpot. Genesis Baker was one of those rare and special people who found pleasure in most all aspects of life.

"I have a new job for you, and you'll never guess who it is with! Are you ready for this?" Too excited to wait for Maddy's answer, she gushed, "None other than Carson Elliot!"

Madison's mouth twisted in thought as she tried to place the name. "I've heard that name before. Who is he, again?"

Genny's voice morphed into a falsetto of jaunty sophistication. "Only the Sisters' most suave and debonair citizen. Our very own version of Fred Astaire."

"Oh, yes, right. The dance instructor. So what's the job?"

"He didn't say. That's why we're meeting him at his house this afternoon."

"We?"

There was a slight hesitation before her friend answered. "He asked that I come along."

"He did?" It wasn't that she doubted her friend's word, but it was an odd request.

"Welllll," Genny said, drawing the word out dubiously, "he said he hoped to see me again very soon, as he handed me directions to his house. I think he just assumed I would bring you."

"I guess since I don't have an office, he assumes I don't have a car, either," Madison scoffed.

Genny was quick to assure her, "You know you are welcome to your booth here for as long as you like."

Until now, that back booth at her friend's restaurant had been her official unofficial office space. Not the best in terms of confidentiality for her clients, but the only thing she could afford.

"And while I do appreciate your generous offer, conducting business from the back booth of a very busy restaurant is not quite the vibe I'm going for."

Genny ignored the sarcasm with her customary optimism. "Your office will be done soon. Nick and Kiki are in here eating. Before the fans got wind of it and swarmed the place, I overheard them saying your office is all but done. Then all hell broke loose when Kaci Gill and Latricia Jefferson burst through the door and rushed over to Kiki, begging for her autograph." There was a great noise in the background, followed by Genny's exaggerated groan. "Oh, great. Now a news crew has shown up. I gotta go, but call me later, okay? We need to be at the dance studio around four."

As her friend hung up the phone, Madison's answer was a weary sigh.

Life in Juliet and Naomi, Texas—collectively known as The Sisters—had forever changed when she signed that contract. Agreeing to be guinea pig for a new home-makeover reality show was the only way she could afford renovating her aging Victorian and making it suitable for a modern-day family. The television show was an instant hit on national TV, thanks in part to Nick Vilardi and Kiki Paretta. The attention was great for businesses in the small towns, especially for Genny's café where much of the off-site filming took place. But the fame, and the fans that came with it, made privacy an issue. Everyone wanted their own fifteen minutes of fame.

"Note to self," she mumbled aloud. "The next time someone offers to remodel my home for free in exchange for doing a TV show, say no. Capital 'N.'"

Madison hummed the alphabet song beneath her breath as she concentrated on filing. She had sung the song hundreds of times when the twins were still infants, hoping to give her children the advantage of knowing the basics long before kindergarten. Blake picked up on the string of letters early, but Bethani struggled with anything past 'g.' It hardly helped that her speech was slurred and most of her words were in gibberish. Her twin brother often had to translate for her, relaying her thoughts to those around them; how he understood was anyone's guess. It was probably one of those uncanny twin things.

Tears misted her eyes. Without Blake and Bethani racing through the house, Granny Bert's old craftsman seemed empty and sad. There was no fighting over the television remote, no arguing about who rode shotgun. Madison found it oddly depressing to flip through the channels at her own leisure. She never thought she would miss going grocery shopping, either, but without her fifteen-year-old son there eating his way through the summer, she had only been to the grocery store once in the past two weeks.

She picked up her phone to text them, asking how things were going in Dallas. She knew both enjoyed visiting with their old friends; not so much with their grandparents.

Not for the first time, she wondered if she had done the right thing by letting Blake and Bethani go for a visit. True, Annette and Charles were their grandparents, and loved the children in their own small, selfish way. In turn, the twins loved the staid older couple in their own open, selfless way. Kids were like that. They loved unconditionally, even when grownups did not deserve it.

Annette Reynolds made no secret of the fact that she disapproved of Madison's life choices. To be completely accurate, she disapproved of Madison. Period. Her latest contention was her daughter-in-law's involvement with a lowly reality show. She pretended it was concern for the twins, claiming national fame exposed them to potential dangers and sexual perverts. But Maddy knew the real reason Annette objected; she felt such common behavior besmirched the memory of her beloved son and the holy Reynolds name.

Madison gave a mirthless snicker. Grayson had done enough to ruin their good name, long before his untimely death last November. Having an affair wasn't even the worst of it. Cheating clients out of their hard-earned money, dodging the IRS, and burning through their life savings had been the greater evil.

Her phone binged with a reply from Blake.

You're still coming Friday, right?

She wrote back with, *Of course.*

Bethani weighed in on the group text. *I'm helping with the decorations for Saturday. Sort of. Grandmother hired a party planner, but she's letting me do some of the table arrangements.*

Madison's mouth turned downward.

How big is this party going to be? she typed.

Pretty huge. You know Grandmother.

Unfortunately, she did. With rumors that the IRS was looking into Gray's business dealings, Annette combatted the slight to their family name the only way she knew how; she was hosting a party. A gala, to be more accurate. She was throwing an extravagant event for Dallas' elite, while throwing a huge amount of cash at a local charity. All in Gray's honor, of course.

Can we go out for pizza before the party? They'll have those tiny little appetizers and dainty portions for dinner. This from Blake.

Madison smiled and typed back her reply. *We'll see. I would hate to see you starve.*

Her phone binged again with his answer. She could practically hear the whine. *You have no idea. It's pretty bad. Headed out now with Toby. Stopping to grab a burger before we meet the rest of the guys for movie and dinner. Gotta go. LYB.*

Madison laughed aloud. It sounded just like her son. *Love you bunches, too. Beth, what are you doing tonight?*

She could imagine her daughter's shrug. *Guess we'll go to the mall.*

Did she detect a bit of boredom in her daughter's lack-luster reply? As little as a year ago, going to the mall had been the highlight of the teen's existence. That was before they moved to Juliet. Before she had tried out for cheerleader and made a new best friend, one who preferred sports and riding horses over movie theaters and malls. Was Bethani truly missing her new life in The Sisters, or was Maddy reading too much into this? She typed a positive reply.

I saw Megan today. She really misses you. She can't wait for you to come home.

There was a long pause before the teenager answered. *Where did you see her?*

Madison knew what she was asking. She wanted to know if it had been in the presence of her best friend's father. Maddy's mouth dipped into another frown.

Sadly enough, seeing Megan had nothing to do with Brash. Between his football camp for underprivileged youth and several law enforcement conferences, Maddy had hardly seen the police chief over the summer.

She typed out a reply to her daughter. *She came by to visit and to bring back your blue-striped top. I think she's just lonely, with her best friend and her dad both out of town.*

There. That should put her fears to rest.

After a few more brief messages, they both signed off and Madison turned her full attention back to work.

When she reached the bottom folder on the stack, she noticed the missing tab. A quick search still left her empty handed. After a moment of hesitation, Madison flipped the folder open. One glance told her that it housed an assortment of files, none of them pertaining to the same client. Most of them did not even share the same initial.

"Oh, Miss Gloria, what did you do?" she groaned aloud. The entire filing system had been a disaster, and now this. What if all the folders were as unorganized and haphazard as this one was? The thought of going through each and every folder was terrifying.

Madison talked herself down off the ledge. "Maybe you put all these in one folder, thinking you would sort through them later," she reckoned. "Maybe this was your time-saving method at the end of the day." A long-suffering sigh escaped her. "No matter. It's up to me to sort them out."

Madison laid the files on the desk to sort them alphabetically. It would make finding their proper homes that much easier. She had barely started when Shawn Bryant called, asking her to locate and bring a particular file to him at the County Courthouse in Riverton.

She scooped the papers back into the folder and stashed the entire mess away for later, deciding this was as good a stopping point as any. Genny had that appointment lined up for her this afternoon with a new client. If she stopped now, she had plenty of time to find and deliver the needed papers and still make their four o'clock meeting. She would sort the files when she returned on Monday.

Assuming, of course, that she survived the weekend in Dallas.

2

"So tell me. Why the fascination with Carson Elliot?" Madison asked, somewhat amused by Genny's excitement. Her friend all but bounced up and down as they turned onto the highway and headed south.

"Are you kidding me? Have you ever seen the man?"

"Not that I am aware of."

"I'd say he's in his mid-sixties, but very well preserved, if you know what I mean. Dark hair, dark skin. I think he must have some Italian or Latino background." Genny flexed her mouth as she pondered his heritage.

"Doesn't sound like anyone I've seen around town. What kind of dance does he teach?"

"You name it, he teaches it. That I am aware of, he offers ballroom dancing, ballet, artistic expression, country line dancing, and modern dance." She ticked each one off on her fingers. "The man is a genius."

"That's quite a range! Where did this guy come from?"

Genny shrugged. "He's a bit mysterious about his past. I know he was in the Army and stationed overseas when he fell in love with an exotic dancer. She's the one who taught him to appreciate dance. He came home minus the girl, studied the art form, and glided his way to fame. He once danced on Broadway, you know. A few years ago he left the Big Apple and came home to Texas. I'm not sure how he settled on The Sisters, but we can always ask." She flashed a dimpled smile.

Madison chuckled at her friend's obvious fascination with the man. "I'm sure you will. What else do you know about him? And how do you know all this?"

"Word of mouth, internet." Another flash of dimples with the guilty admission, "Google search."

"You're really impressed with this guy, aren't you?"

"He's very interesting. Did you know he taught lessons for several people who appeared on *Dancing with Dreams*?"

"I've never watched the show," Madison admitted.

"Not even when John Paul Nobles was on it?" Genny knew Madison had harbored a crush on the movie star since their high school days.

"Not even then. I told you, I don't like reality shows."

"And yet you are the star of this summer's most popular reality series."

Madison rolled her eyes at the irony and muttered, "Figure that one out."

Genesis brushed aside her friend's scornful attitude. "I watch *Dancing with Dreams* all the time. Carson Elliot was even a judge one season."

"So is the guy married? Single? Gay?"

"Single. Actually, he was seeing Gloria Jeffers."

"Miss Gloria, the one who just died? The one who worked for the law office?" She and her filing system were the only reason Madison currently drew a paycheck from *Lone Star Law*.

"That's the one."

"I only met Miss Gloria a time or two, but I thought she was quite a bit older. Her hair was solid white."

Genny's blond head bobbed as she explained, "They said she used to be quite a looker. Glossy dark hair that hung to her waist. Then her husband was killed in an offshore drilling accident and her hair went from brown to solid white, almost overnight. Stress, they said. She almost had a nervous breakdown."

Still unconvinced, Madison frowned. "She even dressed like an old lady."

"So do you."

Madison refused to look down at her outfit. Okay, so polyester wasn't the best choice on a day like today. Despite the stylish new clothes recently hanging in her closet, she often reverted to a favorite old standby. A simple pair of dark slacks and a solid color button-down shirt took less effort than color coordinating an entire ensemble.

"I prefer to call my look classic," she sniffed coolly.

Genny's dimples deepened. "And I prefer to call myself skinny, but it don't make it so, girlfriend."

"Yeah, yeah, yeah." She ignored the ribbing and concentrated on their mission. She nibbled her lip in worry. "Did he say what he wanted to hire me for? I hope he doesn't bring up Miss Gloria's death. I'm not sure I can keep a straight face if he does."

Both women tried to fight it, but the urge to smile, even just a little, was too strong. Amusement tugged at the corners of their lips.

"Okay, I'll say it," Genny finally blurted out. "Never in my life have I heard of anyone dying that way! Bless her heart, I know it's tragic, but it's also just a little bit hilarious."

Madison bit her lip, trying hard not to smile. "I know. It is rather … unique."

The details of Gloria's death were still sketchy, but she had died soon after self-administering a large-capacity enema. According to talk around town, preliminary autopsy reports pointed to extreme levels of alcohol in her bloodstream, even though she was not known as a heavy drinker.

"Unique?" Genny cackled. "I've heard of getting shit-faced drunk, but that's a new low!"

In spite of the seriousness of the situation, both friends burst out in snickers.

"We—We—We're terrible," Madison acknowledged.

"I know. We should be a—ashamed of ourselves." She could barely say the words for laughing so hard.

"If he as much as mentions her name, it could get m—messy!"

After several more wisecracks and a hearty round of laughter, they tampered their humor down to residual giggles. Soon they turned into the long white-rocked road leading up the hill.

Carson Elliot resided in a huge old house atop a high hill several miles from Juliet. Having long since been divided into smaller tracks of land, there was little left of the old cotton plantation, other than the dwelling. The aging structure seemed out of place among the neighboring houses. Most were low-slung brick ranch styles, while others were mobile homes. A few were newer and larger, but none had the style and grace of the old Georgian mansion on the hill.

While smaller and less imposing than the house Madison would soon call home, the house was impressive in its own right. A vibrant federal blue and white color scheme gave the old home an upbeat energy. The grounds were impressive, with a rich riot of colors in all the window boxes and the numerous flowerbeds that edged the walkway and front steps. Despite the oppressive summer heat, the lawn was magnificent.

Before they reached the top step, the door swung open and a handsome gentleman stepped out to greet them. One glance at Carson Elliot, and Madison understood her friend's enthusiasm for coming.

Tall and lanky, the man had the lithe, toned body of a dancer. His every movement was fluid and grace. Dark hair, frosted eloquently with fine strands of silver, pulled back from his face into a long ponytail. He wore flowing white pants and a loose-fitting, black and white shirt that glowed against his dark skin.

Simply put, the man was beautiful.

A delighted smile split his dark face. "Ah, Genesis. You came. And you must be Madison Reynolds. I have heard wonderful things about you."

"Why, thank you. It is a pleasure to meet you."

"The pleasure is all mine." He shook Madison's hand with casual formality. Then he turned to Genny, taking her hand in an intimate gesture and lifting it to his lips. "I had the pleasure of meeting your friend this morning." His smile deepened. "I'm so happy you could make it. Please, do come in."

The entry was as dramatic as the man. Expensive artwork and exotic vases set upon marble pedestals filled the sweeping space. Large archways on either side of the entry led to his dance studios. The one to the left had mirrors and rails, the one to the right had richly appointed walls and crystal chandeliers. It took no imagination to know which was for ballet, which for waltzes.

"Come, we will visit in my personal residence."

He led the way up a curved staircase. Twenty-five years their senior, he took the steps twice as quickly, and twice as gracefully, as either woman.

Double doors led into his private domain. Here the style was less formal and more eclectic. The man obviously appreciated the arts. One-of-a-kind sculptures, signed oil paintings, and intricate porcelain pieces occupied every surface.

Madison felt a bit claustrophobic from the array of color, alone.

She was relieved when they passed through that room into a smaller and more intimate library turned office. Here the decor did a complete one-eighty. The colors and the mood of the room were dark, rich, and somber. Except for the excess of stuffed and mounted heads on the walls, she felt much more at home in this space.

"Can I offer you ladies a drink?" he asked, pausing beside a well-stocked liquor cabinet.

"Nothing for me, thanks."

"I'm good."

"Very well. But before we get down to business, I must ask your opinion on something." He tapped a long tapering finger against his lips. "I am considering donating a dance class to be auctioned off during the fire department's fundraising event this fall. Do you think that is something people in The Sisters would be interested in?"

"Of course!" Genny was the one to answer, her eyes twinkling with pleasure. "I, for one, would definitely bid on lessons."

Carson studied her with intent eyes. Pursing his delicate lips, he made a thorough appraisal before nodding his approval. "You would make a worthy student. Your friend moves with natural grace. But you, my lovely Genesis, have passion." He blew the word from his fingers with a kiss. "I will make this donation, but you, my dear, are welcome here anytime."

Genny squirmed in her seat, obviously embarrassed by the eloquent words. For a man who recently buried his girlfriend, Carson Elliot was openly flirting. Madison tried to keep an open mind. She knew from first-hand experience that life went on, even when one's mate, or marriage, died.

"So what can I do for you, Mr. Elliot?" she asked. "Genny tells me you are interested in retaining our services."

When he was slow to pull his eyes from her friend, Madison somehow knew his answer would not be direct. "I had a most delightful surprise this morning," he proclaimed. "After hearing such good things about the new bakery and café in town, I wanted to try it for myself. Imagine my delight when I discovered not only the lovely proprietor, but the best croissants I've had since leaving Paris." He used the French pronunciation of the pastry, his tongue caressing each letter.

Madison smiled at her friend. "You'll get no argument from me. Genny is a very talented baker."

The man's brow puckered in disapproval. "Why do you insist on calling her Genny? I much prefer the name Genesis. It has such a beautiful ring to it, befitting of its owner." On his theatrical tongue, it did indeed sound special.

His eyes twinkled as he took in Genny's flushed cheeks, but he continued, "During our delightful conversation, Miss Baker mentioned that you are somewhat of an amateur sleuth. I understand you work part time for a private investigator?"

"I'm not sure 'sleuth' is the right word," Madison hedged. "You might say I am curious by nature, and that I like to solve puzzles. And as far as working with a private investigator, I mainly do routine surveillance," she clarified. Code word for *boring*.

"But you have an impressive record in solving cases."

"I'd like to think I helped clear up a few inconsistencies."

Carson Elliot's broad smile was bright against his dark skin. "And that is why I am hiring you, Mrs. Reynolds. You seem perfect for the job."

"What job?" she squeaked.

He continued as if she had not spoken. "Money is not a concern," he assured her. "If Genesis says you are worth it, that is good enough for me."

Was this man for real? Madison had heard about these artistic types—brilliantly talented, but often not in full control of their mental facilities. Carson Elliot wanted to hire her, no questions asked, on the recommendation of someone he met just this morning. Madison wondered about his stability as he opened a desk drawer, took out a ledger, and began writing a check.

"I trust two thousand dollars will be enough to retain your services. If you will submit receipts for reimbursement, I will gladly pay for any research or expenses that you may incur." He spoke as he wrote. With a flourishing movement of his hand, he ripped the check from its bindings and presented it to Madison.

By natural reflex, she reached for the check, even as she protested, "Mr. Elliot, I have no idea what it is you are hiring me to do!"

"Please, do call me Carson."

"Very well, *Carson*. Please tell me why you wish to hire us." *Us* consisted of her and one part-time employee, Derron Mullins.

Carson's expressive mouth turned downward. His eyes no longer twinkled. His elegant frame seemed to shrink as he settled into his chair and spoke in a sad voice. "A friend of mine recently passed away. Her name was Gloria Jeffers."

Madison had been wrong. She did not have the urge to smile when hearing the name. Now face to face with the man who obviously cared for the woman, Madison no longer found the circumstances of her unfortunate death amusing. "I am so sorry for your loss," she said with sincerity. "I did not know Miss Gloria very well, but the few times I was around her, she seemed very nice. Her death was quite a shock."

"What makes it all the more shocking is the fact that Gloria was not a drinker."

Noting how his guests struggled for a suitable reply, the man insisted, "It is true. Gloria did not drink alcohol. It is impossible that she died of alcohol poisoning."

Madison shot a wary look toward her friend. Genesis looked as confused as her.

"I am well aware of what people are saying," Carson continued. "I know what the coroner's preliminary report says. But I also know Gloria. She did not drink. It would be impossible for her to die in such a manner. Not of her own accord."

"Are you… are you suggesting her death may not have been an accident?" Madison ventured to ask.

"That is exactly what I am saying."

"Did you speak with Chief deCordova and tell him of your suspicions?"

18

"I did. He promised to keep my suggestions in mind, but frankly, I think he dismissed me as a grieving lover who was blind to his lady friend's faults."

Despite the dark scowl on his face, Genny spoke softly and asked, "Are you certain that's not the case?"

"I was well aware of Gloria's faults and weaknesses." He met Genny's concerned eyes and elaborated. "She hated summer heat and winter cold. She had no green thumb and could kill a cactus, although she recently became enchanted with plants as an herbal remedy. She was obsessed with reading, particularly those whodunits. When she wasn't reading, she imagined a mystery in everything around her. She loved her theories, as she called them." He paused with an affectionate chuckle. "She wanted to believe that I had a storied past, myself. Something much more exciting than a routine stint in the Army. I was nothing more than a field mechanic, but she wanted to believe I carried out undercover missions. She thought the government kept me from my first love, when in reality, it was the girl's father who would not let her come with me to the States."

The dance instructor kept his soulful eyes intent upon Genny's sympathetic baby blues. "Gloria had her faults, but drinking alcohol was not one of them. As a wine enthusiast myself, I tried to share my hobby with her. She refused to take as much as a sip. So the idea that she drank herself to death is simply ludicrous."

"Surely there is something you could do to contest the autopsy results..." Genny offered.

"There was no autopsy, just a postmortem blood test."

"Can't you request one?"

"*I* can't," he reported sadly. "It has to be done by a member of the family."

Genny tried to recall what little she knew about Gloria Jeffers. "I think she had a son, isn't that correct? Have you spoken to him?"

"Yes, but he has returned to Chicago and has not answered my calls." He turned toward Madison. "And that is where you come in. I want you to find out what really happened to my friend. Examine her lifestyle. Talk to her friends. You will find there is absolutely no evidence Gloria was a drinker."

Earlier, she and Genny had made snide remarks about the poor woman's death. Guilt wracked her conscience. "I—I'm hardly qualified, Mr. Elliot," she protested.

"You are exactly what I need. A smart, curious, meticulous professional who will uncover the truth."

"Mr. Elliot—"

"Carson."

"Carson, there is a huge gap between proving she did not drink and proving that she was murdered. For one thing, you need a suspect. Can you think of any reason that someone might want your friend dead?"

He stood from the desk and paced the room, his loose clothes flowing around his lithe body. Madison had trouble picturing this vibrant man with her vague recollection of the deceased woman.

"As I said, Gloria had quite the imagination. She often got carried away with herself."

"Such as?"

"She had what she called her 'theories.' One such theory was that Moe's Market injected flavor-enhancing and addictive drugs into their meat. She did her own informal investigation, buying the same cuts from different stores. None were as good as the ones she bought at Moe's, so she was convinced it was something he added. Naturally, Moe was less than thrilled with her assessment. And she insisted that my gardener used some secret, highly scientific elixir to keep my lawn this green in the summer."

"She might have had a point there," Madison murmured, remembering the thriving bright colors outside.

He winced and admitted, "When she said it, it sounded much more like an accusation."

"How did that set with your gardener?"

"The way you would imagine. My gardener has quite the ego."

"None of your examples are reason enough for murder," Madison pointed out.

"I'm not asking you to find out who killed her. The police can do that. I merely want you to prove that she could not have drunk herself to death." He pointed to the check in her hand. "I will write you another check for twice that amount if you can convince the police to re-evaluate her death and investigate the matter more thoroughly."

Four thousand dollars? Had she heard him correctly? One glance at Genny's shocked expression, and she knew she heard right.

Before she could convince herself it was a foolish idea, Madison thrust her hand forward. "Agreed. I'll bring a contract for you to sign, first thing in the morning."

3

Before Madison could leave for the weekend in Dallas, she had the contract to deliver, errands to run, and a last minute meeting with her carpenter at the Big House.

She backed out of Granny Bert's drive, mentally reviewing her list of errands. Anything to keep her mind off the dreaded weekend to come.

A large black car zoomed up behind her, stopping cattycorner to block her exit. Half of the car was in the drive, half in the road. Madison slammed on the brakes in time to avoid a collision. The driver's door opened and a man jumped out, striding her way angrily.

Great. Barry Redmond.

For a moment, she was tempted to ignore him. Their sole meeting in the past twenty-one years had not gone well. Barry, however, had no intentions of going ignored. Open palmed, he pounded on the glass until she reluctantly rolled it down.

"Who the hell do you think you are?" he demanded.

Something about the man irritated Madison to no end. It was more than the fact that he was a Redmond, she a Cessna. They had never gotten along in high school. By silent accord, they had agreed to disagree, no matter the topic. Back then, Madison had learned to ignore the spoiled little rich boy who had to buy his friends. She knew she should continue to ignore him, but she could no longer resist goading him. His face turned such an interesting shade of fuchsia when he was angry.

"Why, Barry, is your mind going, along with your hair? I'm Madison, remember? And I live here. You are the one who is trespassing on private property."

"Don't get smart with me, Madison Cessna. You told Lisa to divorce me and file for custody of *my* daughter. You can't do that!" he bellowed.

Her voice remained calm. "And I didn't. Lisa was planning on divorcing you before I ever talked to her."

"You're not a licensed PI! You had no right spying on me like that."

"You're right, I'm not. And I wasn't spying. I merely observed, which is perfectly legal and requires no license."

"You took pictures!"

"Again, perfectly legal."

His face a dark mottled red, Barry leaned down to make certain Madison heard him when he made a low threat. "Stay out of my way, Madison Cessna, or you'll be sorry. If Lisa tries to take Miley from me, I'll hold you personally responsible. She belongs to me!"

"You do realize this is your daughter you're talking about, not a fancy piece of furniture to be haggled over."

"I know exactly what I'm talking about. I'll not pay that scrawny little woman one dime, even if she does take the kid!"

Madison stared at him in horror. He did not care about losing his daughter. He cared only about losing money.

"You have ten seconds to get off my lawn and back into your car." Madison revved the gas pedal before putting the gearshift in reverse. When he stood there glaring at her, she kept her voice devoid of emotion and counted down, "Nine." She got to eight before he turned and stalked away without another word.

Just before he drove away amid a squeal of tires, he shouted back at her. "Stay out of my way!"

"Thanks for coming by, Madison," Nick Vilardi greeted Madison an hour later. She had used the sixty minutes to run her errands and cool down after the altercation with Barry.

As lead carpenter for the network and celebrity star of *Home Again,* Nick was a genius when it came to remodeling. He looked at what *was* and imagined *what could be.* Beneath his gifted hands, even the most weathered wood in the most damaged structure took on new life.

Already, he and his crew had worked miracles at the old mansion, known to locals as the Big House. Rotted boards were replaced. Old woods refurbished. Window sashes were re-fitted, windowpanes upgraded for more efficiency. Plumbing and electrical underwent total re-haul. Every appliance and every fixture was ripped out and updated with something newer, better. All chimneys swept and fireplaces restored to working order. A new third turret took the place of an outdated screened-in porch, making room for new bathrooms on all three floors. The roof was re-shingled, the other four porches reinforced, and each door restored or replaced. Most importantly, the cellar was secured, all secret passages accounted for, and a brand new security system installed.

Madison could not be more thrilled with the progress. She smiled now at the man responsible for it all. "I knew you had some questions before I left for the weekend."

"Kiki should be here any minute. She's running late. Something about traffic problems."

Until *Home Again* came calling, livestock created the biggest traffic hazard in town. Cattle occasionally got loose from The Sisters Sale Barn or someone's pasture. Prior to the County 4-H Show each spring, kids often trained their animals by walking them along the streets of town. The mayor's horse was known to unlatch its own pen and wander through Naomi, and once, her Aunt Lurline's flock of peacocks had marched down Main Street, conducting their own majestic parade. Natural wildlife like deer and feral hogs sometimes created a nuisance, not to mention occasional damage to vehicles. However, there had never been an ongoing traffic problem concerning automobiles. Until recently.

A hit reality show filmed in rural Texas was big news, especially when it came with skeletons, ghosts, and secret passages. The opportunity to be on national television, even as a face in the crowd, was too tempting for most mere mortals to ignore. People flooded into the small sister cities, hoping to catch the camera's lens. And where the people went, the news crews were sure to follow. By the time Kiki arrived, there was a traffic problem on the normally quiet streets. Two new traffic lights, one in each town, were installed to control the steady flow of vehicles coming in and out of The Sisters.

Kiki Paretta was the celebrity designer in charge of decorating the old mansion. A huge phenomenon herself, the star was doing a cross-production remodel that merged *Home Again: Starting Over* with her own hit show, *Kiki's Kustomworks*. If having one television show filmed in The Sisters was stressful, having two filmed there was nothing short of chaotic.

Traffic concerns aside, Madison realized the show's producer was missing. "And Amanda?" she asked.

"She was called away by the network brass. Something about scheduling for next season," Nick said. "We have a few minutes before Kiki arrives. Let's do a walk through and I'll show you what progress we've made this week."

They strolled through the sprawling first floor, examining each room they passed through.

"I can't wait until we're done with the library," Madison admitted. "I need an office terribly."

"We're almost done," Nick assured her. "The floors need one more coat of varnish. The plaster has been repaired and painted, the fireplace is up to code, and all the windows have been replaced. The burled walnut wainscoting was already in excellent shape. All it needed was a light polish."

"And the French doors leading onto the front porch have their own keyed and coded entry, correct? Because I'll have my clients use this entrance, rather than the front door."

"Already taken care of. Honestly, all we're waiting on is the last coat of varnish and the furniture. You can probably be moved in within a couple of weeks."

Madison let out a dreamy sigh. "That will be amazing. I can hardly wait." She looked around the room, imagining where she might place her desk. And Derron's. She had promised her part-time employee a desk of his very own and the opportunity to work his magic as a receptionist.

"This is really happening, isn't it?" she breathed. Excitement sparkled in her hazel eyes and stirred color into her cheeks.

Nick could not help but laugh. He cocked his dark head, listening to the sounds drifting in from adjacent rooms. The whir of an electrical saw drowned out the steady beat from a hammer. Voices carried over the blaring music of a boom box. All around them were the unmistakable sounds of a remodel in progress.

"Yes, Madison, this is really happening. Come on, let's go to the kitchen. I want to show you what we've done in the butler's pantry."

When he held out his hand, Madison hesitated for only a fraction of a second. She still remembered what happened the first time he took her hand. His touch had been electric. To her chagrin, she had literally jumped. The only saving grace to her shame was that he had been affected every bit as much as she.

Not that the attraction between them had a chance. She was in love with Brash. No matter how charismatic Nick was, no matter how unconventionally handsome he might be, she was not interested. She liked the man just fine, respected his talent with his hands, and valued his opinion and expertise. Nick had gone to bat for her more than once, and she suspected he was almost wholly responsible for the remodel being done in the first place, particularly at no cost to her. She even considered him a friend. But nothing more. There was room for only one man in her life, and that man was Chief of Police Brash deCordova.

Madison tucked her hand into Nick's and allowed him to lead her from the room. As they rounded the corner into the parlor, they came face to face with the lawman who had arrested her heart so completely.

"Brash!" she cried in surprise. The delight was evident on her face. She had not expected to see him before she left for Dallas.

"Maddy."

She loved the way he always said her name. His voice would drop to an intimate level, conveying a world of depth and feeling in just one simple utterance.

His eyes fell now to her hand, still clasped within Nick's. Madison saw him stiffen. The lines around his sensuous mouth tightened with displeasure.

Before Maddy thought to pull her hand free, a whirl of activity swept into the room behind Brash. Kiki Paretta made her entrance, stirring the air around her with a sense of awe and inspiration, cloaked by her very own signature fragrance.

"I'm here. I'm finally here," she said with a hint of exasperation, waving her arms in the air. She had a habit of talking with her hands, flashing an odd mix of gaudy costume jewelry, fine diamonds, and brightly painted half-inch nails. For all her diminutive size, everything else about the woman was bigger than life. She loved bright colors, trendy flowing outfits, and killer high heels. Even with three-inch stilettos and the unruly mass of raven-black curls piled atop her head, she did good to hit five and a half feet tall. Yet for all her flair and drama, Kiki's charm and effervescent personality were genuine.

"Madison, where have you been keeping this divine specimen of a man?" Not waiting for an answer, Kiki curled herself around Brash's arm. "I knew I was running late and my foot was just a tad bit heavy on the gas." She pinched her fingers, almost touching, to measure the violation. "This wonderful officer of the law noticed my error right away and corrected me on it. He was kind enough to just give me a warning. As we were talking, we realized we were both headed to the same place, so he more or less gave me a police escort." She beamed up at Brash with a bright smile that was as charming as it was sincere. She hugged his arm as she continued to chatter. "Of course, if I had known Officer deLight would be the one stopping me, I might have sped through town long ago!"

"The name is deCordova." Madison corrected her. She bit her tongue, lest she add 'and he's mine.' She hoped the message came through in the look she threw at Kiki, but the other woman was not even looking. Her eyes were on the tall officer she clung to.

"Brash tells me you and he are high school acquaintances. I bet it's been a blast, catching up on old times. I just love running into former classmates, don't you?" Without pausing to take a breath, much less wait for an answer, the dark little whirlwind spun into a new tale. "Why, just last month, I was in New York at an art gallery opening, and who do you think I saw, but Sarah Jo Fredericks. We went to junior high together in Blanco, of all places! Of course, now she goes by Sari. No last name, simply Sari. But we had the best time, talking about all our old friends and the pranks we used to play in Mrs. Kraus' homeroom." She paused long enough to draw in a breath and glance back and forth between Brash and Madison. "Was it that way with you two? Don't you just love remembering the crazy things we did as teenagers? Tell me what you remember best about Brash, Madison. Come on, something juicy." Her eyes shimmied in delight.

So Brash described us as old friends from high school, did he?

Madison felt the claws all but pop from beneath her nails. She forced herself to relax. Keeping their relationship under wraps had been her idea. Not only did a secret romance insure privacy from the media, it also allowed Bethani time to adjust to the thought of her mother with another man. It made sense at the time, but now, seeing the way Kiki cuddled up to Brash, Madison questioned the wisdom of her suggestion.

It took great effort forcing her voice to come out light and playful, but Madison managed. "Juicy? Well, let's see. I remember a particular Powder Puff football game, when the football players dressed up as cheerleaders while the girls played the game. *Brasha*, as I remember, was quite fetching." Until just now, she had forgotten all about the silly event, but it suddenly popped into her mind with full clarity.

As a fundraiser for their senior trip, Brash and his classmates hosted the popular alternative-style sports event. Even with balloon boobs and yarn hair, the star football-player-turned-cheerleader had stolen her breath away. Beneath a short skirt, his legs were long and lithe in a pair of woefully stretched-out tights. Twenty-something years later, the memory of seeing him like that still did funny things to her breathing.

"A cheerleader?" Kiki clapped her hands together with glee. "I would have loved seeing that!"

"If I remember correctly, you filled out a football uniform quite nicely, too," Brash informed Madison with a mysterious glint in his eyes.

"Yeah, right, like you even noticed me!" she huffed.

"You wore Darren Schultz's uniform. Number thirty-six."

"You—You remember that?" she breathed. "You even *knew* that?" She warmed, just knowing he had noticed her in high school. All these years, she assumed the attraction had been completely one sided.

"I told you, Maddy, the only reason I never asked you out in high school was because I couldn't decide between you or Genny. You were both so different, but both so dad-gum cute." He gave her the same lopsided smile that always melted her heart.

It was true that she and Genesis had always been on opposite ends of the spectrum. Genesis was blond, she was brunette. Her best friend was a cute, compact bundle of energy, while Madison possessed a more serene, understated beauty. Where Genny was generous curves and soft edges, Maddy was all long legs and straight lines. At a slender five foot seven, Maddy could wear most any style and look great, even though she favored simple, tailored lines. Several inches shorter and twenty pounds over vogue, Genny loved ruffles and patterns, even though they did not always love her. One woman had blue eyes, the other hazel. One was energetic and bubbly, the other quiet and more reserved. Definitely opposites, but the best of friends since junior high.

Pretending to be unaffected, Madison waved her hand with a nonchalant air. "Poor Brash. So many girls, so little time."

"Good thing I've learned to slow down and enjoy life." He allowed his gaze to wander over her, lingering on her lips. A delicious thrill shot through her body, especially when he drawled, "One simple pleasure at a time."

Kiki assumed he was kidding and laughed at his wicked flirtation. "Would you two like to be alone?" she teased. "Maybe re-live a few old high school fantasies?"

When Nick stiffened beside her, Maddy realized he still held her hand. She slipped her palm free and sent Brash a meaningful look, admonishing him with her eyes. How could they keep their relationship secret when he looked at her like *that?*

"Actually, I do need to speak with Maddy, but it can wait until you've discussed your business," Brash offered.

"You're welcome to stay."

Madison's quiet invitation was all he needed to hear. He fell in line as they toured the first floor, only half listening as Kiki prattled on with her decorating plans.

They took the back stairs to the second floor, as workers had the main staircase blocked. That staircase had played a deciding factor in Nick's desire to restore the old house. He called it nothing less than a masterpiece, clearly enchanted with the attention to detail that went into creating it. According to him, the different woods used in construction made it all the more valuable, and authenticated its age and worth. The figures he quoted were impressive.

The back staircase was not nearly as grand, but served its purpose just as well. They stepped from the landing, passed the upstairs laundry room, and entered into the suite of rooms that occupied the entire right half of the second floor. This was the master suite, designed specifically for Madison.

"You will be the envy of women everywhere!" Kiki announced. She propped her hands upon her tiny hips and surveyed the master bath, which connected to the upstairs laundry room. "After this, I may be calling Nick in to remodel my own suite."

"It is sumptuous," Madison agreed. Even half finished, it was grander than any bathroom she ever had. Not even their master bath in Dallas had been this extravagant.

"And this closet is to die for!" Kiki flung open the double doors and stepped inside, a dreamy expression upon her face.

Madison had originally protested the double doors. It was a *closet*, after all. Connected to a bathroom, no less. Why the oversized entrance? Nick and Amanda had won that argument, so now there was plenty of room for the four of them to step inside. The storage space was larger than the entire bedroom she currently shared with her daughter at Granny Bert's. In light of all the built-in shelves and clothes racks lining the walls, as well as the bench in the middle of the room, the double doors no longer seemed so ridiculous.

"Too bad I don't have enough clothes to fill even one wall," Madison admitted ruefully.

"Then you know what that means," Kiki said, flashing a bright smile. She held her arms wide and wiggled her entire body. "Shopping spree!"

They crossed into the bed chambers, where the walls were already painted a soft, soothing green. Thank goodness, the rose garden had been ripped from the walls and no trace of the gaudy wallpaper remained.

"I'm thinking lots of soft white and creams, with just a touch of moss green. Perhaps a second color, as well, for emphasis." Kiki tapped her lips as she envisioned the bedding and furniture. "Pink? Coral? What is your favorite?"

Careful not to allow her eyes to betray her, Madison avoided Brash's gaze. She turned her back to him, just in case. "I was thinking something more neutral," she admitted. "Not so feminine."

Kiki's eyes glittered with mischief. "Why, you little dickens, you!"

Maddy flushed a deep scarlet. She could feel Brash's amused smile, so she dared not face him. "I've never been one for frills and frou-frou," she replied as evenly as she could manage.

Kiki burst out laughing. "I'm just teasing you, Maddy! Whether you share this room or keep it all to yourself is none of my concern. But I agree something more neutral suits you best. Not so girlie. So let's think…" She tapped her bright red lips again and tossed out a few ideas. As they discarded them one by one, Madison became frustrated, but Kiki smiled with confidence. "Don't worry, I'll come up with the perfect color scheme."

Madison followed the designer around the room as they discussed placement of furniture.

"I've ordered a magnificent bed, custom designed specifically for you. It will resemble an old iron bedstead, but will have a modern twist. King sized, of course, with adjustable lighting, charging ports, and digital speakers integrated into the ironwork. Four posters, to be used with or without a canopy." She clapped her hands together. "You're going to love it!"

"It sounds fantastic."

Kiki swept across the room, indicating a space near the balcony doors. "There will be a custom table here to match, flanked by upholstered chairs." She crossed the room, into the adjoining sitting room. "A settee in here to pull the look together. Ironwork with upholstered cushions."

"I wanted to talk to you both about the entertainment center," Nick said, stepping forward to join them. "Naturally, there will be room for a television and stereo system, with doors to hide it all when not in use. The question is, do you want it large enough for a computer desk to be on one side?"

"Why would I need a desk in the bedroom? There's a connecting library right there." Maddy pointed to the remaining room of the grand suite. As an avid reader, Juliet Randolph, the original owner of the house, had her own personal library constructed upstairs, separate from the formal library on the first floor. Madison loved the intricate woodwork and cubbyholes that comprised the room. The shelves were still filled with Miss Juliet's books, many of them first editions.

"Just asking to be sure. So let me show you the design I had in mind." Nick opened his iPad and pulled up a computer-generated drawing.

"Oh, Nicky, this is delightful!" Kiki beamed. She bent her dark head over the design, examining every feature.

As she and Nick discussed various options, Madison slipped away and approached Brash. "Sorry about all this," she murmured. "I had no idea you were coming home today."

"I couldn't go another day without seeing you," he said, keeping his voice low. "I thought we both could use some river therapy."

Dismay filled Madison's face. "I leave for Dallas this afternoon, remember?"

He swore softly. "Damn it, I forgot!"

"I thought you were trying to stop cursing," she chided.

"Some things merit a relapse," he growled. From the corner of his mouth, he bewailed, "I was planning a special evening for us, Maddy."

A weary sigh was her only answer. Kiki had turned toward them, an expectant look on her face. "Maddy? Don't you want to see this? Nick has truly outdone himself this time!"

Trying to look enthused, Madison returned to the drawing they ogled. She had to admit, it was impressive.

"I wanted it to be special for you, Madison," Nick said quietly.

"Thank you, Nick."

"Hopefully you'll think of me each time you see it." He murmured the last so the others could not hear. Somehow his fingers brushed against hers as he repositioned the device they both held.

Madison tried to hide her dismay. She had suspected Nick was interested in pursuing their attraction to one another, but he seldom made his intentions so obvious. She wondered if he did so now because of Brash. Men could be so childishly territorial.

All she needed was for Brash to storm over and set Nick straight on which man claimed her heart. Before the lawman got wind of Nick's subtle overture, Maddy discreetly pulled her fingers away and stepped backward. "So is this the wall where it will be?" she asked in a falsely bright voice.

Kiki sent her a quizzical look. "No, I assumed you would want it on the opposite wall. That way you could watch television from the bed or the chairs."

"Of—Of course. Good idea."

"So I can proceed with the design?" Nick confirmed. He was the only one who understood Madison's confused act. "I wanted to start on it this weekend."

"Yes, yes, they're great." She looked down at her watch. "Speaking of this weekend, I really need to start packing. Was there anything else?"

"I need to confirm filming for next Thursday," Kiki clarified. "We'll need to decide on a final color scheme so that I can present it to you on camera. You'll be appropriately undecided, of course, but once you make your choice we'll all be delighted." Her hands shimmied in the air like tambourines.

Madison was still getting accustomed to how 'reality' television worked. In truth, it was actually quite unrealistic and often heavily scripted. The hardest part for her was acting surprised, when she knew good and well what was going to happen. She was not a professional actress and lacked Blake's gift for drama. Granny Bert's, too. *Now there are a couple of natural-born performers for you,* she thought with an internal shake of her head.

"Send me my choices and we'll go from there," Madison answered aloud. "Nick, it really is a great design. Thanks for coming up with it. You and Kiki are doing a great job." She turned her attention to the lawman. "Brash, you needed to talk to me? You can walk me to my car."

"Absolutely."

He followed her home, where they managed to find a few moments alone after a two-week absence.

"I've missed you, Maddy," he murmured into her hair. They snuggled on the sofa, arms entwined.

"I've missed you, too."

"Are you sure you have to go this weekend?" He scattered kisses along her neck. Warm breath fanned across her cheek as he nuzzled her ear. "I could make it worth your while if you stayed."

"Don't tempt me."

"I'd like to try." He turned her into his arms, kissing her with his exceptional persuasive powers.

She came close to giving in, but reason finally returned to her love-addled brain. She pulled slightly away. "I have to go," she whispered sadly.

"I know." His sigh was resigned.

"I don't want to." She twisted so that she could settle against his broad chest and wrap herself in his arms. "Except for bringing the twins home, I'd gladly skip this entire weekend."

"Maybe it won't be so bad." He tried to sound encouraging, but the effort failed.

"I wish I could take you with me," she whispered sorrowfully. "Maybe I could tolerate all the pomp and circumstance if I had you there by my side."

"I don't think Mommy Dearest would appreciate that."

"So you've met my mother-in-law, have you? Because you have her pegged to a tee."

"Come on, surely she's not that bad. You let the kids go up there this summer."

"Only because she is their grandmother and for some insane reason, they happen to love her."

"Warts and all?" Brash teased, trying to lighten the heavy mood that had settled around her shoulders.

"Big, fat, hairy warts. She just keeps them hidden beneath designer clothes and expensive makeup."

Brash rubbed his cheek against hers. "I may not be there in the flesh, but I'll be there in spirit. I'll always have your back, sweetheart."

"I know. And I appreciate that more than you know," she said softly. "Because believe me, this weekend is not going to be pretty."

4

It was already a busy day at the café, even before the tour bus pulled into the parking lot.

Genny watched its progress, wondering if the bus was lost. Not many tours made their way into the tiny towns of Naomi and Juliet, Texas.

One glimpse at the t-shirts, and she knew why they were here. As a swarm of bright yellow-clad women emerged from the specialized van, Genesis grabbed the phone and called her best friend.

"Maddy, you have to get over here. You will never believe what just pulled up at the café."

"Bart McSwain's new truck? The one with the deer horns mounted on the hood and the half-naked woman in camo on the tailgate? I saw it yesterday. The ultimate redneck-mobile."

Genny shook her blond head, even though her friend couldn't see. "Think bigger."

Madison groaned. "Granny Bert didn't really buy a new motor home, did she?" Eighty years young, her grandmother vowed to keep the roads hot this summer, making as many state parks as her busy schedule would allow. She contemplated doing so in a newer model of luxury-on-wheels.

"No. Just come down here and see for yourself!"

"I can't. I've already left for Dallas. I'm a good half-hour out of town. What was it you wanted me to see?"

"Are you ready for this?" Genny cleared her throat, her equivalent to a drumroll. "A tour bus just pulled up. And there's a dozen women inside, all wearing bright yellow t-shirts that say *'Take me to the Big House. I'll serve my time in The Sisters.'*"

After a long silence, Madison managed a strangled, "You've got to be kidding."

"Oh, no. They're about to come through the door as we speak."

"Good luck?" Her tone was as much doubtful as it was encouraging.

"I may need it," Genny said with a rueful purse of her lips. "Now that Shilo Dawne has quit, we're short staffed. Call me later and I'll give you the full scoop."

"On Shilo Dawne or the tour?"

"The tour. There's no scoop on Shilo Dawne. Cutter broke her heart when he told her he wasn't interested, so she's moved away to concentrate on her studies. She's taking a full course at Blinn College this summer." The door dinged and a sea of yellow flowed inside. "I gotta go. Be safe. Call me and let me know how the weekend goes."

"You can count on it!"

Genny welcomed the group of women with a smile that was, for the most part, genuine. A tiny piece of her resented the intrusion of privacy, but each time the negative feelings began to wash over her, she reminded herself of her part in bringing *Home Again* to The Sisters. She and Granny Bert

were the ones to come up with the bright idea of submitting
Madison's house for consideration in the first place.

The group, she discovered, was from Longview. They originally formed as a book club, but recently changed their iden-
tity to an *all-media club*. This, they claimed, broadened their
horizons and allowed them to explore other venues of entertainment. This trip to The Sisters was their first field trip to a
non-literary location.

For the next half-hour, Genny and her staff scuttled
around the café. *New Beginnings* was always crowded during
the noon hour, without an added fifteen guests from the
tour bus.

From the corner of her eye, Genesis saw one of her regular
customers step inside the packed building. He paused with
the door still ajar as he searched for an empty table.

"Hey, Hank, there's a spot open at the bar," she called out
helpfully.

"Thanks, Genny." The older man tottered off to claim the
prized availability.

Genny was amused that the tour group found her café so
exciting. The women chronicled everything with their smart
phones and cameras, from the decor and the people, right
down to their plates when they were delivered.

"Ooh, this looks so delicious," one cooed, snapping a photo of her pan-seared tilapia.

"The presentation is perfect."

"And just taste this risotto. I wonder if she would give us
the recipe."

"She really should offer her own recipe book. I'd buy one.
Wouldn't you, Mary Ann?"

"Absolutely. Oh, look! Look who's coming in the door!"

An excited murmur rippled through the yellow sea. Genny glanced toward the door to see what, or *who*, created such a stir. She gave a knowing smile when Cutter Montgomery stepped inside.

The man faltered as he crossed the threshold. Despite his 'heartthrob' status among females from the ages of three to ninety-three, he always seemed embarrassed by the attention given to his rugged good looks. Even now, as the excited whispers and occasional outburst drifted his way, a faint blush stained his cheeks and he seemed ready to bolt.

His eyes scanned the café. He visibly relaxed when he spotted Genny. As a ready smile engulfed his face, Genny swore she heard half the women in yellow swoon.

"Hey, Genny," he said, joining her at the counter. "What's with the yellow shirts?"

"Believe it or not, we have the honor of being a field trip for the Longview All-Media Club." She flashed her dimples with exaggerated excitement.

"Hmm. How 'bout that."

"So what are you doing here so early? You usually eat later in the day."

"I'm meeting my dad here for lunch."

She looked over his shoulder to the crowded room beyond. "I think there's a booth about to open up by the windows, if you want to hang out here for a few minutes."

"Think I could score a cookie while I wait?" His grin was part mischief, part indulgence. One hundred percent charm.

"I'll see what I can do. And I won't even mention that it might spoil your appetite."

"You know better than that, Genny. I'm never too full to eat your cooking."

Two women from the tour group approached, cameras in hand. "Oh, look, Mary Ann," one of the women squealed. "They are so cute together! Just like on TV."

The other one blurted out, "Excuse me, but can we take your picture?"

Cutter was clearly uncomfortable. He glanced at Genesis for help, but she merely grinned. "Uh, yeah, sure," he mumbled.

Genny started to move away, but the one named Mary Ann stopped her with a hastily waved hand. "No, no, you, too. You make such a cute couple!" she gushed. Her voice dropped to a conspiratorial level. "I don't care what Janet Hatcher says, Barbi and I have known all along that you two are an item."

Barbi nudged her friend's elbow with a huge grin on her face. She did not even attempt a whisper as she said, "Did you see how they just naturally gravitated to one another? Just like they do on camera. If they're in the same room, they wind up side by side, every time!"

While Genny blushed a deep crimson and avoided Cutter's eyes, Mary Ann bobbed her head up and down, all the while grinning at her friend. "I know, I know. Aren't they cute together? Did you see how he dropped his head to talk to her, like she was the only person in the room?"

"It reminded me of that episode when he wore his boots and spurs inside the restaurant and tracked cow crap all over her floor. One look at her face, and he got the broom himself and cleaned it up, then went to whisper an apology in her ear." A giggle accompanied her words. "Wouldn't you love to know what he says to her?"

Their open discussion left Genny mortified. Her faced blazed. *Hello. We're right here.*

Focusing her camera, Mary Ann instructed, "Okay, so scoot in closer. Yes, put your arm around her, just like that."

Both women snapped their cameras. "I can't wait to show this to Janet!" Barbi squealed in delight.

Genny glanced up at the firefighter. To her amazement, he no longer looked embarrassed. He seemed to relish the spotlight as he played up his part in the women's misconception. His arm was tight around her waist, holding her so close to his side that she could feel the restrained laughter bubbling from within his chest. He obviously thought their assumptions were hilarious. Not certain whether she should be amused or insulted, Genny elbowed him in the waist for good measure.

"Cut that out!" he said, flinching where her elbow made contact.

"What? Are you ticklish?" She poked him again, this time with her finger.

Cutter twisted and spun, pulling her with him. He tackled her as he tried to dodge her prodding finger. "I'm serious, Genny, don't do that." His sharp command lost its effectiveness as he made a noise that sounded much like a girlish giggle.

"You are! You are ticklish!" she cried with glee.

They wrestled back and forth playfully, drawing the eyes of half the café. Barbi and Mary Ann captured their antics on digitized film. The overhead cameras for *Home Again* whirred. After a mild scuffle, Cutter got the upper hand. He trapped her against his chest, arms crossed in front of her. She tried stabbing him with her elbow, but he held her hands hostage and squirmed beyond her reach.

"Now I've got you just where I want you," he murmured in her ear. "Stop wiggling and smile pretty for the cameras, darlin'."

"You're asking for it, Cutter Montgomery," she hissed, ignoring the blood zinging through her veins as her body warmed against his.

"This is so awesome!" Barbi gushed. She sounded more like a teenager than the probable mother of one. When Cutter laid his cheek alongside Genny's and flashed his trademark smile, Genny thought the woman might drop the camera from her fluttering hands.

Hamming it up even more, Cutter planted a noisy, exaggerated kiss on Genny's cheek. This time, her elbow made contact with his ribcage, causing him to yelp in her ear.

"What did you do that for?" he cried.

She spoke through a smile. "You're making a spectacle of both of us. What's gotten into you?"

"Just giving the public what they want, Genny darlin'."

Genny wiggled out of his hold. "Why don't you ladies let me take a picture of you with Cutter?" she offered sweetly. She grabbed Mary Ann's camera without waiting for permission. "Stand on either side of him. Cutter, put your arms around them. Yes, that's good. Now everyone smile."

The women cuddled up to the firefighter, clearly in awe. She snapped a few pictures, and then agreed to do a selfie with the four of them. Cutter pulled her front and center and held the camera above them to capture a handful of images that were surely destined for social media.

A line soon formed, as one-by-one the group members came to have their picture taken. By the time the last frame was taken and the women returned to their seats, Genny's cheeks ached from smiling and Cutter's father had arrived.

Shooing Cutter toward the available booth, she followed behind with menus. "Hello, and welcome to *New Beginnings*," she greeted his father. She could not remember Tug Montgomery coming in before now.

The man was a legend in Texas football. Nicknamed for his tugboat shape and strength, he first made a name for himself right here at The Sisters High. He went on to play college ball and to win the Heisman trophy before going pro. His record for unassisted tackles still stood, but it turned out that his heart belonged to ranching, and to pretty little Mary Alice Pierce, more than football. After just a few years, he returned to his roots, his ranch, and his rowdy brood of youngsters. Cutter was the baby boy of the family.

Hardly a baby. He's thirty-one.

The number teased Genny's mind. She had guessed the handsome firefighter as younger; far too young for her own advanced age of thirty-nine. Yet ever since learning his true age, the number had haunted her thoughts...

"And hello to you!" Tug Montgomery's voice boomed from his barrel-shaped chest. Laugh lines crinkled the corners of his eyes and formed pale creases in a face perpetually darkened by the sun. Genesis liked him immediately. "Since this seems to be my son's home away from home, I thought I'd better come check it out for myself." His eyes twinkled with humor. "And right from the get go, I see the attraction. With a pretty little thing like you, doesn't really matter if you can cook or not!"

Genny's blue eyes twinkled in response. "Lucky for you, I actually can."

Cutter broke in with formal introductions. "Dad, this lovely lady and the owner of this fine establishment is Genesis Baker. Genny, my father, Tug Montgomery."

"Delighted to meet you, Mr. Montgomery."

"Please, call me Tug." His hand was huge, dwarfing Genny's as he offered it.

"So what can we get for you two gentlemen today?"

"Son, what do you recommend?"

"Everything." His reply was instant. "Genny makes the best food you've ever tasted."

"Better not let your momma hear you say that, son," Tug advised. He grinned as his eyes flitted back and forth between them, assessing the situation. Something in his knowing gaze made Genny uncomfortable.

Cutter stood his ground. "You always taught me honesty was the best policy."

Tug chuckled aloud. "Yes, but there are certain times in a man's life, like when he's sitting at his mother's dinner table, that he must use the fine art of diplomacy."

"I'll give you a few more minutes, if that will help," Genny offered.

Cutter decided for them both. "Bring us two specials."

"Wait one minute, son. What's on it?" his father asked.

"Doesn't matter," Cutter insisted stubbornly. "It will be the best thing you've ever tasted."

Tug was impressed with his son's steady, challenging stare. He relented with a shrug of his mouth. "You heard the man, then. Two specials."

When she returned five minutes later with their lunch, the men were discussing plans for baling one last cut of hay.

"Be there early in the morning so we can get started," Tug told his son. "It was a darn shame what happened to Ranker's hay field. We need to get ours cut before a fire strikes us, too." He turned his attentions to the plate before him, piled high with food. "Well, the portions are decent," Tug said with approval. He poked around with his fork. "But what's this stuff?"

Cutter knew the answer to this one. "Risotto."

"Riso-who?"

Genny's laugh was one of sheer delight. "You sound exactly like your son, the first time he had it. But it turned out to be delicious, didn't it?"

"I must admit, it was. Then again, it may have had something to do with the fact that you were hand feeding me," Cutter teased. "Do I get the royal treatment again today?"

"With all those camera-happy women sitting over there? Not on your life, buster!"

"Hmm, not bad." Tug shoveled another forkful into his mouth. "Not bad at all."

"Wait until you taste the rest of it," Cutter predicted. "Her rolls taste just like Grandma's. Especially with the special butter she whips up."

"Give me time, son. Give me time," Tug said as he dug into his meal. His mouth already full, he winked at Genny as she excused herself and floated off to the next table.

By the time the tour group left and much of the crowd thinned out, the Montgomery men were ready for their final course.

"Desserts are listed here, but we also have blackberry cobbler, apple turnovers, and a selection of cookies and cupcakes in the bakery case. What can we get for you?"

"How about another one of those cookies you slipped my son earlier? What did you call them?"

"Gennydoodle, my signature cookie."

"I'll take a couple of those and a piece of cobbler. I assume it comes with Blue Bell ice cream?" His eyes twinkled again as he propped thick arms upon the table.

"Of course. Cutter?"

"Do you even have to ask?" he grinned.

Genesis playfully rolled her eyes. "A warm apple turnover with ice cream, coming up. I swear, you're going to turn into an apple turnover one of these days."

When she returned with their desserts, Tug waved to the seat beside his son. "Have a seat. There's something we want to discuss with you."

"Oh?" Curious, she slid into the spot Cutter vacated. He shifted to the inside of the booth, taking his prized dessert with him.

"Mary Alice has a birthday coming up. We want to throw her a party, and Cutter suggested we have it here."

"Oh, I think that's a wonderful idea! I love doing parties!" Genny's blue eyes sparkled.

"The thing is, Mary Alice is a fine cook. Until today, I would have sworn she was the best in the county." Tug gave her a meaningful look. "Much as I love the woman, she's mighty particular about eating other people's cooking."

"You think... she won't approve of mine?"

"Well, now, that's why I came here today. I had to see for myself. Based on what you just fed me, I'm thinking it might take another taste test or two to be sure." His eyes twinkled merrily. "Five or six, at the most."

Realizing he was teasing her, Genesis laughed along with the men. "You might want to do another taste test on Monday," she suggested. "We'll have fried chicken on the special."

"Mark me down for double portions." Tug took a big bite of cobbler. "Mmm. Yes. This, right here. This is what we'll want on the menu for the party."

"You don't want a cake?"

"Cake is her specialty," Cutter informed his father. "She studied in France with some fancy pastry chef. Let her make a cake."

Stuffing his mouth with a cookie, Tug nodded. "Okay, you convinced me. But serve these, too. In fact, maybe we should do one of everything."

Genny's laughter twinkled throughout the restaurant. "I think maybe we should narrow it down a bit," she suggested. "To begin with, do you want a sit-down dinner, or a buffet?"

"Sit-down," he replied promptly. "I want a full meal."

"So what is your wife's favorite food?"

After a minor disagreement over the answer, Cutter called a halt to the discussion. "You know what? Mom likes Italian, but she never makes it herself."

"That might be wise, son, serving something she won't dissect with her own recipe." Tug nodded his approval. "Italian, it is."

"What was that pasta dish we had last week?" Cutter turned to Genny and asked.

She smiled at his use of the word 'we'. He considered himself a permanent fixture at the café. She answered with a nod. "My version of chicken carbonara."

"Make that. It was delicious."

Genny rubbed her hands excitedly. "Perfect." She began to name off several other dishes, most of which the men were unfamiliar. "And we'll finish with the pièce de résistance, a very decadent and delicious tiramisu."

Tug looked skeptical. "Whatever the devil that is."

"Three layers of absolute heaven," she assured the men theatrically. "A bit of chocolate, a bit of rum, a bit of coffee, all layered with rich mascarpone cheese and Italian lady fingers. *Delizioso*," she proclaimed, kissing the tips of her fingers and blowing it into the air, Italian style.

"With a build up like that, it better be," Cutter grinned.

"I promise you, it will be." After a confident smirk, she turned back to business. "How many people are we talking?"

"There are six kids, four spouses, nine grandkids. That's twenty-one, counting Mom and Dad."

"Are you bringing Callie Beth?"

Cutter looked horrified at the suggestion. "No. Definitely not."

"Any grandparents, aunts and uncles, or friends?"

Cutter looked at his father. "Grandma Montgomery. Uncle Willie and Aunt Sharon. What about Aunt Loretta?"

"Maybe we'd better not invite her this time. Your grandfather will be there, you know."

Cutter nodded. "We can't forget our special surprise guest. Sticker."

Genny stared at him, mouth agape. "Your grandfather's name is Sticker?"

"According to my great grandpa, he was the runt of the litter. Born small and a few years after the rest. Doctors said he wouldn't make it through the night, but he was tough and hung on. Just like a sticker burr. Small but tough."

"This is your mom's father?" she guessed. She could not imagine Tug Montgomery having anything less than a giant as a father.

"Yep. Sticker Pierce."

"Sticker Pierce," Genny murmured. "Haven't I heard that name somewhere before?"

"Probably. He's somewhat of a legend in the rodeo world. Has a line of western wear and rodeo rigging."

"Maybe I've seen it on a shirt or something," she agreed. "And that's your grandfather?"

"Yep. Mom doesn't know it, but we're bringing him here as a surprise for her birthday. So that should bring the count to twenty-five."

"I'll plan for thirty, just in case."

"Well, son, this was a fine meal, but that hay ain't rakin' itself. Guess I'd better get back to the ranch." He crammed a cowboy hat onto his head and stood from the table. "Genny, that was a mighty fine meal. And it was a pleasure to meet you."

"It was a pleasure to meet you, too, Mr. Montgomery."

"It's good to know all the things my son told me about you are true. Beautiful, smart, funny, *and* a great cook." He winked at her and grinned. "To be honest, you were beginning to sound too good to be true!"

"Why, thank you, sir."

"While I happen to agree, those weren't my words. They were my son's."

She hated the flush that crawled into her cheeks. "In that case, thank you, Cutter."

"Just telling it like it is, Genny darlin'. Just telling it like it is."

5

"All in all, that went better than I expected."

Madison made the admission to her children as she drove home from Dallas Sunday afternoon. If she overlooked the subtle snubs from her so-called friends and Annette's endless snide remarks, the weekend had not been a total loss.

A meeting with her lawyer revealed good news. The debt she still owed creditors had shrunk considerably, to an amount that was now more manageable. A few more years, and she might be free of the disaster Gray shackled her with. While Annette and Charles might fork out plenty of money to keep their son's name in good standing, their generosity did not extend to rescuing their daughter-in-law from the jaws of bankruptcy. She had to dig out of that hole by herself.

But the best news of all was that the IRS had dropped the investigation into her late husband's business dealings. No doubt her in-laws had something to do with the sudden decision, but Madison did not care. As long as the law did not come after her, she was fine with the older couple paying to keep their precious son's name out of the mud.

That was what this weekend had been all about, even if Annette would never acknowledge as much. She claimed it was a celebration of her son's memory. She insisted the downturn in Gray's business was due to the economy, and that things would have turned around, had he lived.

"The decorations were fabulous. You did a great job helping with them, Beth," Maddy continued, making eye contact with the teen through the rearview mirror.

"Thanks. It was sort of fun."

"I'm glad you had fun," her brother sulked from the front seat. "Because I thought the entire party sucked. Big time."

"Blake." Madison used her best mom-tone on him.

"Hey, I can't help it if the whole thing was one pompous show of 'up-yours.'"

"Blakely Grayson Reynolds, you watch your mouth!"

"Sorry, Mom, but it's true. I loved Dad and thought he was a swell guy, but to hear Grandmother Annette tell it, you would think he was a god. Nobody bought all that crap. She laid it on too thick. It was obvious she was just trying to buy her way into their good graces, and she made us all look like fools in the process." His normal smiling face was replaced with a dark glower.

Madison secretly agreed. She wished Annette could hear her grandson's assessment of the weekend. When Annette told her version of the event, it would be a glowing success and an understated tribute to a most deserving man. *Bleh.*

"Blake, honey, your grandmother was only doing what any mother would do." It galled her to take Annette's side. Not only did she need to keep peace in the family for her children's sake, but in this case, she spoke the truth. "She took up for her son the only way she knew how. I would do the same for you."

"If you had the money," he inserted on a grunt.

"If I had the money," she echoed.

The teen turned toward her from his seat. "The thing is, Mom, it may be the only way she knows, but it's not the only way you know. You know how to express your love without just throwing money around." He peered at his sister over the seat back. "The whole time we were there, did she ever hug you?"

Bethani searched her memory banks. "I don't think so," she finally admitted.

"Yeah, me neither. And she never stepped foot in the kitchen. She never made us cookies or made us our favorite meal. She didn't come in to tell us goodnight or tell us goofy stories about when she was little."

"Hey, I resent that. My stories are not goofy!"

"Some of them are pretty corny, Mom. And they all have some little pearl of wisdom buried in them. It may be buried deep, but if you dig far enough, you'll find it. Kind of like an earthworm."

Inexplicably touched by his odd characterizations of a mother's love, Madison blinked back a tear. "Odd as it seems, I actually missed your smart attitude these last few weeks."

"Does that mean I finally get a home-cooked meal?"

With his broad and charming smile, Blake looked so much like his father that it momentarily took Madison's breath away. It was good to be reminded that she once loved her husband. It kept the guilt at bay for now hating him.

I don't hate him. I don't hate him. Madison repeated the silent mantra to herself. *I'm no longer angry at him. Brash was right, it is a waste of my time and energy, and it eats away at my heart. I can't hate a man I no longer feel anything for.*

"Mom? A home-cooked meal?" he repeated hopefully.

Madison laughed. "I suppose that's your definition of a mother's love."

He looked confused, as if it were a trick question of some sort. "Of course."

"Well, my dear and precious son, it just so happens I already have tonight's menu all planned out. We're stopping by the store on the way home. I'll fire up the—" She stopped mid-sentence, as a thought suddenly occurred to her.

"Mom?" Blake questioned.

"Are you okay?" Bethani could see her mother's expression in the mirror. She was immediately worried.

"Oh." Madison snapped out of her trance with a weak and non-convincing, "Yeah. Yeah, I'm fine. I just thought about a job I'm working on."

"A case for the investigator?" Blake asked, his expression hopeful. He thought it was cool that his mother sometimes worked for a private investigator.

"No," she said slowly.

It suddenly occurred to her that, while sorting through the unlabeled file in the lawyer's office, she had absorbed more information than she thought. She had been concentrating on alphabetizing the names, but inadvertently, she had seen some of the confidential content.

She suddenly knew what they all had in common.

Fire.

Brash picked up his phone on the second ring.

"This is a pleasant surprise," he greeted Madison. "I didn't think you'd call this evening."

"Beth is on the phone with Megan, telling her every detail of the last six weeks. Blake's version is much shorter, but his call list is longer. Apparently we did our catching up in the car, because here I sit, all by my lonesome again. It's almost like they are still gone."

"I could come over and keep you company."

"A generous offer, and one I'm sorely tempted to accept. But not tonight."

"When, Maddy?" She heard the frustration in his voice. "I leave for another conference on Friday."

"This is your last one, isn't it? You've been gone all summer." She could hear the whine in her own voice.

"Believe me, I know, sweetheart. And yes, this is the last one. When I hit town next Wednesday, I don't plan on leaving again anytime soon."

"Just so you know, if you leave again, you'll have a hitch-hiker along for the ride. Me."

She heard his pleased smile. "Now *that* would make packing a suitcase again all worthwhile." Judging from the sounds on the other end of the line, Brash leaned back against the headboard in his bedroom, his knee popping as he unfolded his long legs and stretched out on the mattress. "So where would we go?"

She played along with his game. "Mmm, let's see. What about... Shreveport?" It was the first town to pop into her mind.

"Really?" he sounded surprised. "Why there?"

She laughed at her impromptu answer. "Probably because Granny and Miss Sybille are talking about going gambling. While they're there, they want to swing over to Monroe and see the Duck Commander warehouse. I think they have a crush on the older man that carries around that glass of sweet tea."

"You mean Uncle Si?"

"Does he have a beard?"

"They all do."

"I think that's his name. They argue over him like they might actually have a chance with him. They're like schoolgirls."

"I hate to burst their bubble, but I'm pretty sure the old guy is married."

"They'll be crushed," Madison predicted.

"So we won't go to Shreveport." Brash ruled out that possibility. "I'm not much of a gambler anyway."

"Me either."

"So where else would we run off to?"

"Hmm, not Vegas, either. Mexico?"

"Too hot this time of year."

"Disney World?"

"This isn't a family vacation. Just you and me."

Her mouth watered at the thought. She conjured up the most romantic city she could think of. "Paris?"

"Too bad I don't speak French."

"So you pick."

"What about… New York City?"

She squealed with amusement. "Yeah, I'd love to see you up there with your cowboy boots and cowboy hat, talking all

Texan to their Yankee talk. You might need a translator," she teased.

"That's what you'll be there for, sweetheart."

"I don't speak Yankee, either."

They played their game for several more minutes, suggesting and discarding a dozen cities around the world. Brash ended the game when he made the perfect suggestion.

"I know the perfect place. It has everything we need. A river. A night sky as big as Texas, filled with twinkling overhead stars. A soft breeze. Bullfrogs and crickets, chirping out a sweet, romantic song. No one around but you and me."

Their special spot on the river. Maddy closed her eyes and breathed in the beauty of the dream he painted. "It sounds wonderful."

"I have an idea I'd like to run past you."

"What would that be?"

"When I get back home, how about we plan a family outing? You, Beth, Blake, Megan, and me. Granny Bert and Genny are welcome to come along, too."

"What did you have in mind?"

"We have a nice pond out at the ranch, stocked with catfish. We could spend the afternoon out there fishing, then have a fish fry right there on the banks. The kids can swim and play in the water. Adults, too, for that matter."

"That sounds really nice."

"Bethani has been out to the house a few times with Meg, but I'd like for her to see you and me together, to see how well we complement each other. And I'd like to spend more time with both your kids, getting to know them better."

Madison was touched. "That's really sweet of you, Brash."

"I told you I want a future with you, Maddy. Beth and Blake are a part of that future. And even though it might not be my place to say so, I think Blake could use a male influence in his life right now."

The air squeezed from Madison's lungs. She gripped the phone so hard her knuckles turned white. "Wh—Why? Have you heard something? Has he been getting into some sort of trouble I don't know about?"

"No, sweetheart, nothing like that," Brash was quick to assure her. "Blake is a great kid. So is Bethani. But it's gotta be tough for a fifteen-year-old boy, losing his dad so suddenly. It's not intentional, but girls get more attention in situations like these, because they show their emotions more. Boys hurt just as much, but usually in silence. I just think it might do him good to bond with a male authority figure."

Was this man wonderful, or what? Tears clogged her throat.

"I thought I might even take him dove hunting when season opens in a few weeks, if you don't object."

She could barely get the words out on a whisper. "Not— Not at all."

"I know he'll be starting football soon. As a former player and coach, I strongly encourage sports. It builds leadership qualities, teaches the importance of teamwork, and establishes a strong code of ethics and accountability. But hunting... now that teaches an entirely different skill set. There is nothing like being in the great outdoors, surrounded by nature, learning to depend on yourself. Hunting teaches personal responsibility, firearm safety, sustainability, and common sense practices. And it fosters a need that all men have to provide for their families. If he's interested, I'd be happy to take him with me to South Texas this fall to my deer camp. With your permission, of course."

He could not hear her head nodding.

"Maddy?"

"Yes."

"Are you crying? What's wrong, sweetheart? If you don't want to take him hunting—"

"No, no, it—it's not that!"

"Then, what? Why are you crying, sweetheart?"

"Because-because you're trying. You care. You have no idea how many times Blake begged Gray to take him hunting, or fishing, or just camping. But Gray was always too busy. He never took the time to bond with him. I—I can't believe you're willing to do that for my son."

"I told you, Maddy," Brash said, his voice rough with emotion, "I want Blake to be a part of my future, too."

The words were on the tip of her tongue. It was so hard holding them in, to not voice the sentiments surging through her very being. She loved him. Yet she could not, would not, say the words until they were free to explore their relationship. The tricky part, in her mind, was that it had to be with her children's blessings.

"You have no idea how much I appreciate that, Brash. And he will, too. He'll love it. I can't wait for you to invite him."

"So you like my idea about the family outing?"

"I love it." *Just like I love you.* She spoke the words silently, hoping they reached him through telepathy.

His quietly spoken agreement brought another smile, telling her he understood her message. "Me, too, sweetheart."

Clearing the emotion from her throat, Madison made a conscious effort to change the subject. "So I have a professional question for you..."

"I'm listening."

Something about the jumbled file at *Lone Star Law* still tugged at Madison's mind. Even if Gloria Jeffers was known for her overzealous imagination, she wondered if there was a story there. And the fact that Gloria, a woman Carson Elliot insisted did not drink, compiled the file shortly before she died of alcohol poisoning was too coincidental for Maddy's analytical mind. At the risk of being as dramatic as the deceased woman herself, it was worth looking into.

"How do you go about investigating a cold case?" she asked.

"How cold?"

"Dead and buried. Doubtful it was ever a living creature to begin with."

"Hmm. Well, I suppose the same way you would any case, cold or otherwise. Research. Lots and lots of research."

It was sheer luck that Madison's gig with *Lone Star Law* coincided with the investigation Carson Elliot hired her to do. Being at the law firm offered Madison the perfect opportunity to learn about Gloria's work habits and professional conduct.

According to Shawn Bryant and the few clients Madison spoke with, the woman was well-liked and quite efficient. Absolutely no evidence indicated that the lawyer's late secretary had a drinking problem. Everything in the office — other than the filing system itself — was neat and meticulous. And Madison suspected that no drunk could decipher the way Gloria Jeffers filed. That particular method of organization demanded a clear and sober head.

Yet if the woman was an alcoholic, it stood to reason she had a stash of alcohol hidden in the office. Madison spent a full hour searching for it.

Digging deep into a corner cabinet, Madison did not hear the door chime as it tinkled out the first notes of the *Aggie War Hymn*. Shawn was a proud alumnus of Texas A&M, as evidenced the moment clients stepped through the door. This time, however, Madison never realized someone entered until a voice spoke from behind her.

"Hello? I had an appointment with Mr. Bryant?"

Madison banged her head on the cabinet as she jerked from the dark recess. "Ow!" she cried in surprise. She straightened and whirled, rubbing at the offended spot on the back of her head. "I'm sorry. I did not hear you come in."

Lisa Redmond eyed her dubiously. Several weeks ago, the slender woman had hired *In a Pinch* to provide evidence her husband was cheating on her. Despite rewarding Madison with a bonus for a job well done, she seemed none too pleased to see the would-be sleuth now. Madison wondered if it might be embarrassment. After all, who liked to admit her husband was unfaithful? *She* certainly had trouble discussing Gray's duplicity.

"I have an appointment," Lisa repeated.

"Oh, yes. Certainly." Madison dusted off her hands and shut the cabinet door. It hadn't revealed much more than files and spider webs. Certainly no secret stash of bottles.

"If you'll have a seat, I'll let Mr. Bryant know you've arrived."

"I had no idea you worked here." Lisa's words were as stiff as her body as she perched on the edge of the maroon leather armchair, clearly uncomfortable.

"Just while he's in a pinch." Madison offered the tongue-in-cheek reply as she pressed the intercom and lifted the receiver to her ear.

"Yeah, I heard about the other lady," Lisa murmured, letting her eyes trail over the desk. She seemed to avoid Madison's eyes, choosing to study the filing cabinets and custom built-ins as Madison announced her arrival.

"Mr. Bryant will see you now. Shall I show you to his office?"

"I know the way." Lisa scrambled to her feet and disappeared down the hallway.

Madison noted that her appearance had improved since the first time they met. That first day, she had mistaken the stringy-haired, nervous-acting young woman for a drug addict. With a new haircut and a fashionable outfit, Lisa Redmond looked far more confident of herself now. And despite whatever paranoid beliefs Barry held, this was the first time the two women had seen each other since May.

Making a face to herself, Madison knew that if Barry got wind of Lisa showing up here today, he would read something more into it. He would probably accuse Madison of orchestrating the meeting, or suggesting Lisa hire *Lone Star Law* to handle the divorce.

For all she knew, that was exactly why Lisa was here.

Not that it was any of her concern. She had more pressing matters to worry with. Now that she had a new filing system in place for the law office, her job here would soon be done, which also meant her dual-purpose time was coming to an end.

Something about the jumbled file she had found still bothered her. Something about the fact that all five cases revolved around fire.

Madison knew she walked a fine line.

She had access to the files, but the contents were confidential. Even with Shawn Bryant's permission, she had no legitimate reason to review the cases. Short of contacting each client and obtaining their approval, she could not ethically read the details within.

What she *could* do was examine the names, dates, and brief descriptions used for filing purposes. Before tucking the folders into their proper new homes, she took a few notes.

Jerry Don Peavey vs. Omega Insurance: Fire damage to barn

Ray Sams: Motor Home fire

Tomas Montelongo: Small fire at restaurant, personal liability insurance

William Shanks: Chimney fire

Carson Elliot: House fire

Her eyes backtracked over the last name, making certain she read it correctly. Yes, it was right there in black and white. Carson Elliot.

The list covered three towns, two counties, and five years. The only link of commonality was that they each had something to do with fire.

Was it another of Gloria's contrived conspiracy theories? Or was there a legitimate reason the files were combined into one file? Madison's mind hummed with possibilities.

Perhaps she had been doing research on fires in the community. Considering her gentleman friend was one of the victims, she might have had a personal interest in the outcome of such research.

Perhaps she was gathering information for a class-action suit.

Or researching insurance fraud.

Perhaps Gloria had been drunk at the time she shuffled the files together.

...Gloria did not drink alcohol...

Carson Elliot's words, spoken with such absolute certainty, echoed in Madison's head.

Tempting though it was, reading the files was unethical. But there was nothing unethical about asking questions around town.

Her grandmother had an uncanny inside track to most everything that happened in the twin cities. When it pertained to fire, surely Cutter would be a source of information. And if William Shanks was any relation to her Granny's friend Wanda Shanks, surely Miss Wanda would answer any questions she had. As would Carson himself.

A satisfied smile twitched Maddy's lips. While she might not be free to read the files, she could still find out what they contained.

As Granny Bert was fond of saying, there was more than one way to skin a polecat.

6

Maddy launched a covert operation around the two towns, casually striking up conversations about Gloria Jeffers. She dropped by one store after another, chatting idly as she browsed. Whether it was the proprietor she visited with or another customer, the conversation was largely the same.

Casually bringing up *Lone Star Law* as her latest client offered the perfect lead in. She would marvel over the late secretary's meticulous organizational skills, and then stop to rue the fact that she hadn't known the woman very well. Had they known her well, by chance?

It was a simple question, but not a single person answered with a simple yes or no. Everyone offered their opinion, just as Maddy had known they would.

"No, I'm afraid I didn't. But I heard about how she died. How embarrassing!"

"I've known Gloria since we were knee high to a grasshopper. We went through school together, and let me tell you, that girl was prim and proper to a T. I don't care what the coroner said, Gloria Jeffers did not drink herself to death! She never touched a drop of alcohol in her life."

"Oh, yes, I've known Gloria for years. We went to high school together, right here at Sisters High. Of course, that was before they built the new school. Back then, we didn't need a fancy building like that new one to get a fine education. No ma'am, all we needed was a desk, a chalkboard, and a teacher who wasn't afraid to break out the paddle and pop us on the wumpus when we got out of hand. None of this smart-mouthed disrespect you hear nowadays. Hmph!"

"And you and Gloria remained friends all this time? That's impressive."

"I didn't say we were exactly friends, mind you. I said we knew each other. There was always something flighty about Gloria… When she didn't have her nose stuck in a book, she was stirring up some sort of trouble."

"What kind of trouble?"

"She was always in a tizzy about something. Once, she claimed the butcher doctored his meats to get people addicted. Hmph. He just buys prime beef is all. Corn-fed, the best kind. I hear Mo buys most of it straight from deCordova Ranch. Those deCordova brothers know how to raise a fine herd of cattle, let me tell you."

"That doesn't sound so bad…"

"That wasn't all! She swore there was something fishy about Ellen McDaniel's new housecleaning business. I say if the woman is industrial enough to start up her own business, more power to her. Lord knows she don't keep her own house very clean, but maybe she does better when she's being paid. Gloria was just being spiteful. I think she was jealous, because everyone knew Ellen was looking for more than dance lessons out at Carson Elliot's place."

"I understand Miss Gloria and Mr. Elliot were an item?"

"That was another thing. Gloria was always carrying on about his past, claiming he was some sort of important spy for the Army. I know for a fact he was in the Navy, not the Army, so why should I believe the rest of her claims? Some nonsense about a girl he loved but the government keeping them apart because of her ties to the Russians. All just a bunch of hooey, if you ask me. Just like their so-called 'romance.' Those two were no more suited for each other than me and Brad Pitt. They were good friends, I'll give you that, but I don't think it ever crossed into the bedroom, if you know what I mean. I don't mean to speak ill of the dead, but poor Gloria was simply too plain for a man like Carson Elliot. And now we find out she was a lush! Like I said, she was always flighty."

"Bull feathers! I know what they're saying. But the woman didn't even drink real coffee, just that decaffeinated stuff made to look like the real thing. You can't tell me someone who don't drink caffeine is gonna turn around and drink themselves into an alcoholic stupor and die!"

"Gloria was the sweetest, kindest soul I knew. At least, she was before Claude died. Losing him took something out of her. Who knows? Maybe that's when she started drinking."

"Oh, of course I knew Miss Gloria. She taught my Sunday school class when I was little. It was so sad what happened to her. And so shocking. I never thought she would drink a single sip, much less enough to kill her. Just goes to show, you never know about people...."

"Gloria Jeffers? Of course I knew her! That was so tragic about what happened to her. I guess she took after her momma's uncle. He was always a little too fond of the bottle, too. A mean drunk, they said. Why, I remember my daddy telling about the time..."

"Why, yes, Mrs. Jeffers had been coming in here to the pharmacy for years. Then a few months ago, she all but stopped. Bless her heart, she even came in to apologize. She said she was trying all-natural cures for her ailments now, but she didn't want us thinking she was mad at us. Doesn't that just sound like her? Always so sweet and thoughtful."

"I heard about someone else who died that way. Accidentally ingested some sort of poisoning and literally pooped their intestines out. Poor Gloria. What a way to go. The only consolation is that maybe she was too drunk to feel anything."

"Who? Oh, yes, the woman who... well, you know. Such an undignified death. No, I never met her."

"She was in here getting her hair done, not two days before the deed. All I had to do for the service was give it a good going over."

"Did you notice anything different about her that last time?"

"Well, that very last time, I did notice that she was dead. But you mean the last time she was in here? Not really. She was working on some new theory she had, something about some fires in the area. That was Gloria, always working on one of her theories. I always told her *she* should be the one writing those books she kept her nose stuck in."

"What was her theory about fires?"

"To be quite honest, I didn't usually pay her theories much never-mind. She was always working on uncovering some big mystery, which usually amounted to nothing more than an oversized imagination and a bunch of malarkey."

"I found several notes on her desk," Madison fibbed. "I understand she had been using herbal remedies lately."

"Yep. If fact, it all started with one of those books she was reading. It sounded so interesting that she decided to look into them herself. I think it might be one of the few times one of her theories actually held water."

The client in the beautician's chair joined the conversation with a loud harrumph. "I don't know about that. She gave me a recipe for herbal tea. It was supposed to provide energy and stamina, but all it gave me was constipation."

"You must have written it down wrong, Earline. Everyone knows Gloria had enough trouble in that department without adding to it!"

"She wrote the recipe down herself, so there! *I* didn't do it wrong."

"Then you must have made it wrong," the beautician insisted.

"Or it could be that her handwriting was sloppy."

Breaking into their argument, Madison protested, "Based on everything I've seen at the office, Miss Gloria had excellent penmanship."

"No, I distinctly recall that I had trouble deciding if she had written a '2' or a '3.'"

"Maybe she was drinking when she wrote out the recipe?" Madison offered.

Both women were aghast. On this, they agreed.

"Gloria did not drink!"

"Oh, heaven's no! She was definitely a teetotaler. Probably because of what happened to her uncle on her momma's side. I'm sure you've heard *that* story a time or two!"

"Knew her well," the old black man nodded. Jolly Dewberry still ran his service station the old-fashioned way; he offered *service*, along with the gasoline. He elaborated as he cleaned Madison's windshield. "Never knowed her to drink, but I did notice her staggering a bit the last time she left. Almost fell getting back in her car."

"When was that?"

He scrubbed on a stubborn smudge left by a bug meeting the windshield at seventy miles an hour. "Now that you mention it, I believe it was that same day she died. Asked me to fill 'er up, then decided to come inside and get a coke. She liked my old-timey dispenser. Said drinks from those cans just didn't taste the same as glass bottles. And that the aluminum would eventually eat into our brains and cause cancer."

"Do you remember which kind of soda she liked?" In Texas, 'coke' was a generic name for all soft drinks, not a brand.

"Mostly Sprite, but she favored root beer if I had the kind with no caffeine. See? That's another thing that don't add up. If Miss Gloria didn't drink caffeine, why would she take up drinking liquor?" He shook his graying head. "Don't make no sense."

$$\mathcal{D}$$

Madison glanced around nervously. "Are you sure we have permission to do this?" Her voice held the warble of worry. It seemed like old times, back when they were in high school. Genny as the instigator, Maddy as the faithful sidekick.

Even now, it was Genny who turned the key into the lock. "I don't see why not. Carson Elliot gave us the key to Miss Gloria's house, so it's not breaking and entering. And since her death was more or less ruled an alcohol overdose, we aren't tampering with an investigation. We should be good."

"Should be," Madison grumbled, following her friend over the threshold. "I just hope Brash sees it that way."

"It's not like we're going to take anything. We're just looking around."

Still, it felt strange, walking into the home of a deceased woman they barely knew.

Despite her confident jargon, Genny stalled near the door. The house still had that lived-in feel, despite the eerie silence that echoed throughout the space. "It looks like she could return at any moment," Genny whispered.

It was a cozy scene. A plaid chair in the corner of the room, its fabric frayed and its seat cushion creased from frequent use. A worn ottoman stood nearby. A half-read paperback lay face down upon it, the pages splayed to mark reading progress. The shade on the lamp cocked to one side, offering optimal light for reading. Even while they stood there, the digital recorder on the television whirred to life, the timer set to record a favorite program. All that was missing was the owner of the house.

"Probably recording one of her soap operas," Genny guessed, glancing at the clock on the wall. "I think that may have been one of the reasons Carson hired you. He said Gloria was a huge fan of Caress and was thrilled when you vindicated her death."

Caress Ellingsworth had been Naomi's very own resident soap queen. The fact that she retired years ago did not diminish her glory. Devoted fans still reeled from her untimely death this past spring.

"So we'll just take a quick look around," Madison said, getting into the spirit of their expedition. "Look for evidence that proves she was a closet alcoholic."

They prowled through the living room, searching in every drawer and cabinet, beneath every piece of furniture, inside every potted plant. Neither found a single drop of alcohol, hidden or otherwise.

"At least someone cleaned out the refrigerator," Madison commented as she ventured into the kitchen. Everything was neat and tidy. "It's possible they could have thrown out any open bottles of wine, but there's not even a corkscrew in her drawers. No wine glasses in the cupboards. No indication that the woman drank anything stronger than coffee. And decaffeinated, at that."

"I hope they cleaned the bathroom, too," Genny muttered. When Madison shot her a warning glare, Genny shrugged. "Hey. Just saying."

Madison exhaled with a guilty sigh. "Okay, so I agree. And I guess there's just one way to find out." She took a deep breath of courage as she stepped into the hall and went in search of the bathroom.

Genesis crowded behind her for moral support.

The room still reeked of bleach. The heavy smell of sanitation was almost overpowering.

"So I guess this is where they found her?" Genny murmured. She tried not to imagine the poor woman, lying prostrate beside the commode on the cold tiled floor.

They wandered around the spacious bathroom, each poking through a different area. It was an old bathroom in an old house. Instead of built-in cabinetry, it featured a wall sink and a decorative skirt to hide the plumbing. Storage was a freestanding cabinet and a wooden table in the corner. The table was outfitted with a skirt to match the one at the sink.

"Looks like Miss Gloria was into natural herbs," Genny mused, seeing an array of jars and bottles with handwritten labels. "Look at all of these. White Oak. Raspberry Leaf. Slippery Elm. Agrimony. Comfrey. Cayenne."

"Remember? Carson said she could kill a cactus but had recently gotten into the healing power of plants. I heard the same thing around town and down at the pharmacy. Mrs. Shubert said she hardly came in at all anymore, now that she was into natural healing."

Genny studied a jar of dried leaves. "Wonder if she buys her herbs from Myrna Lewis?"

"Why Myrna?"

"Didn't you know? Myrna started up a business. She does yards now, and started cultivating and selling her own flowers and herbs. I heard business was so good she hired part-time help."

"Huh. I had no idea." Madison shrugged as she made a learn-something-new-everyday face and turned back to her snooping.

"I've never heard of some of these herbs. Like Marshmallow Root. Wonder what all these were for?"

Madison glanced around the bathroom, her eyes darting back to the commode. "Given the circumstances of her death, maybe constipation?" she suggested timidly.

A smile quirked the side of Genny's mouth, but she was determined not to laugh. "Maybe so," she said. She leaned down to peek beneath the skirt. "Oh, my."

"What is it?"

"Uhm, her supply."

"Of alcohol?" Madison squeaked. "This is where she kept her stash of liquor?" Yet on second thought, it would make sense. Few people would think to look in a bathroom for booze.

"Not alcohol." Genny pulled the curtain aside so her friend had a clear view to the shelf below. Bottles of liquid, at least a half dozen in all, were lined up in neat rows.

"Are those what I think they are?" Madison asked with rounded eyes.

"That depends. Do you think these are disposable enema bottles?"

"Yes."

"Then, yes, they're what you think they are. But it looks like she refilled them with her own solution." Genny's lips curled in distaste and she dropped the curtain, dusting her fingers as if tainted.

"Maybe it's some sort of herbal remedy."

"Maybe. But anyone needing that many enemas has a serious medical condition."

Madison made a face. "According to Molly Schubert, enema sales have dropped dramatically since Miss Gloria started using her herb remedies. They had to run a special, in fact, to get rid of back stock. Apparently she kept them in business, at least on that front. And in case you are wondering, she preferred the up-close-and-personal method over laxatives. Too unpredictable, she claimed."

"Believe me, I was *not* wondering. In fact, this definitely falls under the 'more information than I ever wanted to know' category." Genesis placed her hands over her ears, even though the damage had already been done.

"You and I might find this all rather amusing, even if in a morbid sort of way, but you would be surprised how many people knew that Gloria suffered from frequent bouts of constipation. Apparently there are certain people, particularly within her age bracket, that feel discussing bowel habits is a perfectly acceptable topic of conversation. Much to my dismay, at least four of those people went into detail, one of them quite graphically, I might add, about how they suffer from the malady far worse than our friend Gloria."

"All righty then." Taking a moment to rid herself of the mental images that dared peep into her head, Genny winced. "I can see life as a private investigator must be full of glamorous insights such as this."

"You would be amazed."

When Genny would have scurried from the room, Madison stopped her. "Wait a minute. All those bottles don't make sense."

"What do you mean?"

"According to the death report, she died after giving herself a 'large-capacity' enema, the kind with a bag. So why all the bottles?"

Genny threw up her hands in a gesture of innocence. "Don't ask me. I eat plenty of bran and fiber. So in case *you're* wondering, I don't need these things."

After Genny slipped from the room, Madison lingered long enough to snap a few pictures with her phone. She photographed the neatly aligned bottles and the names of the herbs. After looking for hidden alcohol, she searched the medicine cabinet for anything that may have pointed to depression or a serious medical condition. By all indications, and the lack of prescribed medications, Gloria Jeffers was quite healthy for a woman her age. Like the druggist said, she seemed to rely upon all-natural herbal remedies.

"Are you finding anything?" Madison asked as she joined Genny in the bedroom.

"Nothing. And if Carson ever stayed over, he didn't leave anything behind. No clothes, no hairbrush, not even a stray sock. And there was only one toothbrush in the bathroom."

Madison absently fingered the dresser. "I can't get a feel for their relationship. Do you think they were lovers, or just friends?"

Genny looked surprised at the question. "I don't know," she admitted with a frown. "I guess I just assumed they were lovers, even though they didn't seem to be a matched set, so to speak. Carson is so suave and sophisticated, and she was so..." She spread her hand wide, indicating the mundane room. The bedspread was from a different decade, as was the color scheme. While neat and orderly, the style of the house was outdated and worn. Stagnant. And a huge contrast from Carson Elliot's elegant home.

"I know opposites attract, but I just don't get the feeling they were intimately involved. If they were, he certainly bounced back fast, judging by the interest he is showing in you. And there's no need to blush. It's obvious he's attracted to you."

"There is a huge gap in our ages," Genny pointed out.

"I keep telling you, age doesn't matter. You and Cutter are the perfect example." When Genny would have protested, and loudly so, Madison waved her comments aside. "And no matter what their actual ages were, I still say Miss Gloria just *seemed* so much older than Carson."

Letting the comments about her and the fire chief slide, Genny stuck to the topic at hand. "They say alcohol ages you. Maybe she wasn't as old as she looked."

"And that's another thing. We haven't found a single drop of alcohol! If she drank herself into a stupor and died, wouldn't there be some sign of a drinking problem?"

"Maybe it's what you said. Someone—like whoever cleaned out her refrigerator—threw out all the liquor."

"Maybe," Madison mused. "But if they did, they searched the place from top to bottom and got rid of it all. Because we haven't found a drop."

"So here's the four thousand dollar question. If Miss Gloria was a teetotaler like Carson claims, how did she get so much alcohol into her bloodstream?"

Eyes narrowed in thought, Madison shook her head. "I have no idea. But I keep thinking the answer might just be in her latest 'theory' and that file I found. Some way or another, I have to find out more about those fires."

7

"Why the snacks?" Bethani asked as she watched her mother arrange chips around a bowl of artichoke dip.

"I invited Aunt Genny over to watch the show with us tonight."

The teen eyed the decorative platter that was considered fashionable a decade or two before her birth. "You don't usually break out Granny Bert's best plastic. What's the occasion?" A look of suspicion crossed her face. "Is Mr. de coming?"

"No, he's out of town again for another law convention." She hoped she did not sound as despondent as she felt. "But I did invite Cutter to join us tonight."

Bethani stared at her mother. "Cutter?" she squealed. "Cutter Montgomery is coming *here*, to our house?"

Madison was confused by the reaction. "Yes, he's coming here, to our house."

"And you're just now *telling* me?" the teen wailed. Her hands flew up to her long blond tresses. "I have to wash my hair! The show starts in a little over an hour, and I don't have a thing to wear! Mom, why didn't you *tell* me he was coming over tonight?"

"Because I just asked him today, when I saw him at *New Beginnings*. What is wrong with you? What does Cutter have to do with your hair and wardrobe?"

"Mo—om! He's the hottest guy in the entire two towns combined. The entire county. Maybe the state. He's like a movie star and a rock legend, all rolled up in one." She patted her head, as if searching for unseen curlers. "I don't have time to wash my hair," she fretted. "I've got to see if my Miss Me jeans are clean. And I've got to call Meg. She can come, too, can't she, Mom? What about Kaci? She has a huge crush on Cutter. Oh my gosh, just wait until my friends hear about this!"

"Megan is always welcome here, but let's keep it to just us, okay? Cutter's coming over to help me with a potential case, not to be ogled by a bunch of admirers."

"Like that doesn't happen to him every single day," the teen scoffed, but she let the protest die. She clapped her hands together in excitement. "Oh my gosh, I can't believe he's coming to *our* house!"

As Bethani flew off in a flurry of activity, Maddy shook her head and laughed. She saw Cutter on a regular basis and considered him within her circle of friends. It never occurred to her that the twins did not know him half as well and were seldom included in their visits.

A short time later, Genny knocked on the front door. Stepping inside, she called out, "Yoo-hoo, we're here."

Madison heard Bethani's excited squeal from the bedroom.

"I'm in the kitchen," Madison called back. "Make yourself at home. I'll be right out."

HOME AGAIN: STARTING OVER

By the time she carried out the tray of refreshments, Genny and Cutter were seated on the couch, engaged in a good-natured argument about baseball.

"There's no way the Rangers are going to win the series. The Astros will take them in two games," Genesis predicted.

"Wanna bet?"

"Sure do."

"Fine. You're on. If there is a third game, you and I are going. Your treat."

"Done." Genny extended her hand to shake on it. "Not that I have to worry about it, though, because there won't be a third game."

Cutter bumped his shoulder into hers, grinning mischievously. "*When* we go to the game, you have to buy me a hot dog. And popcorn. A great big buttery tub of it."

"What if there isn't a third game? What do I get?"

He considered it for a moment. "I'll take you to the movies," he decided. "And I'll buy you a hot dog and a big, buttery popcorn."

"I'll start scouting out movies, because we'll be going to the theater, not the ballpark."

Madison broke into their banter. "Okay, you two. You sound like Bethani and Blake."

Cutter grinned and bumped Genny's shoulder again. "She started it," he imitated a whine. While Madison pretended to scowl, he asked, "So what's up?"

Madison turned her focus to the man perched alongside her best friend. "I have a few questions I'd like to ask you, if you don't mind."

Cutter nodded his concurrence. "Shoot."

"To begin with, what can you tell me about a fire out at Jerry Don Peavey's place about four years ago?"

The fireman had traded his standard cowboy hat for a ball cap tonight. The Texas Rangers logo had sparked the point of contention between him and Genny moments ago. As he pushed the bill upward, he rubbed his forehead in thought. "Yeah, I think I remember that. It was late in the year, around Thanksgiving. A deer hunter spotted a small fire while he was on the stand. By the time he called it in and we responded, it had spread over the entire pasture. I think Peavey lost his barn." As the details slowly came to mind, Cutter nodded. "Yeah, I remember now. The barn wasn't a total loss, but he had a heck of a time getting his money from the insurance company. He had the whole thing insured for three times as much as it was worth, and they balked about the payout. Said it wasn't worth it. He had to get the bank involved and prove he had mortgaged it for the same amount."

"Do you know if they ever came to a resolution?"

"I'm not sure. I do know the barn he re-built in its place wasn't nearly as big."

"What about a fire the next year at *Montelongo's*?"

"That one I remember. A grease fire started in the kitchen. We contained it before it spread to the front of the restaurant, but it did a lot of smoke damage. They were closed for several days." He looked down at Genny. "That was before you opened. I almost starved to death that week."

"Have you ever thought of learning to cook?" the blonde beside him suggested.

"I can cook," he informed her. "I simply prefer to keep the local eateries in business."

Madison ignored their repartee. The file noted personal liability insurance. Perhaps Cutter knew about that, as well.

"Do you happen to know if anyone was hurt during the fire?" she asked.

"Bernie Havlicek claimed to be. He worked there at the time. In fact, he was the one to start the fire. He claimed to burn his hand, but I saw him a few days later and he was feeling no pain, if you get my drift. I think faking an injury was his way of covering up his own negligence."

"By calling attention to himself? That doesn't sound too smart," Genesis frowned.

"This is Bernie we're talking about. He doesn't believe in hard work. If there's an easy way to make a dollar, he's the first in line. He probably figured there was more money in an insurance claim than in getting his job back, once they reopened."

"I never pegged him for the food industry type."

"As far as I know, that was his one and only stab at being a cook. He had only worked there a couple of weeks when the accident happened."

"Hmm," Madison said thoughtfully. "I don't suppose you would know anything about Ray Sams, losing his RV just across the county line?" Madison asked.

"Sure. That sucker went up like a roman candle. He had an auxiliary fuel tank attached to it, full of gasoline. After the initial explosion, the whole thing melted like a cheap candle. It was one of those high-dollar jobs, too, with all the slide outs and upgrades. I hope he had it insured, because it was a total loss and then some."

"What causes a fire like that?"

Cutter shrugged. "Could be anything. An electrical short, faulty wiring, someone tossing out a cigarette, leaving an appliance turned on inside..."

Genesis scooped a tortilla chip into the cheesy dip concoction on the coffee table. "Mmm, this is delicious."

"Thanks. It's your recipe," Madison grinned.

"In that case, I'll have one," Cutter said. When he opened his mouth expectantly, Genny grunted in objection. She complied by stuffing a loaded chip inside and deliberately smearing some of the dip around his lips. He made a face and swiped it away with his thumb.

"Serves you right for being lazy," she muttered.

Madison watched their interaction with amusement. They weren't exactly flirting, but they seemed completely comfortable with one another. Somewhere along the way, there had been a subtle shift in their relationship. She made a mental note to ask Genny about it later.

Cutter got the next chip himself. "Why all the questions about old fires?"

"It may be nothing. But I ran across some information," she chose her words carefully, "that I think warrants a closer look. I'm not at liberty to say much, but I hope you'll indulge me and tell me what you know."

"Sure, anything to help." He ate a third helping. "This is really good."

"Do you happen to remember a chimney fire at William Shank's house? I'm guessing that must be Miss Wanda's late husband?"

"Oh, she's not a widow," Cutter corrected her. "They got a divorce a few years ago, after being married for over fifty years."

"Why would you stay married to someone for that long and then all of a sudden get a divorce? That doesn't even make sense," Genny commented.

"Could have something to do with finding him in bed with another woman."

"You have got to be kidding!"

"Nope. Miss Wanda caught them together, walked into the living room, took a shotgun down from the gun case, and walked back in the bedroom without saying a word. Pearl Simpson ran out of the house, butt naked, waving her hands in the air and screaming at the top of her lungs."

They all laughed at the mental image of the woman running down the street without any clothes. According to Blake, simply seeing Wanda Shanks in her bathing suit while doing granny aerobics was enough to scar his young eyes forever. Madison could not imagine the trauma of him seeing Pearl Simpson, already at least seventy at the time of the incident, in all her wrinkled glory.

When their laughter had settled down, Madison returned to her line of questioning. "So was the chimney fire before or after the divorce? I think it may have been about five years ago."

"Before, because it was the house Miss Wanda still lives in. She has a gas insert now. I check it out for her, every fall."

"Are you thinking this is insurance fraud?" Genesis prodded.

"Honestly, I don't know what I'm thinking," Madison admitted. "But something feels off."

"You should always trust your instincts," Cutter advised.

"There was another one. Carson Elliot."

Genny's eyes flew to her friend. "*Our* Carson?" she asked, clearly shocked. This was the first she had heard of it.

"I would say he's definitely more *yours* than mine," Madison smirked.

A deep frown burrowed Cutter's forehead. "Wait a minute. He's that guy that teaches dance lessons."

"Yes, we know."

He looked from Madison's smug smile to Genny's flushed face. His scowl turned suspicious. "He's not some sort of old pervert, is he? Has he been giving you trouble, Genny?"

"No, no, nothing like that."

"But he did invite her to come for lessons," Maddy teased. "*Private* lessons."

"He did not!" Genny protested. She made a fluttering motion with her hands, batting the attention away from herself. "Go on with your questions, Maddy. I had no idea Carson's home burned. When was this?"

"About five years ago. It was a brand new house, too."

"Yeah, over in Riverton," Cutter said. He was slow to answer, his mind apparently still stuck on the matter of inappropriate private dance lessons. Eying Genny with skepticism, he answered Madison's original question. "They called us for backup, but it was completely engulfed by the time we got there. All we could do was keep it from spreading."

"I always hate to hear about house fires," Madison murmured. "I can't imagine losing everything you have, all in a matter of minutes."

"He was one of the luckier ones. It was a new house and he hadn't moved in yet. Total loss on the house, but at least he still had his possessions."

Genny cocked her head. "Why would a new house just burn down like that?"

Cutter shrugged, the action pulling at the seams of his pale blue western shirt. The color reflected in his chameleon eyes. "Same reasons a motor home would burn up. Any home, really."

"Do you think you could find out more about the details on any of these? Maybe from the fire inspector or something?" Maddy asked hopefully.

"I can try. I may have a few notes in my files down at the station. If the fires were in our jurisdiction, that is."

"That would be great. And I just have one last question," Madison promised.

He loaded a chip with dip and motioned for her to continue.

"I understand you were the first to respond to the 911 call on Gloria Jeffers."

In spite of himself, his nose wrinkled slightly. "That's right."

"What can you tell me about that night?"

The normally confident young man looked uncomfortable as he realigned his baseball cap. "Not a lot," he said slowly. "Confidentiality, and all that. Her friend—Carson Elliot, actually—was the one to find her."

"I understand she died of alcohol poisoning?"

"That's what they say."

"Did you see any signs of alcohol that night? Any bottles of whiskey or wine? Anything?"

His handsome face scrunched into a scowl. "Now that you mention it, no. I didn't see a single bottle."

"Do you think Carson may have moved them? Hidden the evidence, thinking he was sparing her reputation?"

"Could be," Cutter acknowledged. "You know, I've attended a lot of strange and embarrassing-situation deaths. A married man, dying of a heart attack in his mistress' bed. Car wrecks and fires when the victim isn't where they're supposed to be or is with a person they aren't supposed to be with. Overdoses that come as a complete shock because loved ones had no idea the person was a junkie. Most deaths are ugly to begin with. But that poor woman had to have suffered the most undignified death I have ever seen."

"Her friend insists she was not an alcoholic. That she didn't even drink," Madison said.

"Yet the tox screen tells a different story. From what I understand, she had astronomically large levels of alcohol in her system."

"But there were no bottles at the scene of her death," Genny pointed out.

"Again, I wasn't looking for them."

They were all silent for a long moment, contemplating the situation. Finally, Cutter stuffed a chip into his mouth, loaded another one, and handed it to Genny. "Don't make me eat all this by myself." He lightened the mood by teasing her. "Unless you think it will slow down your dance moves."

"Very funny. And I advise you to eat all you can now, before Blake gets a whiff of it."

"Isn't that the truth!" Maddy laughed. Hearing the oven buzzer go off, she unfolded her long legs and stood. "Oops, excuse me. That would be the second bowl of dip. If the girls are lucky, Blake might share with them."

"Girls?" Genny asked.

"Megan's on her way," Maddy said over her shoulder.

With a wince, Genny peeked over at Cutter. "Be warned. I have it on good authority that both girls think you are the hottest thing in Wranglers."

"They're just kids!" he cried in protest.

"So?" she shrugged. "Even kids have valid opinions."

His grin was playfully naughty. "Does that mean you agree with them?" he teased.

Color infused her face. Before she could come up with a smart denial, Cutter gave her a break. "Hey, seeing your face turn red reminds me. You've got to see this new app I have. It's hilarious."

He fished into his pocket and pulled out his cell phone. Turning it to selfie mode, he aligned the screen with his face and tapped. "Look at this." Another tap distorted his image into an elongated version that bore little resemblance to his handsome face.

"Oh, that's awful!" Genny hooted with laughter.

"Look at this one. It gives me big red spots."

"You look like you have a case of giant chicken pox!"

"Think that's funny? Look at this one." His image puffed and swelled, his jaws drooping with the visual weight. "Here, let's do you. Open your mouth and see what happens."

They played on the phone, howling with mirth at the images that appeared on the screen. Madison could hear them as she took the dip from the oven.

"What in the world is going on in there?" Granny Bert asked as she wandered into the kitchen.

"Cutter and Genny are playing on their phones. They sound like a couple of teenagers, don't they?"

"I hate to say it, but Cutter laughs like a girl."

Madison shrugged. "It's good to know he has at least one fault. According to most every female in town, he's near perfect."

Granny Bert peered through the opened doorway of the kitchen and the living room beyond. Even with a dining room between them, she had a clear view of the couch and the two people sitting on it, heads bent close as they took selfies together and broke out in unrestrained laughter. Through peals of merriment, Genny wiped tears from her eyes.

Granny Bert turned back to Madison in confusion. She cocked her gray head toward the living room. "When did that happen?"

Madison understood the question. "I don't think they even know that it has."

"Humph," her grandmother snorted. "They need to get a mirror." Another gale of laughter floated through the rooms. Granny saw Cutter lay his cheek against Genny's and snap a photo. "And a room."

"Psst. Mom."

Bethani's loud whisper drew their attention. She stood at the edge of the hallway, striking a pose in her stylish ripped jeans and cute shirt. "Does this look okay?"

"You look beautiful, sweetheart," Madison assured the teen.

"I'm not overdressed, am I?" she worried.

"Your jeans look like they got caught in a weed-eater," Granny Bert harrumphed. "You're not overdressed to take the trash out."

"These jeans are the latest style," the teen protested.

Madison averted her face from her daughter. "She wants to make a good impression on our company," she told her grandmother, sending a silent code through her raised eyebrows.

Granny Bert glanced back at the cozy couple on the couch. They still giggled in glee, lost in the camera and their own little world.

"I'm not sure he'll notice."

8

When the show was over and their company gone, Granny Bert helped Madison with cleanup.

"I am plumb disgusted with myself," the older woman proclaimed as she wiped the counter clean.

"Why is that?" Maddy asked.

"I must be slipping. I thought I had my finger on the pulse of this community, but here I've missed the hottest romance of all! I guess I was so focused on you and Brash, I completely missed what was happening with your best friend. And right beneath my nose." She shook her head in self-deprecation. "I'm definitely losing my edge."

"Don't be so hard on yourself, Granny. Nothing has actually happened between them. Genny thinks she's too old for him. The truth is, he's older than he looks. When she thought he was only twenty-five or so, she looked at it as a harmless crush. Finding out he's thirty-one and only eight years younger than herself has her freaked out."

Granny Bert gave a wise shake of her gray head. "No, no. Eight years is just the right age span. Men aren't as tough as us women. Their bodies wear out long before ours do, even without childbirth. It's best to get a younger man that will see you through your golden years." Seeing the frown pop out on her granddaughter's forehead, she was quick to amend, "Brash might be the exception. He's a fine specimen of man and healthy as a horse. Don't get ideas about replacing him with a younger model. But Genny? She should latch onto that Montgomery boy with both hands."

"I'll be sure to pass along the message."

"You do that. I don't want her to face the same heartache I did."

Madison was sympathetic to her plight. "I know you've been lonely since Grandpa died. Even though you stay busy, I know it's not the same."

"I miss that man every day. There wasn't a better man on God's green earth than Joe Cessna, and I loved him with every fiber of my being. But your grandfather was not my first love."

Madison's head snapped up from the dish she washed. "What? You had a sweetheart before Grandpa Joe? Why haven't I ever heard this before?"

"Well, for one thing, your grandfather was powerful jealous, and he didn't like me talking about other men. And just for the record, I had several fellas before Joe. But only one that I loved."

"Really? Who was it? Anyone I know?"

Granny shook her head. A note of sorrow slipped into her voice. "He left town when I broke it off. You see, he was younger than me. Shorter, too. I had some foolish notion that the man was supposed to be the big, tall, elder of a couple. A few of my friends teased me about dating a little boy, and I was fool enough to listen. It wasn't until he was gone that

I realized how stupid I was. He was a fine young man, but I judged him by numbers. I let a ruler and a calendar convince me he wasn't worthy of my love. Stupidest thing I ever did."

"But... you loved Grandpa Joe!" Madison protested. "You were happy with him."

"Of course I was. The smartest thing I ever did was learn from my mistakes. It took awhile, but I pieced my heart back together and gave it to your grandfather, cracks and all. He made it whole again. I had fifty-three wonderful years and three sons with that man. But he was almost ten years older than me, and I've been a widow now for eight years. Genesis would be wise to marry a man younger than her. It will save her some heartache and lonely years later on."

Madison protested. "I don't know about marriage. But it definitely looks like some sort of relationship is in the making."

Granny Bert offered one of her characteristic snorts. "Neither one of you girls are getting any younger. If it's not already, marriage should be on both your minds!"

Madison nibbled on her lower lip. "You know," she murmured aloud, "I think I might sympathize with Bethani a little more than I did. I always thought of you and Grandpa Joe as having the ultimate marriage, the ultimate love. Knowing you loved someone else makes me feel a little queasy. It—It sort of shakes my foundation, you know?" She sucked in her breath, touching a hand to her stomach. "I think that must be how Beth feels. She thought Gray and I had the perfect marriage. Seeing me with Brash must make her feel the same way." It was a hard realization. Her heart felt as uneasy as her stomach.

Bertha Hamilton Cessna shook a crooked finger in her granddaughter's face and spoke sternly. "Don't think for one minute that I didn't love my Joe. I doted on that man. I loved him completely, with my whole heart and soul. Not once did I think of another man when I was with your grandfather. Not once did I compare the two or think of what might have been. Not once did I regret the way my life turned out. But the heart is an amazing thing. It's big enough to love more than just one person. Look at how much you love each of your children. What you feel for one doesn't take away from the other. It multiplies your love. It's a wise woman who knows that and lets herself love again."

Madison dropped her eyes. "You're telling me not to feel guilty for loving Brash."

"Exactly. Even if Gray hadn't messed up and ruined your marriage long before he died last fall, you have every right to get on with your life. You deserve to be happy. You deserve to find love again. And there aren't many men as fine and decent as Brash deCordova."

A dreamy smile lit Madison's face. "He wants to take the kids fishing. He even offered to take Blake hunting. How wonderful is that?"

Granny Bert cackled with glee. "I knew the two of you were more serious than you've been letting on! Has he popped the question yet?"

"Granny! Of course not! We're not even officially dating."

"What's that got to do with anything? The whole concept of dating is just a getting-to-know-you-better period. When you find the right person and know it, you can skip the audition and move right on to the main show. Your grandfather proposed to me on our second date."

"I bet you didn't accept that quickly though, did you?"

Her grandmother's smile was sly. "No, but not because I wasn't keen on the idea. I wanted to make him sweat it out a little. No need in letting a man get all cocky, right from the get go."

Maddy laughed, imagining the heartache her grandmother must have dished out to any man brave enough to trust her with his heart. She was thankful Joe Cessna was one of those men, even if he was not the first.

"But we weren't talking about me," Granny Bert said, getting back on topic. "We were talking about Genny and Cutter, and how I completely missed this one. How can I be your partner if I'm losing my edge?"

Madison was almost afraid to ask. "My partner?"

Again, Granny's gray head bobbed up and down. "Sure. You're working for that private investigator now. You said yourself, after a year you can even get your own license. Either way, I figure you need me as a backup. We'll make a great team, you and me. Beauty and brains. And don't worry, you have plenty to offer to the partnership, as well." She patted her granddaughter's hand.

Madison snorted at the obvious slight. "Thanks a lot!"

"But this worries me, not seeing their little romance brewing right under my nose."

Seeing how the older woman truly did look troubled, Maddy spoke on a whim. "Okay, so I'll give you the chance to redeem yourself. I'm investigating something. Maybe you can shed some light on it."

Granny Bert rubbed her hands together with exuberance. "Hot dog, we've got a case!"

"*I* have a case," Maddy corrected. "But I would appreciate your input."

"Is this about the scam at the Gold and Silver Exchange?"

"What? No. I don't even know what you're talking about."

"The way Janet McSwain 'misplaced' her favorite recliner?" Madison frowned in confusion. How did a person misplace a chair that size? "No."

"The illegal cock fights still floating around town? You can tell your boyfriend he might want to show up at Billy Blackburn's this Saturday night if he wants to catch them in the act."

"How do you— Never mind. No, that's not it."

"That new car Howie Morse is driving, even though he lost his life savings on his last trip to Shreveport and the check he wrote for twenty dollars for the offering plate last Sunday bounced like a rubber ball?"

Madison stared at her grandmother. "And you worry you're slipping? I bet you even know who Barry Redmond has been messing around with."

The older woman never batted an eye. "Angie Jones thinks she'll be wife number five. Then again, so does Marla Hedrick. But I'm guessing neither one of them knows about his late-night visits to the adult video store over in Riverton and the pretty little woman who runs it."

Madison shook her head in a mixture of horror and awe. "You are amazing. And that is not necessarily a compliment. But never mind the town gossip. I want to ask you about some fires that happened in the area over the last five or six years."

"I had nothing to do with Ray Sams' motor home going up in smoke," her grandmother was quick to say. "We had a friendly competition going on is all. Nothing worth setting a fire over."

"What are you talking about?" Madison cried.

Her grandmother frowned. "That's not the fire you were asking about?"

"Actually, it is one of them, but what did you have to do with it?"

"Nothing! That's what I'm trying to tell you."

"What are you—" Madison stopped herself mid-sentence, throwing up her hands. "You know what? Never mind. Let's just skip this one. Tell me what you know about a kitchen fire over at *Montelongo's*."

"For some fool reason, Tomas and Maria hired that no-count Bernie Havlicek to work in the restaurant. He's about as useful as a screen door on a submarine. He hadn't been there a good two weeks before he set fire to the kitchen. Claimed he burned his hand, but I figure he did that cooking up a batch of meth. Tried to sue and get some money out of the whole sorry mess."

"Was he successful?"

"They settled out of court. Tomas had to hock the restaurant and get a loan, just to pay off that lazy rascal."

"Hmm." Madison filed away the information in her mind. "What do you know about Jerry Don Peavey's barn burning down?"

"Just that he had it insured for more than it was worth. Might have been a smart move, except that the bank gobbled up most of the money to satisfy his mortgage. He was lucky to get out with enough to rebuild, even if it was half the size of his old one."

"What about a chimney fire over at Miss Wanda's? Apparently, it was when she was still married."

"That sorry, no-good-for-nothing, two-timing buzzard she was married to blamed near burned their house down," her grandmother grumbled. "Too lazy to clean out their fireplace.

Too cheap to hire a chimney sweep. The whole mess caught fire, burned part of their roof and smoked up the entire house. Good thing they were home, or the whole thing would have burned down."

"Did they have problems getting their insurance to pay?"

"Only because they had the bank listed as the first payee, and Willie had fallen behind on payments. They had to get Asa Bryant's grandson to sort it all out. He took over the law practice after his grandpa died."

"Yes, I've been doing some work for him recently, remember?"

"That's right, so you are. Since Gloria up and died so suddenly, it kindly left him in a pickle, didn't it? Well, it should all be in the files. You can read up on it. But by the time it was all said and done, they barely had enough to fix the roof and buy one of those gas inserts. Not one of those nice, full-size ones, either. Just a little rinky-dink version, but Wanda uses it for her main heat source. If it gets really cold, down into the twenties for a few days at a time, she has to crank up space heaters all around the house."

Madison corrected the other woman's misconception. "I can't read other people's files, Granny. It would be unethical."

She should have kept her mouth shut. Granny Bert's knowing gaze was cunning. "So that's what this is all about. You came fishing with me, because you can't look at the files. Not with a clear conscience, anyway."

"Maybe," she hedged.

"I think it's more than any maybe," Granny Bert said on a harrumph. "I'll bet Newly McArdle wasn't on your list, was he?"

"No. Why would he be?"

"Because he had a fire, too. But he wasn't represented by a lawyer or by an insurance company. Went belly up after his repair service burned to the ground."

"Where was this?" Madison questioned.

"Over on Beacon Street in Naomi. That was several years ago, right where the taxidermist is today."

"You're right, that wasn't on my list." Madison mulled the information over in her head, trying to see a connection between the fires. Nothing came to mind.

"Granny? You mentioned Miss Gloria. How well did you know her?"

Her grandmother snorted. "Apparently, not as well as I thought! I had no idea she was a souse. I always took her for a teetotaler."

Her grandmother's candor caused her to grimace. "That's not a very nice way to speak of the dead."

"The truth ain't always pretty, girl. I don't know how she managed to keep her drinking a secret all these years, but the truth came out in the end." She snickered at her own unintentional joke. "Hey, that was a pretty good one, huh? It came out in the end!"

"Granny, you're incorrigible!" Madison tried her best to keep a stern look on her face, but a smile wiggled through.

Her grandmother made several remarks, some of them rather crude. And most, Madison had to admit, were also quite funny. Before she succumbed to outright laughter and further encouraged the old woman's antics, Madison pleaded exhaustion and said goodnight.

As she reached the doorway, Granny Bert said, "Tell Brash I said hello."

Madison whirled around and saw her grandmother's smirk. She hadn't missed their romance, for sure. Rather than argue, Maddy just smiled. "Will do. G'night."

9

"Tell me again. What is it we're looking for?" Genny asked as she and Madison walked into the records room at the county courthouse.

They were surrounded by filing cabinets and bookcases, every one of them stuffed to overflowing with the official records of River County. Madison's head spun with the enormity of their mission.

"Anything and everything we can find connected to the names and businesses on this paper. Miss Gloria had discovered something that tied them together. Look for anything you can and we'll see what pops."

Genesis grinned at her friend. "Look at you, already talking like a real private eye."

Madison wrinkled her nose at her friend's teasing. "I watch a lot of detective shows."

"Not tonight, you won't. Our eyes will be permanently crossed," Genny predicted, gaping at all the filing cabinets before them. "If we survive this day, you owe me dinner and a couple of margaritas at *Montelongo's*."

"It's a deal," Madison readily agreed. "I know this isn't how you wanted to spend your day off."

"Hey, jury duty was canceled, so I'm all yours." Genny flashed her dimpled smile. "Torture me as you will."

"Great. You take the first two names on the list, I'll take the next two. First one through gets the last name."

"I'm sure you've been thinking what I've been thinking. If Carson Elliot is right and Miss Gloria's death wasn't an accident..."

Madison nodded and finished her friend's thought, "... then maybe she was on to something, and someone wanted to keep her silent." She looked pointedly at all the filing cabinets. "But first, we have to figure out what that something was."

They worked in silence most of the morning. Switching between computerized records, microfiche film, and paper files, Madison and Genny looked for all public records pertaining to their list of names. A few other people drifted in and out of the room, but for the most part, the two had the space to themselves.

"Is this anything?" Genesis asked around noon. "After the fire at *Montelongo's*, the State Fire Marshal fined the company that serviced their suppression system. They protested, insisting the equipment had been tampered with."

"I don't know. Who was the company?"

"*A+ Fire Systems* out of Giddings. They actually gave me a bid when I opened, but I went with someone else."

"Jot their name down. We can see if there's anything else on them."

"You do realize this list is getting longer, not shorter."

"I know, but what choice do we have? We need to see who all the players are so we can get an overall picture of the situation."

"I see the situation. It's one big mess."

Madison blew out a sigh. "I hate to say it, but I think I agree." She looked around at the scattered files and multiple legal pads, scrawled with notes and names and possible leads. Her frustration mounted. "Maybe we're chasing a dead end here. Maybe there was never a case to begin with. Miss Gloria may have just been experimenting with a new filing system. Who knows? I haven't figured out her rationale for most of her other filings, either. Maybe this is all for naught."

"Or maybe not."

Madison perked up when she heard the note of excitement in her friend's voice. "You found something?"

"Possibly. I went to the website for *A+ Fire Systems*. They specialize in restaurant equipment and mobile food trucks. Which led to their newest endeavor, pairing up with a manufacturer to create a revolutionary new vent system, currently installed only in food trucks and upper-end motor homes, listed here by brand name." She looked up from her computer screen with a triumphant air. "Ray Sams had one of these brands."

"So we have our first connection. At least two of our fire victims have ties to *A+ Fire Systems*."

"I could call them, pretend I'm not happy with the system I have. I could ask about their different models and get the conversation flowing where we want it. When we go to *Montelongo's* tonight, I'll find out what kind they have."

"Maybe we could start with that, and work our way around to the fire itself. Until I know there's something concrete going on, I hate to question the victims outright."

"That's the second time you've called them victims. You suspect arson, don't you?"

Madison's shrug was vague. "You can be the victim of a fire, without arson being involved."

"True. Have you talked to Shawn Bryant about any of this? Maybe he knows why the files were together."

"No. I don't want him to think I've been snooping around, doing something unethical. He might fire me, or give me a bad recommendation."

"But without looking into those files, we don't even know which insurance companies were involved."

"That's on the docket, so to speak, for this afternoon." Madison waved a hand at the massive filing system toward the back of the room. "We'll be searching through court records, seeing which cases were on the court room docket for these dates. If they went to trial, they are a matter of public record."

Genny gave her best friend an exaggerated glare. "Did I say you're buying a *couple* of margaritas tonight? This is quickly becoming a three-margarita day."

Madison just laughed. "All in all, I'd say you're pretty cheap labor. That was a good lead you found about the fire extinguishers. Well worth three margaritas."

Tomas Montelongo gladly spoke with them about his experience with *A+ Fire Systems*.

"I was very pleased with the work they did," the restaurant owner acknowledged. "I don't know what went wrong. We had just been serviced a few days before the fire. Everything checked out fine. The fire department said a wire was unhooked, but *A+* insisted it was impossible. They claimed someone had to have tampered with it, but who would do such a thing? My insurance company refused to pay when one of my employees filed a suit against me. It was a big mess. I had to get the lawyers involved and take out a huge mortgage before it was all over."

"Oh, goodness," Genny murmured in sympathy. In truth, she did empathize with the man's plight. She could very well be in the same situation herself one day. "Do you remember the name of the technician who came out? Maybe I should ask for someone else, just in case he was at fault."

"His name is Tiny. But it's a funny. In truth, he's a big, huge, old German guy." He held out both arms in a circle to indicate the other man's girth.

"That should be easy to remember."

"And maybe you should ask about the insurance carrier, as well," Madison suggested. "You certainly don't want to use the same one."

He was quick to supply the answer. "Magnus. Magnus Insurance. Whatever you do, steer clear of them. They do not honor their claims."

"So what actually happened?" Genesis asked. "I heard you were closed for several days."

"Even one day would have been too long. Three almost put us out of business." His face turned dark. "At a weak moment, my Maria hired that fool Bernie Havlicek. He was nothing but trouble. Lazy as a hound dog. He was already on probation when he started the fire. He claimed his sleeve caught fire while he was frying, but other workers told a different story. No matter, he flung his coat off and the fire spread. Then the idiot tried to put it out with water. You know what happened then." He spread his arms to mimic a mushroom effect. "Then, to top it all off, he had the nerve to sue me. Said we had unsafe work conditions!" Even though Tomas Montelongo spoke excellent English, he slipped into his native tongue to unleash a string of angry curse words. Both women knew just enough Spanish to pick up on the theme of his rant.

After a few more questions, Genesis smiled at the fellow restaurant owner. "Thank you for taking the time to speak with us. You've been very helpful."

"It has been my pleasure. And do not even think of paying. Your meal is on the house."

"Oh no, we couldn't let you do that," Madison protested. "I'm treating Genny tonight, for helping me with a project I'm working on."

"The meal is paid for," he insisted. "You can buy the drinks."

"Very well. Thank you, then, for your generosity."

"Yes, Tomas, thank you so much," Genny agreed.

"It is my pleasure. Shall I send another round of margaritas?"

"Oh, yes. And make mine a *grande* this time." Genny's eyes twinkled with mischief. If Madison was only paying for drinks, she might as well splurge.

Madison wasted no time in researching Magnus Insurance. It came as no real surprise to discover they had numerous complaints against them and had been fined several times. But with none of their indiscretions significant enough to have their license pulled, the company was still in business.

It took half a day of searching, but Madison finally unearthed another link. Magnus was a subsidiary of a larger, more prominent insurance company. Madison was familiar with Omega Insurance, even without the link to Jerry Don Peavey. She often did temp work for their agent in the area.

It seemed the perfect time to drop in on her associate.

While Madison had no qualms approaching the namesake of the Dean Lewis Insurance Company, his wife was a different story. Madison did not care for the opinionated and bitter woman. It amazed her how a polite, affable man such as Dean could be shackled to a mean, spiteful woman such as Myrna. If it were up to his wife, their agency would never use *In a Pinch* again, but Dean was pleased with the work Madison did and insisted on calling her each time they were, indeed, in a pinch.

Myrna Lewis fancied herself something of a horticultural expert. Her yard was her pride and joy. Woe be to anyone, man or beast, who dared to trample it. Shortly after coming to town, Madison and Bethani had witnessed her wrath firsthand when a 4-H show goat escaped its lead rope and dined upon her prized cabbage roses. Bethani filmed the entire escapade on her phone, including the part when Myrna came flying out of her house with a broom. The video went viral, Bethani became a hero to the very kids she mocked, and Myrna confronted the teen in a showdown that brought out Madison's momma-bear instincts.

It was their first confrontation, but hardly their last. The worst had been when Madison uncovered the fact that Myrna's sister, Darla Mullins, led a secret life. Myrna still held Madison responsible for Darla's death, even though her claims were preposterous. Even Darla's son knew the truth. Derron not only worked for Madison, but he was also her friend.

Scouting to see if the coast was clear, Madison drove past the Lewis residence en route to the insurance agency. Sure enough, Myrna was at home. And outside.

Locals often talked about Myrna's method of gardening, but this was the first time Madison witnessed it for herself. Had she been thinking straight, Maddy would have pulled out her camera and snapped a few pictures to share with Bethani, but the sight before her was so outrageous that all she could do was stare in astonishment. Her foot slipped from the gas pedal and the car rolled to a stop as she ogled the woman clipping her yard by hand.

Part of the hilarity was the woman, herself. Myrna Lewis had the misfortune of having no discernible shape. She was like one solid chunk. A block with awkward arms and short, chubby legs, and topped by a head. No neck. No visible breasts. No waist. And no fashion sense, whatsoever.

Beside Myrna, Madison felt like a glamorous model. Madison, whose wardrobe still left much to be desired, even after a much-needed shopping trip with Derron. After weeks of badgering from her fashion-conscious friend, she had agreed to let him select a handful of new outfits for her. She wore one of them today. Khaki walking shorts, stylish sandals, cream scooped-neck tee, topped by a plaid shirt that doubled as a jacket. Muted blues and greens crisscrossed over a khaki background to pull her casual and stylish look together.

In contrast, Myrna wore mustard-colored knit shorts that did nothing for her squat figure. Nor did the garish orange and black athletic shoes and cuffed black socks against her pale skin. Her t-shirt was red, oversized, and at odds with the rest of her outfit. Mid-way down her body, presumably near her waist, was her ever-present fanny pack, this one specifically geared for gardening.

But the most amusing part of the spectacle was the position from which Myrna clipped her flowerbed. She lay upon the bed of grass, using shears and a measuring tape to perfect the cut. When she was satisfied with one section, she rolled to another.

Madison watched in fascination as Myrna reached around into her fanny pack and whipped out a pair of ordinary household scissors. She worked on a troublesome spot, trimming the edges of the flowerbed to an acceptable height. She measured twice, just to be certain. Then she was rolling again, a solid mass of color contradictions and sharp utensils.

"Something is so wrong with this scene," Madison muttered aloud. She shook her head in wonderment.

A jogger happened down the street at that moment. Myrna began waving her arms in warning, long before the man reached her. "Stay away from my grass!" she bellowed. "Don't you dare step foot on my lawn!"

The runner kept coming, paying her no heed. Ear plug connections dangled from either side of his flushed face, blocking the sound of the woman's bitter rant.

Madison recognized Barry Redmond at the same moment he looked up and saw her. His entire demeanor changed, and for a moment his feet faltered. Then he began running full speed, directly toward Madison.

It was not until that moment that Madison realized she had stopped in the middle of the street. She started to accelerate, but Barry slammed into the side of her car. She jerked to a stop, giving herself a mild case of whiplash.

"What? Are you stalking me now?" the man raged through the glass, palms thrust against it.

Just for spite, Madison rolled the window down. Barry surged forward, smacking his forehead on the doorframe. The metal—sizzling from the Texas sun—left a red slash across his skin.

"Keep touching my car and you'll owe me a car wash to get the sweaty palm prints off."

"I asked if you were stalking me!"

"Believe me, I have better things to do than stalk you, Barry Redmond."

"Then what are you doing down this street? You don't live here."

"Nor do you. And this is a public thoroughfare. I have every right to drive down this street, just as you have every right to jog down this sidewalk."

From behind them, Myrna Lewis added her bellowed remarks. "Neither one of you have the right to destroy my yard! Shoo! Get away from here. Your exhaust fumes will wilt my petunias. And your sweat better not fall on my grass, Barry Redmond! The salt will ruin my lawn." Her remarks might have been more effective, had she not been wallowing around on the grass, trying to get her feet beneath her in an attempt to stand.

As it was, both parties ignored her. Madison consulted the watch dangling from her slender wrist. "Shouldn't you be at work this time of afternoon?"

"You forget. I'm president of the bank. I set my own hours."

"Ah, yes, banker's hours. So much for the old adage *an honest day's pay for an honest day's work.*" She snapped her fingers in an 'ah, shucks' gesture.

"I've warned you, Madison Cessna," he snarled. "Don't mess with me."

"Barry, Barry. You are so paranoid. And so forgetful. I married years ago. My name is Madison Reynolds now."

"You are a Cessna, through and through. And a Hamilton!" he spat the name in distaste. "Your great grandmother sided with Juliet Randolph, making us enemies before we were ever born."

Madison stared at him, shocked that he still harbored that old grudge. "That was a hundred years ago. Literally. We celebrate the towns' centennials this year. Get over it, Barry. And grow up."

"And get off my sidewalk!" Myrna finally managed to pull herself upright. She charged over to the car and the bickering couple, brandishing her scissors like a weapon.

"This isn't your sidewalk, old woman. Go back to wallowing on your grass."

"Why, you arrogant, pompous ass!"

Myrna swung her arm, making as if to strike him with the scissors. Barry was quicker and stronger than she. He easily grabbed her hand and twisted, popping the instrument right out of her hand. It skidded down her solid body, bounced inward, and left a long red scratch down one leg before clattering onto the sidewalk. Myrna cried out, either in anger or in pain. Perhaps both.

"Don't you dare." Barry's voice was low and menacing, but Madison had no trouble hearing the words from where she sat in the car. "I think you are forgetting a certain business arrangement we have, one that your husband knows nothing about. Don't make me call in your loan."

"You—You can't do that!" Myrna sputtered, her face losing its color. "I'm current on my payments."

"I can do anything I please. I'm president of the bank."

For once, the obnoxious woman had nothing to say. While she stood there with her double chins quivering, Madison spoke up in her defense. Differences with Myrna aside for the moment, she told the banker, "Keep running, Barry. Since you hate the town of Juliet so much, go back to your side of the tracks and leave us alone."

"Gladly. I've had enough slumming for one day." Before releasing Myrna Lewis' hand, he gave it a painful twist and hissed, "Remember what I said. Don't cross me or you'll be sorry." He dropped her hand then, and glared down at Madison. "And that goes for you, too. Stay out of my face."

"No problem. And I agree with Myrna." Myrna, who made a hasty retreat into the house, moving remarkably fast on her short, compact legs. "Don't drip your sweat all over her grass."

With that, Madison sped away. She glanced into the rear-view mirror, watching as Barry swiped his foot through the woman's manicured flowerbed. The crushed blooms were evident from twenty yards away. As a final insult, the banker made a wide, sweeping turn through her prized lawn, tromping childishly across the grass before jogging away.

10

Arriving at the insurance office, Madison did not mention the incident to Dean Lewis. As hard as it was to imagine, she actually felt sorry for his wife. Even though the woman had a knack for antagonizing everyone she knew, not even she deserved the treatment Barry Redmond had dished out.

"What can I do for you today, Madison?" Dean smiled in greeting. "Are you here to buy that policy we talked about?"

The question drew her back on track and she promptly forgot the problems with the bitter banker.

"Not today, I'm afraid. I'm here on another matter entirely. I've been doing some work for a private investigator out of Houston, Murray Archer. Perhaps you've heard of him. No? Well, no matter. If you would be so kind, I have a few questions I would like to ask you pertaining to insurance." It wasn't a direct lie. She did do work for Archer. It simply had nothing to do with why she was here now. Seeing the concern that filled Dean's eyes, Madison was quick to assure him. "Nothing that would compromise confidentiality or your trust with your clients."

"Very well then. What would you like to know?"

"You are an agent for Omega Insurance, aren't you? I remember handling some of their claims while working here."

"So obviously you already know the answer to that question."

"Good point. Okay, so what about a subsidiary of theirs, Magnus Insurance?"

"I don't handle that division," Dean Lewis told her. "Omega is the parent company, but they have several smaller divisions under their umbrella. Most of them concentrate on specific areas, such as the medical field, industrial, food industry, that sort of thing. I prefer to deal with Omega as it has a comprehensive, one-size-fits-all offering."

"I've checked into some complaints concerning Magnus."

Dean nodded. "I've heard they have some problems within that division. I think it comes from management, and not training their representatives properly. Some of their agents are more concerned with making the sale than fully explaining their policies."

"I imagine that is often the case with many things," Madison agreed. "I spoke with Tomas Montelongo last night. He mentioned something about that. I didn't think to ask him, but do you happen to know if there is an agent that serves this area?"

"Yes, I believe so. A fellow by the name of Hanson, over in Giddings."

"Giddings?" That was where *A+ Fire Systems* was located.

"I probably have his number here somewhere…"

"Magnus denied the claim, saying the suppression system was faulty, even though it passed inspection just before the fire. Is denying a claim like that a common practice?"

"All insurance agencies send out their own claim adjusters and, if need be, their own investigators. They typically base their final decision upon the investigator's recommendations."

"Why not hold the company that serviced the system responsible, instead of denying Tomas' claim?"

"My guess would be because it is easier to deny a claim than to turn around and sue a third party."

"Is there anything you can tell me about a barn fire at Jerry Don Peavey's about four years ago? He sued Omega Insurance when they tried to deny his claim. Something about inflated value."

"As you probably know, the claim was eventually paid."

"But not to Mr. Peavey. Most of it went to the bank."

"I'm afraid that's beyond the scope of my involvement."

"What about a similar claim with William Shanks? I understand Omega had that policy, as well."

"William Shanks." He tried the name out before recognizing it. "Oh, yes, Wanda Shanks. A chimney fire that did quite a bit of smoke damage. Again, the policy was bound by terms of mortgage liens against the property."

"Meaning what, exactly?"

"If a property is mortgaged, all reimbursement checks must bear the names of the lien holder as well as the policy holder. Hypothetically speaking, if a person is not current on their loan, the mortgage holder might not sign over the funds in full to the policy holder. I'm not saying this happened in either case, but hypothetically, it could."

"How would a policy holder pay for damages if he received only a portion of the reimbursement?"

"I'm not sure. I suppose there are several alternatives. Shop around for cheaper repair rates, re-build on a smaller scale, take out a second mortgage; those would be my first suggestions. The last resort would be to sue the insurance company. Unfortunately, often the easiest solution is to sell the property and be free of the damage, and the debt, altogether."

"I don't suppose you could disclose the lien holder in either of these cases?" Madison asked hopefully.

"If you did not find it in a public records search, you won't find it here."

Madison smiled. "I appreciate your professionalism. And I won't insult you again by asking you to compromise it." She stood to go. "Thank you for your time."

"Here's the card for the Magnus agent. And this one is for the chief investigator for all the Omega companies. Big ole German fella that goes by the nickname Slim. Truth is, he's anything but." Dean chuckled at the irony of the moniker.

"Do you happen to know where this Slim is based out of?"

"I think he lives somewhere in the Giddings area."

The facts were too coincidental. *A+ Fire Systems* was based out of Giddings. Their technician was a large German man that went by the name Tiny. Magnus Insurance was located in Giddings. The chief investigator for the company was another large German man called Slim, who was also from the small town of Giddings.

An idea formed in Madison's mind. "Dean? Would it be unethical for an insurance adjuster to investigate a company his relative worked for?"

"It may not be unethical, technically speaking, although it might fall under suspicion. As long as the relative did not play a role in the incident and was not a deciding factor in the outcome of the investigation, I don't think there would be a problem."

It was worth looking into. Unfortunately, it was too late to do so today. By the time she drove to Giddings, the business offices would be closed.

That did not mean, however, that her investigation was at a standstill. As Madison saw herself out, she looked up Wanda Shanks' telephone number.

Wanda Shanks was more than willing to speak with Madison. At length.

Her ears were still ringing the next morning as she and Granny Bert drove to Giddings. With Genesis working back at the restaurant today, Madison reluctantly invited her grandmother along.

"Remind me to never mention William Shanks' name again in front of Miss Wanda," Madison groaned. "She railed against him for hours. I heard more details than anyone should ever have to know about their personal lives." A shudder ran through her shoulders as she recalled some of the more graphic details.

"You forget, I'm one of her closest friends. I know most of those details, and I agree. They ain't pretty." Even her grandmother winced as a similar shudder echoed through her frame.

"She is very bitter. Understandably so, but she gets a bit carried away. Between the rants and the stories from the last fifty years, I'm afraid I didn't get much useful information from her. I can tell you this, though. I will never look at a turkey baster in the same light again." Another shudder racked her body. "But enough of that. Let's go over the game plan for today. What's our cover?"

"We're checking out fire suppression systems on Genny's behalf. She's too busy to come herself, so being the sweet and loving friends that we are, we agreed to help out."

"You're adlibbing again," Madison warned.

Her grandmother shrugged. "Close enough."

"Fine, but remember. We're just asking questions. Be subtle."

"Of course. Subtle is my middle name."

"So this is the model you suggest for my friend's restaurant?" Madison pretended to peruse the brochure in her hand. It touted a long list of the benefits to choosing that particular brand.

"Absolutely. Anything less would be inadequate, anything more would be overkill," the large man called Tiny replied.

"You see, Madison?" Granny Bert beamed. "I told you we needed to talk directly to the man who installs them. That salesman up front would have sold us more than we needed, just to make the commission. I say you can't ever go wrong, talking to the main man like Tiny here."

Madison still looked unconvinced. "And you service them, too, correct? Because that's what my friend is most interested in."

"Absolutely. That's my service area, so I'll be the one making quarterly inspections."

Granny Bert sidled up against the man and spoke with a conspiratorial air. "They didn't show it on television, you know, but there was an *incident* at the café. Could have been bad, but luckily that good-looking fireman was there at the time. Took care of the flame before it burned the whole place down."

"You don't say."

Instead of moving away, Granny Bert remained close. She stared up at him, her eyes filled with what appeared to be admiration. "Tell me, Tiny. Are you married?"

An amused smile played across his lips. Tiny Libenthal had a big, beefy body, set upon a sturdy frame no less than six feet tall. With no hair left on his bald head, it was hard to determine his exact age, but Madison guessed him in his late sixties. Shackled with a squared head, thick neck, and blunt features, the man had not been blessed with good looks. "As a matter of fact, I am single," he confirmed.

"You don't say."

"Granny Bert!" Madison blushed at the insinuation in her grandmother's voice. Was she playing matchmaker?

"What? I'm not asking for you; I'm asking for me!" She placed a wrinkled hand upon his fleshy arm, which would easily make two of her own. "I just love a man who makes me feel all small and dainty. I'm a bit on the taller side, you know, and most of the men I know are stooped over like a humpback whale. It's nice to have a tall, handsome man such as yourself towering over me." She ran her hand up and down his bulging biceps. "You remind me so much of someone else I know, but for the life of me, I can't figure it out. Surely there can't be two men as big and handsome as yourself."

"Sure there can," Tiny grinned. "I have a twin brother. They call him Slim."

"Slim?" Her tone was incredulous. "The one who does insurance adjustments? *That* Slim? He's your twin? He can't be!" She swatted at his arm in feigned disbelief.

Tiny nodded vigorously. "Most folks have trouble telling us apart."

"But you're so much more handsome than he is. And you look five years younger!" She peered at him closely. "Yes, I see the resemblance now. And I reckon that's who I was thinking of, but I never would have taken you two for twins. Maddy, you remember Slim, don't you? He helped me out with that claim for my motor home." She offered a sheepish smile for the big man. "He knew I would come out on the short-end of an insurance claim, so we worked a little deal on the side."

Tiny laughed. "That sounds about like my brother. Always trying to make an extra dime. Then he goes and spends it on fast women and cheap liquor."

"I resent how you make that sound like a bad thing," Granny Bert huffed.

"Uh… Uhm…" he stammered, clearly at a loss for words. His eyes flew to Madison for guidance, but her stunned expression offered no help.

The older woman ignored them both and continued. "He said the problem was most likely the electric martini shaker I left plugged in, but he put it down as a faulty oven exhaust. Said there were known problems with the model I had and no one would question his ruling, especially since the same thing had happened to some other schmuck just before me. That one really was the exhaust. Between that and the axillary fuel tank, he said that sucker melted like a wax candle."

"Yeah, I saw that one," Tiny grinned. "Before and after."

"Before?"

Realizing his slip, Tiny started to recant, but Granny Bert ran her hand along his arm again and cooed, "Why you little dickens, you! You're as sneaky as your brother, aren't you?"

"Maybe." The questionable way he said the word neither denied nor confirmed her claim. But his grin spoke volumes, punctuated by his sly wink. "For the right price."

Granny Bert gave a gleeful peal of laughter. "Maddy, girl, I think we've found just the men we were looking for!"

"I think so," Madison agreed. It took her a while, but she had finally caught on to her grandmother's game.

"Is your friend's café in some sort of trouble? Because between the two of us, we could help her out," Tiny offered. "Sometimes a wire comes mysteriously undone... A claim can be approved or denied, depending what the customer is paying for..."

"Things are good for now, but once they quit filming, you never know what will happen." Granny Bert shrugged for good measure. "But it sure is good to know we have options, just in case things go south." She patted Tiny's arm. "Maddy, I think we've taken up enough of this man's valuable time. I know he has more important things to do than entertain an old woman and her fantasies."

She followed Madison to the door, but turned to smile over her shoulder. "Tiny, the next time you're in The Sisters, you be sure and look me up, you hear?"

"I might just do that," the man grinned.

As they hurried out to the car, Madison hissed, "You were flirting shamelessly with that man! I thought you said your middle name was *Subtle*."

"It is." She flashed a wicked grin as she ducked into the car. "And my first name is *Anything But*."

The next stop was the insurance agent's office. The agent represented several lines, Magnus included. Did the ladies need new auto insurance, by chance? Could he interest Madison in life insurance? What about a cancer policy? Granny Bert might want to hear about a burial policy he had. And everyone needed more home insurance coverage these days.

When Madison explained they were specifically interested in a Magnus policy, he looked genuinely perplexed. Their rates, he explained, were generally a bit higher than those of their competitors. The company specialized in commercial policies.

"We've heard good things about them," Madison lied. "We've heard several restaurants use them and are impressed with how quickly they process a claim."

Granny Bert added her own, "They say the adjuster comes out lickety split. A real nice fella they call Slim."

"Slim Libenthal? Nice?" His eyes bugged. "I could think of a lot of names to call Slim Libenthal, but nice would not be one of them. The man is about as friendly as a porcupine."

The older woman shrugged. "Maybe they were on the right end of his decision."

"Not without some money under the table, they weren't," the man snorted. He looked up, realizing they heard the muttered words. "I'm sorry. I shouldn't have said that."

"That's okay. We heard Slim could be swayed by a wad of bills and a pretty face." She winked her eye. "If we have a problem, Madison here has the cash, I have the face."

"My grandmother is kidding," Madison quickly assured the agent. "We would never do such a thing."

The insurance agent sighed. "I've often suspected Slim was on the take, but I can never prove it. Too many of his cases have had controversial results. He backs them with the right paperwork, all the right citations and such, but still..."

"Have you reported him to the company?"

"Unfortunately, he's seen as something as an expert in the field of fire suppression equipment, even with other insurance companies. They applaud his 'invaluable insight and uncanny talent in detecting faulty equipment and hazardous conditions.' Especially when it saves them money."

"It sounds like you've made the complaint more than once."

"I hate seeing my clients devastated by a claim that has been denied."

"In a worse-case scenario, what usually happens to those clients?" Madison inquired.

"They go broke. Some file bankruptcy, some sell out, some just cut their losses and close down their business."

"There's nothing you can do?"

The man answered with a wry smile. "I can suggest my clients go with another company, just as I'm doing with you. Let me get you some information on *TriState Insurance*."

A call to Slim Libenthal's office went to voicemail. Deciding to kill some time before trying him again, Madison and Granny Bert hit a few of the antique stores Giddings was known for. After two hours of shopping, a long lunch, and still no answer at the adjuster's office, they admitted defeat and headed back to Juliet.

"I'm still thinking about that hall tree I saw at *Whistle Stop*," Madison said wistfully. "It would be perfect for the ladies' parlor, don't you think?"

"Which parlor is that again? Miss Juliet had one for every purpose."

"The parlor on the right, between the foyer and the library."

"I never did understand my friend and all her airs," Granny Bert confessed. "Front parlor, ladies parlor, small parlor. Formal dining room, breakfast nook. Formal library and personal library. She had too many dad-blamed rooms to begin with. I still say you should have knocked down a few of those walls."

"There were structural issues. Not to mention Nick's obsession with staying historically correct."

"Is that anything like politically correct?"

"If it is, you would know nothing about it. I still can't believe you said some of the things you said today."

"But I got results, now didn't I, girl?" Her grandmother preened as they drove through the winding back roads that connected Lee County to The Sisters. "So recap for me. What have we got so far?"

"Five fires, none of them the same. Two have connections to *A+ Fire Systems*. At least three had coverage with Omega or one of their subsidiaries. We also know that the installer for

A+ and the adjuster for Omega, parent company of Magnus, are brothers who can be easily bribed."

"A bit of coincidence that Omega keeps popping up in all of this."

"My thoughts, exactly."

"So you're thinking Omega denies the claims to keep from making a payoff?"

Madison pursed her lips. "That was my original thought, but it really doesn't make sense," she admitted. "They didn't always deny the claims. They denied the one at *Montelongo's*, but they paid out for Jerry Don Peavey and Miss Wanda."

"Who did Ray Sams have insurance with?"

"I don't know. But the vent system in his motor home was designed, in part, by *A+*. I don't know if Slim was there on behalf of the manufacturer or the insurance company, but he was the one to determine the outcome of the claim."

"Which was?" Granny Bert asked.

"I was hoping you knew."

"Don't look at me like that. I told you, I had nothing to do with that fire!"

"I never said you did. But you obviously know this Sams fellow. Do you know him well enough to ask him about the outcome of the fire?"

Granny Bert squirmed in her seat. "I know him well enough to know not to call him! We have what you might call a competitive history."

"Competitive? Or combative?"

"Could be both," her grandmother admitted.

"You might as well tell me."

"Ray is part of the group I travel with. We all have our own RVs, but we go together because it's more fun that way.

Once Ray's wife died, he got the notion he was somewhat of a lady's man. He tried sparking with me a few times, but I wasn't interested. The man's a sloppy kisser, if the truth be known. When I showed more interest in Merv Mullins than I did in him, he got his shorts all in a wad and decided to show me up. Next camping trip, he took along Dolly Mac Crowder because he knew good and well we had a rivalry going in high school. The next time it was Dorian Nettles, who was running against me for mayor of Juliet."

Madison listened in amazement. Apparently, the love life and drama among seniors wasn't much different than that of teenagers. This sounded suspiciously like one of Bethani's stories.

"When he realized I wasn't jealous, he went for the jugular. He insulted my wheels. Challenged me to a road race. Made disparaging remarks about ole' Brown Betty. You remember my motor home before this one, don't you?"

"I think so."

"I loved that ole' gal. We had some fine times together. Traveled many a mile, seeing the countryside." With an affection smile on her face, Granny Bert reminisced about the vehicle as if it were an old friend. The smile faded and her voice turned hard. "Then one day, out of the blue, she quit on me. We were over in deep East Texas at the time, back in the Piney Woods. Ray made another pass at me, I turned him down flat, and the next morning Brown Betty wouldn't start. The mechanic mentioned something about a contaminated fuel source that gummed up the whole engine. I had to trade her in, right there on the spot." She shook her gray head in regret.

"But you have a really nice one now," Madison offered in consolation.

"True. Sassy and I have a lot of good travels, but I still miss Brown Betty. 'Course, when Ray saw I bought a brand new model, he had to have one better. He bought the latest and greatest, with all the fancy slide outs to double the size. Darn fool spent thousands of dollars, just trying to outdo me. I heard he borrowed from his life insurance, just to make the down payment."

"Sounds like he's a sore loser."

"You don't know the half of it, girl. He would park his rig next to mine, as far over to the side as he could, so that when he opened the slides they would hang over into my space. While we were driving, he would try to pass me every time. Nearly caused two wrecks, pulling out in front of other vehicles just to go around me. Challenged me to another race. When I left him in the dust, he went out and bought an axillary tank and filled it with some sort of rocket fuel. I hear that's what caused all the fireworks when the rig caught fire."

"So that's why you were so quick to say you had nothing to do with the fire, the first time I asked about it."

"Ray put up a big squawk, pointing a finger at me for the blaze. Said I probably set the fire out of jealousy."

"Why would you be jealous, if you won the race?"

Her grandmother shrugged. "Because he went out and got that fancy fuel tank. And he started seeing Sybille."

Madison was surprised. "Miss Sybille, your best friend?"

"It didn't last long. She sided with me and he vowed eternal revenge against the both of us." She sounded slightly amused.

"Really? You don't seem too upset about it. Aren't you afraid of what he'll do next?"

"Nah. Since he was such a *good catch*," she used air quotes to emphasize her mocking tone, "Dorian snatched him up and married him before he had the sense to see what was happening. Now she has him so busy with honey-do lists and driving her to church every time the doors open that he doesn't have time to plot his revenge against me and Sybille. And we figure being married to Dorian is the worst punishment of all, seeing as she's already been through four husbands, each one of them deader than the next. So we're good." She finished with a brilliant smile.

Madison, too, wore a smile. "I'm learning all kinds of things about you, Granny. I never realized you were such a *femme fatal*. First, your mystery man before Grandpa Joe, now this Ray Sams and whoever Merv is. How many other men don't I know about?" she teased.

"There are a few others," her grandmother acknowledged. She gazed out at the passing countryside. "But you know about the ones that matter."

11

"I think it's time to visit your friend again," Madison informed Genny the next day at the restaurant. They indulged in a cup of coffee and pastries.

Genesis waved her fork in the air. "Luckily for me, I have more than one friend. Be more specific."

"Carson Elliot."

Genny wrinkled her nose. "I don't think I like the way you keep referring to him as *my* friend."

"Why?" Madison teased. "Is Cutter getting jealous?"

"Cutter? What does this have to do with Cutter?"

"I saw the way he reacted when he thought Carson made a move on you. He was clearly jealous."

"You're delusional," Genny snorted, clearly unamused.

Madison allowed her friend a moment of respite as she finished off her pastry. "So do you want to come with me, or not?"

"Will I hear the end of it if I do?"

Madison grinned. "From me, or Cutter?"

"You're certainly in a good mood today. Did you sneak out to see Brash last night or something?"

"Shh!" Madison's eyes flew around guiltily. She knew the cameras did not cover the back booth, but there could be ears nearby. Thankfully, no one was close enough to overhear their conversation. "Keep your voice down."

"I could say the same to you," Genesis replied in a surly voice.

"Okay, okay. And in answer to your question, no, I did not sneak out." A smile broke across her face. "But I do get to spend some time with him next weekend. You know about the fish fry, right? And you're coming?"

"Sure, count me in. It's been too long since I've just goofed off and splashed around in the water. And I love fried fish, especially when someone else is doing the frying."

"We'll plan the menu on the way out to Carson's. When can you leave?"

Genny looked around the near-vacant café. "Let me tell the staff I'm leaving and grab my purse. Oh, and can we go in your car this time? Mine is acting up again."

"Too bad I finished my gig at *Cessna Motors*, or I could get you a sweet deal on a new ride."

"You still have connections," Genny pointed out. "Your uncle owns the dealership."

"We can stop by on our way back," she offered.

"Nah, I'm not ready to buy a new car just yet. It's probably just the battery or something." She hopped up from the booth. "Okay, I'll be right back."

"I'll pull around back and pick you up there."

After telling the staff her plans, Genny stopped by her office to grab her purse. When she stepped hastily into the hall, she ran headlong into a solid body. She bounced backward from the impact, blinking up in surprise.

"I've had it, Genesis!" the man snarled. Barry Redmond's lip curled in anger, reminding her of a pit bull. His face had an odd pinkish purple hue.

"What—What are you talking about?" Her eyes narrowed. "And what are you doing here? Cutter threw you out a couple of months ago."

"That kid can't throw me out of here! Who does he think he is?"

Genny put her hands on her hips, showing more bravado than she felt. "Doesn't matter," she insisted. "I'm the owner, and *I'm* throwing you out."

"Not before I deliver my message." Barry shoved a finger in her face, almost touching her nose. "You tell your friend to stay the hell out of my business! This is my last warning. If she doesn't, you're both going to be sorry."

Genesis swatted his finger away like a pesky gnat. "I assume you are referring to Madison."

"Of course I'm referring to Madison. The two of you are like opposites sides of a bad penny. And not worth a single cent, combined!"

"If we're so worthless, what's the fuss all about?" Genny asked coolly.

"She knows damn well what the fuss is about. You tell her to mind her own business."

"I'm not your messenger, Barry Redmond. If you were half the man you *think* you are, you'd be man enough to deliver your own messages."

"Don't worry, little Genny, she'll get the message," he threatened darkly. His voice was a snarl. "She messes with what's mine, I'll come after what's hers."

"That sounds distinctly like a threat."

"Take it how you want. Just watch your back."

"Get out," she ordered. "And this time, stay out."

She shoved past him and marched out the back door. Menu plans for the fish fry were forgotten as she climbed in the car and relayed the episode to Madison.

"I'm sorry, Maddy. I should never have said what I did, telling him to deliver his own message to you. I don't want him anywhere near you. To tell you the truth, I think the man is unstable."

"I've wondered about that myself. He probably found out Lisa met with Shawn Bryant the other day, but I had nothing to do with it. I have no idea why Barry thinks I'm still meddling in his affairs."

"Maybe all that moldy money has released toxic fumes and eaten his brain," Genny mused. "And it must be wreaking havoc on his blood pressure, too. Because you're right. He turns an interesting shade of purple when he gets angry."

"My, my. Two visits in two weeks. I am, indeed, a lucky man."

Carson greeted them with his customary warmth and grace. Today he wore a pale blue linen outfit, loose and comfortable and totally out of place in River County, Texas. On him, the look worked.

"I'm sorry to drop in on you on such short notice," Madison said. She had called while waiting on Genny.

"No problem. I have just finished my last class of the afternoon. I have another this evening, but you have my undivided attention for the next hour and a half." When his eyes fell upon Genny, Madison somehow doubted his claim.

BECKI WILLIS

"I promise not to take that long. I just have a few questions I wanted to ask you."

"Certainly." With a sweeping arm movement, he ushered the women inside and up the stairs.

Once they were settled again in his private study, Madison told him the reason for her visit. He was so busy ogling Genny, she wasn't sure he listened.

"I wanted to ask you about a fire you experienced about five years ago. I understand you lost your new home to the blaze?"

"Yes." One word, but his heavy sigh said so much more. "The touch-up paint was still wet. I did the walk-through that afternoon, signed the papers, and took the key. I planned to move in the very next morning. That night, the entire house burned to the ground."

"That's horrible!" Genny's soft cry was filled with empathy.

"What was the cause of your fire?" Madison asked.

"Faulty wiring in the exhaust vent over the stove."

Madison perked up at the mention of the vent. It sounded much like the case with *Montelongo's* and Ray Sams' motor home. "Oh? Do you happen to know who the manufacturer was?"

"Absolutely. *Allied Industries.* I took them to court and won. It seems they had installed an experimental exhaust system without my knowledge. They had applied for a patent on the product but it was still in the approval stages and not fully tested for residential use. Long story short, I lost my house but won the lawsuit."

Allied Industries. Her research revealed they were partners with *A+ Fire Systems* on a revolutionary new system that turned out to be not-so-revolutionary.

"I'm very sorry for your troubles," Madison murmured. "I suppose you had insurance?"

"Yes, absolutely. It was a condition of my loan, actually. My policy covered litigation costs, so in the long run, I came out ahead, at least financially."

"Yet you did not build again on the same lot."

His expressive mouth turned downward in a frown. "That turned out to an odd situation. After everything was said and done, the bank came back with a claim that the lot ownership reverted to them. It was a small clause, buried deep within the boilerplate of the contract, that said if for any reason the intended use of the property was changed or altered, I had thirty days to notify the bank in writing. Without the proper notification, the land used as collateral would revert to the bank."

"That's awful!" Genny cried.

"To be honest, after the fire and the trial and all that was involved, I was glad to be rid of the place. I had more than enough money to relocate elsewhere." He flashed a bright smile as he spread his arms wide. "As you can see, it turned out quite well for me."

"So what made you choose Juliet?" Genny asked. "I believe I read somewhere that you grew up in the Panhandle?"

He smiled, obviously pleased that she had researched him. "That is correct, I was born in the Panhandle and lived there until I was in grade school. I much prefer this area of Texas, however, with its gently rolling hills and many rivers. And the people here are so delightful." He flashed her a flirtatious look.

"So the fire was a blessing in disguise, luring you away from Riverton and closer to Juliet and The Sisters," she murmured.

"It would definitely seem that way."

Madison mentally rolled her eyes. *First Granny, now Genny. I can't take these two anywhere!*

"Mr. Elliot—" she began.

"Carson."

"Carson, do you know what, if anything, your fire had in common with a handful of other fires in the area over the past few years?"

His brow puckered in thought. "You know, Gloria asked me the same thing. But I'll tell you what I told her. I have no idea. I had just moved to the area when my house burned."

"So Gloria never mentioned anything specific about these fires to you?"

He had the grace to look ashamed. "I must admit, I thought she was overacting, as she was prone to do. Gloria insisted there was a bigger mystery behind the fire that took my home, but I'm afraid I did not take her seriously." He pursed his lips in thought. "I do recall that one of the people she mentioned was Ray Sams. I talked with him before the trial. He had a fire similar to mine in his motor home."

Madison leaned forward in interest. "What can you tell me about that?"

"I know they settled out of court and the company paid handsomely to keep their name out of the news. Launching a new product line as they were, they could not afford the negative publicity."

"Probably not," she agreed. So, Ray Sams had received a settlement.

Carson's eyes grew worried. "Are you thinking Gloria was right? Was she close to uncovering something?"

Madison nodded slowly. "I think it might be a possibility."

12

A cook called in sick, so Genny returned to the restaurant to cover the dinner rush. A few hours later, she gladly flipped the sign on the door and proclaimed the restaurant *Closed.* Twenty minutes after her last employee left, she had the cash register settled, the bank deposit made out, and all alarms set for the night.

She drove one block to the Naomi State Bank and dropped the bag into the night deposit. As she pulled away and circled through the parking lot, her car sputtered.

"Ah, come on, not now!" she wailed, banging on the dashboard. The motor responded with a giant shudder and promptly died. "Great. Just great," she muttered. She manhandled the steering wheel, coaxing the vehicle halfway into a parking space before the wheels locked.

She grabbed her phone and was about to call for help when a familiar truck drove up beside her.

"Problems?" Cutter asked through the opened window of his pickup.

"My car just died!"

"I'll have a look," he offered. Leaving his own diesel engine running, he jumped from the cab and came around to Genny's much smaller sedan. "Pop the hood."

After several minutes of poking and prodding around the engine, Cutter admitted defeat. "We'll get Jolly Dewberry to come out in the morning and see what the problem is. Just leave it here tonight. I'll give you a ride home."

"Are you sure?"

"I'm going right by your house, on the way to mine," he assured her with an easy smile. He opened her car door and helped her transfer into his truck. A few minutes later, they roared out of town.

Halfway down the ribbon of asphalt, the radio on Cutter's belt squawked to life. He groaned when he heard the familiar tone out. The series of unique tones was followed by the dispatcher's voice.

"River County SO to The Sisters Fire Department. Sisters Fire, there is a large grass fire reported off County Road 238, approximately five miles north of the Naomi city limit. The caller advises there is a barn filled with hay within two hundred yards of the fire. Repeat. A large grass fire off County Road 238, five miles north of Naomi city limits."

"That's Bob Peterson's place." Cutter pulled his radio out and barked into the receiver, "Unit 339 responding. I'll grab a brush truck and head that way."

"10-4, 339. The caller advises the fire is moving quickly and has already covered about five acres. It's approaching a heavily wooded tree line, as well as the barn filled with hay."

"Go ahead and tone out Riverton Fire Department for assistance," Cutter instructed the dispatcher.

Instead of slowing down to make a U-turn, he sped up as they continued down the road. "Turn around, Cutter," Genny urged. "I can find a ride home."

"We're more than halfway to your house. I'll drop you off and come back to town."

"Are you sure?"

The radio toned out again. "River County Sheriff's Office to The Sisters Fire Department. Sisters Fire, be advised the grass fire on County Road 238 is growing rapidly and has almost reached the tree line. The landowner's employee tried to cut a perimeter around the barn but was overcome with smoke. The tractor is now fully engulfed and the fire is within a hundred feet of the barn. We have Riverton Fire en route for assistance."

Cutter edged the speedometer needle upward.

"Turn around. Honestly, I don't mind," she said.

"I'm seeing you home, Genny."

"Then at least drop me at the road. I can walk to the house."

"Absolutely not. I'm seeing you inside."

"Cutter, that fire is moving fast." The road curved, giving them a clear view of the red-tinged night sky. "And it looks huge."

More traffic on the radio demanded his attention. By the time he listened to the update, he swung into her driveway and pulled up to the house. "I'll wait until you're inside," he compromised. "Flash your porch light and lock your door."

"Yes, Daddy," she agreed with false sweetness. She paused as she opened her door and hopped out. "Seriously, Cutter, be careful tonight. That fire sounds dangerous."

Genny heard sirens all through the night, racing back and forth to the fire. The turn-off for County Road 238 was a half mile from her house, so the clang and clatter of fire trucks, heavy equipment, and emergency personnel echoed especially loud in the still of night. She was awake much of it, worrying. She glanced out her window often, thinking of Cutter and the other men and women who put their lives in harm's way to save a neighbor's property. The telltale glow in the sky confirmed her fears; the fire still raged.

By morning, a lingering haze muddled the air and smoke rode in on the southern breeze. She hadn't talked to Cutter since he dropped her off the night before. She wanted to know that he and the other firefighters were safe, but of course her peace of mind took a backseat to fighting fire.

She was on her second cup of coffee when the doorbell rang.

"Who is dropping by at this time of morning?" she muttered. A glance at the clock told her it was a few minutes shy of eight o'clock. Just before she swung the door open, she thought to glance out the side window.

"Cutter!" she exclaimed as she worked the locks free.

The firefighter stood on her doorstep, looking haggard and worn. He had on the bottom half of his bunker gear, a rumpled shirt she remembered from last night, and a cloak of weariness. Smoke, smudge, and a five o'clock shadow darkened his face.

"Come in, come in," she insisted, opening the door wider. "You look terrible, by the way." *And sexy. Incredibly sexy, soot and all.*

He glanced down at his attire and shook his head. "I'm a mess. I just thought I'd stop by, see if you wanted that ride into town when I drop off the firetruck. We can call Jolly and have him meet us there."

"You've been out all night?" she cried in dismay.

He nodded confirmation. "We finally got it under control. We had to call in the Forestry Service, but it's ninety percent contained now. We handed it over to a fresh crew from Riverton and we're headed in to rest."

"So you haven't eaten?"

"Someone brought donuts out to the command center early this morning, but they were gone by the time I got off the truck."

"Then get in here. I'll cook you breakfast." She tugged on his arm.

"I can't. I'll make a mess on your floor."

She peered at his bunker gear. "Do you have jeans on under there?"

"Of course."

"Take off the grungy pants and the boots," she ordered. "I'll start breakfast." She turned away before he could argue.

Shedding the filthy clothes on her front porch, Cutter padded inside on his stockinged feet. Seeing no signs of her in the neatly arranged living room, he wandered into the hall and found the bathroom, where he washed his face and hands. By the time he was done, he simply followed his nose to the kitchen. Hints of cinnamon and frying bacon floated on the air, pulling him forward like a puppet on a string.

He stopped at the kitchen door, taking in the sight of Genesis in her domain. The room was rather small and dated, and not at all what he expected of a professional chef. Yet somehow the knotty pine cabinets and cheery blue and yellow checkered curtains suited her. The red cherry motif scattered across the room had a vintage look and feel, and was a perfect match for the rest of the space. It was impossible to step into the room and not feel uplifted, particularly with Genny in the picture. She was like a ray of sunshine, filling the small space with her energy. Still dressed in her nightclothes, a flimsy t-shirt that said *Instant Human: Just Add Coffee*, a pair of white sleep shorts, and turquoise toenail polish, her blond hair was mussed and her face devoid of makeup. Cutter had never seen a more beautiful woman.

"It's almost done," she promised, smiling over her shoulder. "Help yourself to the coffee. Cups are in that cabinet there."

Cutter poured them each a cup of the dark aromatic brew and carried it to the table, a yellow Formica and chrome dinette set straight out of the 50s.

"It's not fancy, but it should fill you up," she proclaimed as she plated their food. His plate had several slices of bacon and a huge pile of fluffy scrambled eggs, spiked with chunks of ham and cheddar cheese. Her plate held half as much. A third platter boasted a small stack of thickly sliced French toast.

His mouth watered as he looked at the feast before him. "This is enough for the whole department."

"Invite them over and I'll feed them, too," Genny offered. She moved back to the stove and swirled a pat of butter into the maple syrup she heated.

"Are you kidding? I'm not sharing you with them!"

She poured the buttery mixture into a gravy boat and brought it to the table. "Milk or orange juice?"

"Milk. And quit hopping around. Come sit down and eat with me."

"Go ahead and start. I'll just get the milk."

Cutter groaned with satisfaction as he took the first few bites of his meal. "Don't tell me I could have been eating this for breakfast every morning at the restaurant and just now realized it."

"This is the home version," she assured him.

"This is heaven. Pure heaven." He closed his eyes and savored his second slice of French toast. A hint of brown sugar, cinnamon, and nutmeg mingled with the buttered maple syrup to delight his taste buds.

"The secret is pure maple syrup from Vermont."

"The secret is Genesis Baker. When I'm not so tired, remind me to propose to you." He stuffed another generous bite into his mouth.

"I'll make a note."

"Remind me to tell you how beautiful you look, too."

Genny made light of his compliment. "I'll underline that reminder in red."

"These eggs are fantastic. I guess these are the home version, too, huh?"

"Special reserve for special guests."

His hazel eyes twinkled, despite his weariness. "So what time should I be here tomorrow morning?"

"Sorry, Charlie. You're out of luck." She refilled his empty coffee cup.

"I'm free next Sunday. Pencil me in." He washed down his bacon with a gulp of coffee. "Forget the pencil. Use a permanent marker."

"How can you do that?" she asked, not for the first time. "Doesn't that burn when you take such a huge gulp?"

Cutter flashed a grin. "I'm a firefighter, Genny darlin'. Burn is the name of the game."

"Speaking of burn… It was a bad one last night, huh?"

The twinkle in his eyes wafted into smoke. His shoulders sagged with exhaustion. "It got the barn and about three hundred bales of hay. The tractor and a few small pieces of equipment scattered around the barn. We called the Forestry Department when it hit the trees. It's not going anywhere, but it will probably flare up for a couple of days."

"What started it?"

"That's the thing. It looks like someone may have deliberately set it."

Genny frowned. "That doesn't sound like Bob."

"I agree. Especially when he's in Galveston on vacation."

"So who would do such a thing?"

"Good question."

"Here, you eat the last piece of toast while I go throw on some clothes. You look like you're about to fall asleep at the table."

Cutter cleaned his plate while Genny slipped from the room. When she returned five minutes later in jeans and a t-shirt, she found him sound asleep, his head slumped forward where he sat upright in the chair.

Her heart swelled with admiration. He had been up all night, helping fight a fire because it was the right thing to do. No one paid him to be a fireman. No one paid him to risk his life in the line of duty. He did it because he was a good man.

Genny touched his shoulder to wake him. Her hand lingered.

He awoke with bleary eyes. His hand came up to cover hers on his shoulder. "Genny darlin'," he slurred, his smile crooked and completely captivating.

He had only recently started calling her that, but Genny liked it. Perhaps a bit too well. "Would you like to crash here at my house for a while?" she offered. "I know you're exhausted."

He came wider awake, slinging the fatigue from his mind with a vigorous shake of his head. "Nah, I gotta take the truck back. Thanks for breakfast. That hit the spot." He patted the hand still under his.

"My small contribution to the department," she smiled.

"Small but mighty. Just like you." He pushed away from the table. "Ready? Do I need to help you with the dishes before we go?"

"That might be fun to see. Cutter Montgomery in the kitchen." She grinned, imagining him in a frilly apron and cowboy hat. "Somehow, I can't quite picture you with dishpan hands."

"I can wash with the best of them. My mama didn't raise no fool." He grinned as he put his hand on her waist and ushered her toward the door. "It's a known fact. No man has ever been shot while doing the dishes."

13

"What tornado struck in here?" Granny Bert demanded when she walked in and saw her dining room table.

Bethani and Megan had the entire table covered with art supplies. Posters and handheld signs, all in various stages of creativity, littered the entire surface. Jars of poster paint, brushes, markers, scissors, and tubes of glitter and glue scattered from the table to the floor.

"Oh, hi, Granny Bert," Bethani said casually, waving a blue-speckled hand in greeting. "We're making posters for the cheerleading squad."

"Are you painting the posters, my table, or yourself?" her great grandmother asked wryly.

Megan, her face streaked with blue, yellow, and one bright blotch of pink, grinned and confessed, "Maybe all three. But it's washable paint, so it's all good."

Granny Bert's loud harrumph begged to differ, but she didn't say another word as she continued to the kitchen. Another mess greeted her there.

"I see you've been in the kitchen, too."

"That was Blake and his friends. They stopped by for a snack before going to Jamil's for lunch."

Granny Bert grumbled as she set about cleaning up the mess. She made noise about them eating her out of house and home, complained no one knew how to clean up after themselves, and pretended great distress over the steady stream of teenagers that trailed in and out of her house. But inside, her heart was happy. It felt good to have young people underfoot again.

"I'll come help you, Granny Bert," Megan offered.

"Looks to me like you'd better supervise your friend, before she goes and paints my walls."

Megan giggled and left Bethani in her artistic attempt to draw a crown atop a cotton bale. The school mascot was the Cotton King, a leftover nod to the glory days of cotton plantations and the renowned Randolph Blakely. Without his legendary feuding daughters, there would be no such towns as Naomi and Juliet.

"You don't have to help," Granny Bert told the teenager. "Lord knows no one else bothers to."

Lowering her voice, Megan said, "I wanted to talk to you, without Beth hearing me."

"What's on your mind, child?"

Megan went through the motions of tying the bread wrapper closed as she articulated her thoughts. "It's my dad."

Granny Bert listened in concern. "Something's wrong with Brash?"

"He's not sick or anything. He's just sad."

"Sad?"

"Or maybe he is sick. Lovesick, that is. He's crazy about Miss Maddy. And I've seen the way she looks at him. They think no one knows, but I can tell how they feel about each other."

"You and me both, sister. And half the world, to boot."

Megan continued to twist the tie, knotting it unmercifully as her lips puckered into a pout. "The problem is Bethani." She shot a look into the dining room, where the problem she spoke of was busy with her creation.

"How is she a problem?" Granny Bert asked, pretending not to know the answer.

"She doesn't want them getting together. It's not that she doesn't like my dad. It's just that she doesn't like him with her mom."

"Bethani has been through quite a bit this past year, Megan. Her father died unexpectedly. She had to move away from her friends and her home to a new town, a new school. She's still trying to adjust."

"And I totally get that. I do. But her dad is gone now. And her mom deserves to keep living." Her voice took on a sulking tone. "She gets really upset when I try to tell her that."

"She just needs some time."

"I don't like seeing her sad. But I don't like seeing my dad sad, either. I think we could all be happy if Bethani would just give them a chance. But my dad is so caught up in doing what's right and what's honorable, and all that other hokey stuff, that he'll put her happiness before his. I know him," she insisted irritably. "He won't date Miss Maddy unless Bethani gives them her blessings."

Granny Bert acknowledged the words with a glower. "You have a point. So what do you think I can do about it?"

"Are you kidding?" Megan's face broke out in a wide smile. "You're like a legend. You can do anything!"

Touched by the teenager's claim but too proud to admit it, Granny Bert shoved a package of cookies into her hands. "Take these out there and stop your worrying, child. These things have a way of working themselves out." Seeing the teen hesitate, Granny Bert patted her arm and went back to complaining. "Go on, now. Shoo. I have a mess to clean up. Lord knows those heathen boys won't clean up after themselves. No, that's what they have me for."

Megan recognized her gruff facade for what it was. "You're the best, Granny Bert!" she whispered, before scampering back to her friend, cookie package in hand.

A smile lingered on the old woman's face as she filled the sink with dishwater.

"Granny!" Bethani wailed from the dining room. "This package is empty! The human garbage disposal must have eaten them all."

"I guess you girls will just have to help me make a batch of our own."

She heard giggles and high fives from the other room. "Granny Bert, you're the best!" the girls called in unison.

Granny Bert chuckled. Hearing such a claim never got old.

While the paint dried on both the posters and the girls, spices and laughter sweetened the kitchen air.

"You should see yourself!" Bethani giggled at her friend. "You have four colors of paint on your face, flour in your hair, and grease smudged on your glasses."

"Try looking through these smudges at yourself," Megan retorted. "You're like a fuzzy blur of color. I sure hope that blue paint comes out of your blond hair."

"If not, at least I'll be fashionable. Vivid hair color is all the rage these days."

"I know. I wanted to get my hair streaked, but my mom said no. She said with dark auburn hair like mine, no telling what color it might come out to be."

"You've got your daddy's hair, that's for sure." Granny Bert wormed into the conversation, steering it onto the path she wanted to take. "That thick, dark hair of his is part of what makes him such a looker. That and those gorgeous blue eyes. Whew. Hot stuff." She fanned herself with the recipe card they loosely followed. The girls were adding a few touches of their own, like adding peanut butter chips in with the chocolate ones, and substituting macadamia nuts for the pecans.

Scandalized, Bethani cried in chagrin, "Granny!"

"What?" she asked innocently. "Brash deCordova is what your mom's generation called a stud muffin."

"A *what?*"

"A stud muffin. A hunk. What you girls now call a hottie." She flapped the card for more air. "No matter what you call it, your daddy is one fine specimen of a man."

"I guess I should say... thank you?" The uncertainty in Megan's voice made it a question.

"I know it gets bothersome, having all those women fawn over him the way they do."

Unsure of where this was going, Megan tried a timid, "Well—"

"Oh, we all know it's true. And I've come to the conclusion that Bethani is right. Your dad would be best off, not getting too interested in her mom."

"What?" Megan cried, practically jumping from her chair. This wasn't at all what she asked Granny Bert to say.

Bethani cut her eyes at her great grandmother, surprised to hear this change of attitude. She always got the impression that Granny Bert was one of Mr. de's biggest supporters.

"Well, with them all going off to college in a few years, your dad would be left behind, nursing a broken heart," Granny Bert explained. She sounded completely sincere. "He might as well play the field now, while he still has his looks. No reason to get involved with Maddy and then have her move away."

"Wait. Mom's planning on moving?" Bethani was clearly confused by the announcement.

"Of course. You don't want her rattling around in that big old house all by herself, do you? No, no. She'll go off to college with you and your brother."

"Uh...uhm... college?"

Granny Bert clapped her hands together in manufactured glee. "I'm sure she'll find some cute little apartment, close to campus. That way she can be involved in all your sorority parties and get to know all your friends. It will be best this way. While all the other kids are going to wild parties and binge drinking and getting the whole *college experience*"—this with air quotes—"you and Blake will be spending Saturday nights on your mom's couch, watching all your favorite TV shows and making scrapbooks of your freshman year." Her face beamed as she added, "And I'll be sure and come down every Sunday, so we can make cookies and deliver them to all your professors!"

"Oh. Well, uh..." Looking slightly ill, and more than just a little panicked, Bethani tried to find a graceful way out of her great grandmother's plans.

Getting into the spirit of the charade, Megan nodded. "You know, Granny, I think you're right. If our parents started dating now, they might get too fond of each other. It might be hard for Miss Maddy to move away and leave my dad after dating him for a couple of years. And I know how Daddy is. He would want her with him on the weekends, not hosting some college frat party."

Granny Bert looked suitably mournful. "Even if they didn't break up right at first, they would eventually. I saw a Lifetime movie about that, just the other day. A mom went away to college with her daughter and ended up falling in love with the girl's math professor. Of course, when that ended badly, he flunked the girl and she ended up dropping out of college altogether."

Sneaking a calculated look at the teenager and noting her panicked expression, the old woman pretended to cover her thoughtless blunder. Patting Bethani's hand, she was quick to say, "Oh, I'm not suggesting that could ever happen to you, dear. After all, your mom doesn't really like the math types."

"Maybe we should try to set my dad up with someone," Megan said thoughtfully, drumming sticky, paint-splashed fingers against the table. "I know he's interested in Miss Maddy, but you're right; it wouldn't last. Not with her going away to college with Blake and Bethani." She turned to her friend with a crafty, wistful expression. "Gee, you're lucky, Beth. My mom would never do that for me. Just think. You can eat home-cooked meals every night, instead of having to eat in the common areas like the rest of us. Instead of all the noise and the music and the craziness that is college nightlife, you'll be all snug and cozy at your mom's apartment. You are so lucky!"

"Enough of this!" Bethani finally exploded. "I'm barely in high school, and the two of you already have my college life all mapped out for me!"

Madison came through the door at that very moment, her arms full of groceries. "Hi, Megan. Hi, Beth. Mmm, something smells great. What's this about college?"

Bethani jumped from her chair and pushed past her mother. "Nothing! Just drop it!" she said irritably. She got to the doorway, whirled around, and jabbed her finger toward her mother. "And you are NOT going away to college with me and Blake!"

Bethani stormed from the room, leaving Granny Bert and Megan to dissolve into laughter. Brow puckered and completely confused, Madison frowned. "What did I miss?"

14

It was more testosterone than any one booth should be allowed to hold. Two of the area's finest and most handsome men, sitting across the table from one another in the back booth of *New Beginnings*. Brash and Cutter enjoyed a late lunch while the noisy clatter of other guests dwindled to a low and occasional murmur.

"So you suspect the fire was set," Brash said, lifting his glass for a long draw of sweet iced tea.

"It appears that way. We found a bottle of accelerant in the ashes of a wood pile, near the initial flash site."

"And you don't think Peterson had anything to do with it?"

"I don't. He was away at the time of the fire, visiting his daughter who lives on the coast. He sent a ranch hand out to check on things when he got the call. The hand tried to save the barn and ended up getting the tractor caught in the crosswinds. Peterson cut his vacation short and came home. I heard him tell his banker he might have to sell. His insurance wouldn't cover enough for him to replace everything."

"That's a shame. I always liked Bob. No one deserves to lose his place like that to fire, even when it's an act of nature. Knowing someone may have started the fire makes it that much worse. Any idea who might have done it?"

"None at all. Bob Peterson may have a few funny ways, but none of them bad enough to incite this sort of hatred."

"Well, if it was arson, someone had a reason for setting the fire." Brash stabbed a piece of chicken fried steak and dipped it in gravy. "First thing we need to do is see who might benefit from the fire."

"Unless someone is trying to run him off his land, I don't see where anyone could benefit."

"What about that fire earlier in the summer, the one that destroyed part of the old Crowder place? Did y'all ever figure out the cause of that one?"

The firefighter shook his head. "Couldn't find a thing. The grass was still green; earth still damp from recent rain. No visible reason a fire should have spread that fast." He leaned forward and admitted in a confidential tone, "I suspected the landowner may have started it. It was that fella from Odessa who lost his business when the oil industry fell flat. I figured he needed the insurance payoff. I told Dean Lewis as much, but he didn't seem too concerned. I hear the guy collected the insurance, sold out, and moved on."

"That sort of thing seems to happen all too often," Brash agreed. "You would think the insurance companies would do more thorough investigations."

"You would think," Cutter agreed. "I know they didn't bother investigating when Dugan Rankers' hay field burned last month."

Both men mulled over the problem as they finished their meal. Genesis arrived with a smile and a refill of sweet iced tea.

"Could I interest either of you gentlemen in dessert?"

"Not me," Brash said, rubbing a hand over his flat stomach. "Buttons hardly meet as it is," he claimed.

A smile broke out across Cutter's face as he tugged on his shirt and bragged, "Still plenty of room in mine. I'll take a couple of turnovers and try to fill the gap."

"Somehow I knew I could depend on you," Genesis teased. She tapped on the tabletop between them. "What about booth rental? Either of you fellas in need of an office? Now that the remodel is almost done on Maddy's office, she won't be needing my back booth anymore."

"They threw a stuffy little office in with the chief of police title, so I'm good."

"A nice big drafty space came with the chief of the fire department title, so I'm good, too."

Genny shrugged. "Guess I'll just use it to serve meals."

Brash lowered his voice, conscious of the nearby cameras and other customers. "Redmond hasn't given you any more trouble, has he?"

Cutter caught the name and frowned, his face as dark as a stormy sky. "I threw him out of here weeks ago. Has he been back?"

"He stopped by the other day," she admitted.

"I guess I didn't make myself clear to him the first time. What did he want?" Cutter demanded.

She lifted a shoulder. "Just stirring up a ruckus, as usual. Nothing to be concerned over."

"I told him he wasn't welcome, Genny. I don't want him bothering you."

"It was just the one time. Seriously, Cutter, it was nothing. I'll be right back with your dessert."

A few moments later, she returned to slide a plate in front of the fireman, complete with a generous scoop of ice cream. "Ah, you are the woman of my dreams," Cutter sighed, inhaling a deep breath of the pastries' spicy apple fragrance.

Ignoring the antics of his companion, Brash asked Genny, "You're still coming tomorrow night, right? Swimming, fishing, fish fry?"

"Absolutely. I'm bringing the potato salad." She flashed her dimples. "And a dessert."

Brash turned toward Cutter. "Before you ask, I know there's a burn ban. No open flame. And you're welcome to come. It's just an informal get together, mostly family. Maddy and the twins, Shannon and Matt, Genny, Megan, my parents if they get back from Bryan in time, and maybe Granny Bert. According to her, it depends on if she gets a better offer," he laughed. "If not, she might bring Miss Sybille with her."

What started as an intimate gathering for him, Madison, and their children had mushroomed, but Madison thought it was best this way. She promised the next time it could be just the five of them. Brash was so focused on knowing there would be a next time that he had not argued.

Cutter scooped up a large bite of apple turnover and shoved it in his mouth. "If Genny's bringing dessert, I'm definitely in."

Brash retrieved his Stetson from the seat beside him and settled it upon his head. "Well then, since I'm providing supper tomorrow night, I'll let you buy our lunches today."

❧

The deCordova Ranch was roughly three thousand acres of prime river-bottom soil. Gifted to Andrew deCordova from Bertram Randolph himself, the land was once part of the famed Randolph Plantation.

Upon his death, the undisputed cotton baron of the Brazos Valley—and, some claimed, the entire state—deeded the property to his most loyal and devoted employee. The fertile soil deserved to be cared for and nurtured, and Bertram knew that neither of his spoiled and bickering daughters would treat it with the respect it deserved. To them, he gave their own namesake towns: Juliet to the south of the railroad tracks, Naomi to the north. His most prized possession he gave to his ranch foreman.

Along with his sons, Andrew deCordova built the ranch into a legend in its own right, known for producing generous crops and a fine line of registered Limousin cattle. Cotton and milo still grew in the lower fields, a pecan orchard graced a sloping hillside, and the ranch was known for its top-quality hay.

The deCordova clan had been good to the land, and the land had been good to them.

Brash grew up on the ranch. His parents lived in the original old farmhouse and Brash, himself, had remodeled one of the old bunkhouses into a rustic and simple home that suited his needs. His job as police chief required him to live in town, so he rented a small house in Juliet, with plans to one day build his own home on the ranch. There was ample room for another house, despite the fact that several members of his family already lived there, including siblings, cousins, and aunts and uncles.

Even with the abundance of space, it did not always equate to privacy. A party for one often meant a party for all. So it was with the fish fry. Family members drifted by to visit or throw a hook in the water. By the time the meal was served, Brash invited three ranch employees and at least eight extra relatives to join the festivities.

With no better offers on the table, Granny Bert brought not only Miss Sybille, but Wanda Shanks, as well.

Andy and Lydia deCordova arrived just in time to eat. Having never officially met the couple before, Madison was admittedly nervous when Brash took her elbow and guided her over for the introductions. She was thankful his hand remained lightly upon her back during the exchange, offering not only moral support for her, but a subtle message for his parents. Along with the way he said her name, the touch meant that this woman was important to him.

The fish was fried to a golden brown and served with potato salad, slaw, hushpuppies, and homemade tartar sauce. A large array of desserts followed. While the rest of the group fussed over the sinful selections and brought out the makings for s'mores, Brash and Maddy slipped away with the cover of darkness.

They did not go far. They could still hear the laughter and the varied conversations taking place beyond the trees, but were buried deep enough in the woods to have privacy.

"Tonight has been wonderful, Brash," Maddy beamed. "The kids are loving it."

"Blake is a born fisherman! I might ask him to join my team for the fishing tournament this fall."

"What tournament?"

"We have a fishing tournament every year during Founder's Week. This year's celebration will be extra special, since it is the centennial of The Sisters."

Maddy all but groaned. "Nick is determined to be through with the house by then. It is supposed to be the grand finale of the show, coinciding with live coverage of the celebration. And believe me; the end can't come soon enough."

He put his arm around her waist and tugged her closer to his side. "Has it really been that bad?" he asked.

"Let's see. We discovered a skeleton in a secret room beneath the basement. At least five hidden passages. The plumbing was a nightmare, as was the ancient wiring. I've lost all semblance of privacy and my personal life is splashed across national television every Tuesday night. Someone tried to kill me because they were afraid I would uncover their secret drug operation, no matter how loosely it was tied to the Big House." She ticked the problems off on her fingers. "The show producer has designs on my man, and sometimes I have to wonder if Kiki doesn't, as well. She certainly likes to hang on your arm and gaze up at you with her big, adoring eyes." When he would have protested, she swatted his arm. "I'm not through. My life is like a carnival sideshow. On days they're filming, I can hardly get in the gate of my own house. Reporters camp out on in our front yard. The whole town has gone crazy, trying to claim their fifteen minutes of fame. Have I forgotten anything?"

"Two things. One, all your renovations are being done for free."

"If I hadn't already suspected it, I now know—nothing in life is free." Her voice was mournful. "There's always some stipulation. In this case, a reality television series about my life. A nightmare on film."

They walked on a few steps before she thought to ask, "What was the second thing?"

Brash stopped immediately and pulled her around to face him. Arms hooked at her waist, he reeled her in close. "That your man is just that. *Yours.* Even if Amanda or Kiki or some fancy movie star has designs on me, I am only interested in one woman. And I am about to kiss her, right this instant."

"Then hurry up," Madison murmured, winding her arms around his neck.

Long moments later, Brash lifted his head. "Ah, Maddy, this is where you belong."

She smiled and guessed, "In your arms?"

"That, too. But I meant here, with me. On the ranch. With my family. My parents loved you, I could tell. And so did my sister."

"Today has been wonderful. I've had such a good time. And your family has made me feel very welcome."

"They know we're a couple. I didn't tell them, but they know."

"If they didn't before now, our thirty-minute absence will be a good clue."

"Thirty minutes? Good, we still have fifteen minutes left." He nuzzled her neck. "And I know just how we can spend it."

Maddy angled her neck for better access. "I like how you think, Chief deCordova."

When his hands moved in the dark, sliding over her with delicious promise, Maddy groaned. "Brash, not—not out here." It was hard to articulate a denial, when everything he did felt so perfect.

"Don't worry, sweetheart. Our first time won't be in the woods with our families on the other side of the trees." As his hands traveled slowly over her body, she had a moment of true confusion, trying to see the problem with such a scenario. Then sanity returned to her brain, as he continued to murmur against her lips, "I'm thinking a big, fluffy bed. Rose petals. Candlelight. A ring on your finger."

The words slowly penetrated the fog of desire that clouded her brain. She finally gasped and pulled away. "Wh—What did you say?"

"Shh. Come back here. We still have five minutes left."

"But you—"

He silenced her with a kiss. "Sorry. I have a way of getting ahead of myself. Let's take advantage of our last five minutes, and then we need to get back, before they send a search party in after us."

Maybe she had heard him wrong. Maybe he hadn't almost proposed marriage. Or maybe he was testing the waters. Maddy's head spun with the possibilities.

When they exited the woods, they did not go immediately into the ring of friends. They stood in the shadows, watching the interaction of the others. Bethani and Megan giggled over a messy tower of stacked s'mores. Blake showed the younger boys how to toast marshmallows on the grill and how to get the end of a stick to glow red without catching flame. Small clusters of adults were scattered around, each caught up in conversation. Genny chatted with his sister Laura, while Shannon visited with her former mother-in-law. Some might think it strange that he and his ex-wife were still friends, but in fact, it wasn't until the divorce that their relationship took a positive turn. He still loved Shannon, but the truth was, he had never loved her the way a man should love his wife. Not the way his father loved his mother. And Brash was no longer satisfied to settle for less.

He looked over at the woman by his side and smiled tenderly. What he felt for Madison was already stronger, and truer, than anything he had ever felt for the mother of his child.

"Thank you, Brash," she said softly, slipping her hand into his.

Caught with his feelings shimmering in his eyes, he had to clear the emotion from his throat before speaking. "Thank you for coming."

"I don't know about you, but I could use some more of your mom's sweet tea."

When she tugged on his hand to pull him along, he looked down at their clasped hands. He lifted his eyes to hers, a question in their depths. "Are you sure?"

Madison looked back at her children. Blake's face glowed, and it wasn't from the grill's flame. This was his dream day, including all the things he most loved: fishing, swimming, eating, shooting, even a game of tag football. A day in the sun and water with plenty of good food. Heaven on earth for her fifteen-year-old son.

Even Bethani looked completely happy. Lydia deCordova had joined the girls to inspect their layered creation. Bethani chatted effortlessly with Brash's mother, even when Megan skipped off to refill her tea glass. Madison could hear the teen bragging about catching the biggest fish of the day. Brash had helped her reel it in, and then showed her how to take it off the hook and re-bait for the next cast. Seeing them together had warmed Madison's heart and made her eyes misty.

This was the sort of quality family time she wanted for her children, the kind they had never gotten from the Reynolds side of the family. With sudden clarity, Madison knew this was, indeed, the place she—and her children—belonged.

She smiled up at the man by her side. Firelight shimmered on the ends of his dark auburn hair. Moonlight reflected in his smiling blue eyes. Her heart felt as soft and gooey as the gigantic s'more their daughters created. Her life was twice as sweet. And her love for this man was staggering.

"Yes, Brash," she said softly. "I'm sure. Hold my hand."

"I would be honored. Shall we?"

They proceeded across the clearing, hands casually clasped, pretending not to notice how the others noticed. When Blake came racing toward them, chased by three younger boys, they laughed and separated, but their hands remained together.

"Beep, beep, coming through!" Blake warned, ducking to clear the human arch. Three giggling boys followed, the last one crashing into Maddy's legs. She wobbled and almost fell, but Brash caught her. His arm lingered at her waist as they approached Bethani and Lydia.

To her credit, the teen did not make a scene. She even started up a conversation about fishing with Brash, asking when they could come out again. In Madison's estimation, it was the best endorsement they were going to receive from her daughter, but she would take it. For now, it was enough.

By the time they drove home from the ranch, they were all tired, happy, and sported varied shades of a slight sunburn.

Madison's heart was full.

15

Blake was still on a country high, stoked from the day of fishing. He chattered all through breakfast, reliving the high points from the day before and planning more outings in the near future.

"Just remember, your free time is about to come to an end," Madison reminded the youth. "Two-a-days may have already started, but school starts tomorrow morning. We'll see if you can even lift a rod and reel after your first game."

"I am Hercules," the boy joked, bulking up his muscle and posing like a body builder. "I am strong. I am mighty."

Bethani walked by and punched her brother in the stomach. "You am a wimp."

He merely grinned at her. "Didn't feel a thing," he claimed.

"Okay, you two," Madison cautioned. "Knock it off and get ready for church." She noticed that her grandmother was still in her robe and slippers. "Are you feeling all right this morning? You're usually half-dressed by now."

"My stomach's a bit upset this morning," Granny Bert confessed. "Must have been something I ate last night."

Or how much you ate, Maddy thought. She had noticed her grandmother's plate, heaped high with extra helpings of everything. And that was before dessert. "Do you feel like going to church?"

"I think I'd better sit this one out. I don't move as fast as I used to, and I might not make it to the bathroom in time."

"Can I get you anything?" Madison offered in concern.

"I think I'll mix me up a smoothie. I'll throw in some binding agents, like agrimony and blackberry leaf, maybe a little black walnut. That should do the trick." She rummaged through the cabinets. "Ought to be right tasty, too."

"What the heck is agrimony?" Bethani asked.

"That pretty yellow plant I have growing in the blue pot outside. It has some fine medicinal purposes."

Blake looked skeptical. "*Yellow plant* isn't code word for *weed,* is it? They say marijuana has medicinal purposes, too, you know."

"This isn't pot, silly boy. And marijuana isn't the only plant that can get you high, nor the only one with healing powers. The earth is filled with natural cures for most anything that ails you." Granny Bert opened a small jar and sprinkled a few flakes of a crushed substance into the blender. "Hand me that clover honey, will you, Beth?"

"Is that what makes your smoothies taste so funny? All those plants and weeds and flowers?"

Taking offense, Granny Bert frowned as she tossed in a handful of strawberries. "Who says my smoothies taste funny? They're delicious. You just wait and taste this one."

Watching her add a few drops of a clear oily substance, a dollop of honey, and finely crushed leaves, Bethani curled her nose. "I think I'll pass."

"Plants and herbs have been used for centuries to cure a passel of health problems. This one, agrimony, is good for sore throats, diarrhea, gallbladder ailments, even a runny nose. You can make a paste of it and apply it to your skin to get rid of zits and warts. Good for swelling, too."

"In that case, slather that girl down!" Blake called. "Her warty, zitty face needs all the help it can get."

As Bethani chased her brother from the kitchen and their playful shrieks faded down the hallway, soon punctuated with two distinctly slamming doors, Madison cleared the breakfast table.

"Speaking of herbs, Genny told me Myrna Lewis started her own business. She sells flowers and herbs, and even has a lawn service. Did you know that?"

Seeing the look her grandmother gave her, Madison laughed at her own foolishness. "Of course you knew that. You know everything that happens in The Sisters."

"Where do you think I got half of these herbs I'm using? It's too much trouble to go all the way to Bryan-College Station to find them. Besides, I prefer to buy local whenever I can."

"Myrna is so obsessed with winning Yard of the Year that I'm surprised she's willing to help other people with theirs. But you should see Carson Elliot's lawn. It turns out Myrna is his gardener, and the place is magnificent."

"I heard Dean told her she had to get a job, to help pay off her credit card debt. Most of the charges were at nurseries and garden supply stores. And of course for that gigantic fountain she had installed on their front lawn. That thing is—" When Granny Bert jabbed the puree button, the whir of the blender drowned out her grumbles, but Madison picked up the gist of the complaint.

"I would think starting a business would take money, as well," Madison remarked, more to herself than to her grandmother. As she wiped down the table, she recalled the conversation between Myrna and Barry Redmond. Something about a loan that Dean was unaware of. She idly wondered if Myrna had borrowed money to start her business. A business intended to pay off other borrowed money.

She clicked her tongue. "Always a mad cycle," she muttered.

"What was that?" Granny Bert asked.

"Oh, nothing. I just realized how late it is. I'd better hurry or I'll be late for church."

"Want some?" her grandmother offered, pouring her smoothie into a glass and taking a big gulp.

The mixture looked disgusting. Madison shook her head and backed away. "No, but I hope it makes you feel better."

As a cramp hit her stomach, her grandmother flinched. "I just hope it works soon."

ॐ

"Thanks, Cutter," Madison said as the young fire chief ushered her into the station. Housed in the old cotton gin, the station was large and drafty. Their voices echoed through the towering space.

"No problem. I'm not sure you'll find what you're looking for, but you're welcome to look through the files. My office is back here."

They stepped into a spacious but sparse office. Filing cabinets flanked one wall, a worn couch rested against another, and a long table occupied a third, its surface scattered with handheld equipment, two-way radios, and assorted paraphernalia. Most of the walls were bare metal, but one sported Sheetrock and paint. Maps and charts covered the wall, vying for space with framed awards and diplomas. Bulletin boards brimmed with newspaper clippings, handwritten thank you notes, photographs, and participation ribbons for various chili cook-offs and barbecue contests. Madison noted that most of the ribbons were either blue or red.

In the center of the room was a large messy desk and a couple of chairs. Cutter took the chair behind the desk and rifled through a bottom drawer. "It might take me a few minutes to locate all the files."

"Today was the first day of school. As long as I'm done in time to pick the kids up after practice and hear how their day went, I'm good."

"First football game is Friday night, huh?" She could hear the hum of excitement in his voice.

If Madison had forgotten what Friday nights were like in small towns, she had been quickly reminded. People here lived and breathed for high school football. Each week, the storefronts around town blasted the current rival and vowed eternal loyalty to the Fighting Cotton Kings of The Sisters High. On Friday afternoons, half the town attended the pep rally at school. By evening, the bleachers at the football field were always packed. Those who could not attend the game waited at home to hear the final score. A few may have joined the Space Age and kept up with scores via the internet, but Madison knew most depended on the after-news sports program on television or their favorite radio recap to keep up with local teams. On Saturday mornings, the game was rehashed in detail. Referees were either scorned or praised; scores were either celebrated or best forgotten. And on Monday, it all started over again.

"That's right," she nodded. "Personally, I think it's too hot for those kids to be out there in full uniform, but nobody asked me." She crinkled her nose before her expression turned melancholy. "I can't believe I'll be there watching both my babies." Even though her son favored baseball, Blake's athletic prowess secured him a spot on the varsity football team. Bethani was a cheerleader.

"I hear Blake will be a running back."

"Yes, I think that's right. Did you play in high school?"

"I'm Tug Montgomery's son. What do you think?" Cutter smirked.

"You played."

"All four years. But my favorite sport was rodeo."

"I played basketball."

"I can see that. You have the height for it. What about Genny? Did she play?"

"Genny was the cheerleader."

Cutter's hazel eyes sparkled. "I can see that, too." He turned his attention back to the files and plopped a heavy folder onto the desk.

"Is that all of them?"

Cutter's laugh was dry. "That's only for this year. The rest are in those filing cabinets. You needed to go back... what, five years?"

"Yes."

He pushed away from his desk and crossed to the filing cabinets. After jerking open several drawers and extracting numerous folders, he gave Maddy a sympathetic smile.

"I'm not sure what you're looking for, but here you go."

"I'm not sure what I'm looking for, either, but maybe something will jump out at me."

"Good luck."

16

The birthday party for Mary Alice Montgomery was that evening. Normally, Tuesday nights were not busy at the café. But most Tuesday nights did not include twenty-eight members of the Montgomery family.

With tables lined end to end, Genny decorated the party with rustic elegance. She fashioned centerpieces from mason jars, flickering candles, bits of burlap and raffia, and trailing ivy. Set upon white cloths, the look was full of shabby chic charm.

By the time Tug arrived with the guest of honor, the rest of the party was seated and waiting. The former local beauty queen and one-time contestant in the Miss Texas Pageant was so touched by the surprise party that she broke down in tears.

While Genny and her staff bustled around to serve the guests, she caught bits and pieces of their conversations. A half dozen topics floated around the table. Mary Alice traveled down memory lane, with Tug and some of their children adding favorite stories of their own. Football stats blended into a lively discussion over the newest X-Box game. One end of the table discussed cows and hay, while the other end exchanged ideas seen on Pinterest. Someone else was planning a trip to Paris, while further down the table the topic was deer season.

It must be nice, Genny thought as she circled the table, *to have a big family.* As an only child, she had never had this. *This* was loud and confusing and at times chaotic, but it was nice, nonetheless. She knew some of Cutter's family, but keeping up with all of them was a bit confusing. Doing the best she could, Genny concentrated more on service than conversation.

Fifteen minutes after the party started, an older gentleman walked through the door. Genny knew in an instance that it had to be Cutter's grandfather.

Small, wiry, and whip-cord thin, Sticker Pierce was the epitome of a rodeo cowboy. Just like in all the old westerns, his legs were bowed and bent from too many years spent in the saddle. A pair of well-worn jeans encased his legs and disappeared into boots that came high on his calf. Genny noted the fancy stitchery along the red leather uppers and the flowing red initials embroidered onto the pocket of his shirt. Above the biggest belt buckle she had ever seen, his pearl-snap western shirt was starched and neat, and a match to the shirt Cutter wore. With a full head of hair, its color long since faded away, and a snow-white handlebar mustache, Sticker Pierce was still a handsome man. Leathered and tan, he was an older and more wrinkled version of Cutter.

When Mary Alice saw her father, she flew to her feet. "Daddy? Daddy, is that you?"

Genny had been away from the South for several years, but it never stuck her as odd that a sixty-year-old woman still referred to her father as 'Daddy.' Most men could be fathers. Only the special ones could forever be a daddy.

After hugs and kisses all around, Sticker Montgomery settled in and the meal began. When Genny delivered a plate to the older gentleman, he eyed her with hazel eyes still clear and sharp.

"And who is this beautiful little thing?" he chuckled.

"That's Cutter's friend, and she owns this place." Cutter's sister Constance spoke loud enough that her grandfather—and everyone else in the restaurant—could hear. "Genesis, this is our grandfather, Sticker Pierce. Sticker, Genesis Baker."

"Pleased to meet you, little lady," he said, taking her hand and brushing it with a kiss. His eyes sought his grandson and he winked. "Good job, boy."

"Oh, we're not—" Genny protested, but her words were swept away when one of the children overturned his drink. She rushed to clean up the mess, forgetting to explain their relationship.

"Genesis, where is your plate?" Mary Alice asked after grace was said and everyone began to eat.

"Oh, I'm not—"

Again, her protest was lost in a sea of murmurs. Chairs scooted and people shifted.

"Seriously, I can't join you."

"Of course you can! Sit down, right here!" This came from Cooper's wife, Briana. Not only was she a regular at the café, Genny had gone to high school with her. "That way I can talk you into giving me this recipe. It is delicious."

With everyone chanting "Sit! Sit! Sit!" Genny reluctantly did so. She was soon caught up in all the camaraderie and all the noise that was the Montgomery family. She enjoyed visiting with Cutter's brothers and sisters and hearing their family stories. Sticker, particularly, was a gifted storyteller.

"Your grandfather is a hoot," she told Cutter at one point. "Where has he been all these years?"

"Riding the circuit."

"Still? He must be at least seventy-five! He doesn't look it, but since your mom is sixty…"

"He's almost seventy-eight. When he got too old to ride the stock, he started providing it. The Blazing P Brand is highly regarded in the rodeo world as having some of the best stock in the business."

"Where does he live? When he's not on the circuit, I mean."

Cutter shrugged. "He has ranches in Colorado, Montana, Oklahoma, and Texas. He roams between them."

Genny had to frown. "That seems rather sad, not having one special place to call home. What about your grandmother? Is she still living?"

"She passed away several years ago, but they haven't been married since my mom was little. There have been several wives since then, a few of which I can't even remember."

Genny looked across the table to the vibrant man engaged in a lively conversation with his son-in-law. He seemed to be of good health and sound mind, but she wondered what sort of shape his heart was in; not his ticker, but his *heart*. Leading a free and nomadic lifestyle might sound fun and exciting, but it had to be lonely.

"That's too bad," she murmured. "He's such a charming man." A glance around the table revealed that everyone was through eating. "Oops. Looks like it's time for dessert."

"This tira-mousse better be as good as you promised, or you'll owe me big time. I'm thinking apple turnovers for the rest of my life."

"It's tiramisu, and have no worry. You will love it." She gave him a playful tap on the nose as a reprimand.

His nephew saw the exchange and teased him about it. "Aw, Uncle Cutter is in trouble!"

Genny disappeared into the kitchen. Moments later, she and two members of her staff returned, pushing a cart filled with individual dishes of the decadent tiramisu. Mary Alice's portion sat in a pedestal dish and boasted six slender candles pushed into the creamy layers.

As the family sang *Happy Birthday*, Genny and her staff quickly distributed the other desserts. A second cart rolled out, carrying plates piled high with cannoli, freshly brewed coffee, and cold milk. As Genny placed the cannoli randomly along the tables, she watched people's reactions to the tiramisu.

She watched Cutter as he took his first bite. After a skeptical perusal of the dessert, poking it a few times with his fork and disturbing the chocolate shavings sprinkled on top, he hesitantly slid the first bite into his mouth. Genny knew the moment the flavors hit his taste buds. A look of surprise crossed his handsome face, followed closely by pleasure. As he lifted a second forkful to his mouth, his eyes found hers. A slow smile slid across his face, reflected in his eyes, as he tipped his fork in silent salute.

That look, Genny thought happily. It was what made the job worth it. Every chef, every cook, strived to bring that unique pleasure to their epicure. It made all the hard work of preparing a dish worthwhile.

She looked around for reaction from the others. Tug's dessert had all but disappeared. Mary Alice had her eyes closed as she savored the distinct flavors swirled within the many layers. Constance and sister-in-law Penny oohed as they held their dishes to the light, examining the dessert as if to discover its magical formula. A few of the children were more impressed with the cannoli rolls—some filled with sprinkles, some with fruit mixtures, some dipped in chocolate, some left plain— than with the tiramisu, but the adults were enthralled. Even Sticker looked impressed.

As the end of the evening drew near, Mary Alice stood and thanked her guests for coming and for sharing her special day. She extended a particularly warm thankyou to Genesis.

"It has been my pleasure," Genny assured her with a genuine smile.

Tug caught her eye and winked in approval. Before the party broke up, all four sons and one grandson had done the same.

Genny threw back her head in delight, her dimples deepening and her eyes twinkling. The entire Montgomery family was thoroughly enchanting. And the men were lady killers, right down to the toddlers.

She collected hugs as they filed out the doors. Cutter was one of the last to shuffle past.

"Genny darlin', what can I say? You outdid yourself tonight. Thank you." He gave her a warm hug.

"Kiss her, Uncle Cutter," little Houston insisted from behind him. "Grand Tug did, and so did Sticker."

Genny grinned at Cutter, tapping her cheek. "Sure did," she confirmed with twinkling eyes.

"I can do better than that," he mumbled. Before she realized what he intended, Cutter swooped in and brushed a kiss onto her lips. It was quick and light, but Genny was not immune to the magic. It felt like stardust had fallen around her.

His voice was a low rumble against her lips. "Good night, Genny darlin'. And thanks again. Just like you, the party was perfect."

17

It was a big day for the Reynolds family. A big day for
HOME television network. And, being that the towns-
people took such a personal interest and pride in their
small part in the success of *Home Again: Starting Over*, it was a
big day for The Sisters.

Today, they were filming their first 'reveal' episode for the
show. One room was officially complete.

Television cameras shadowed Madison, Bethani and Blake
up the cobblestone walkway. Amanda coached them on what
not to wear—nothing solid brown or solid beige, nothing red
or orange, nothing too matchy-matchy, nothing too flashy.

"I'm nervous," Bethani confided.

"Me, too, honey," Madison admitted. "Kiki banned me
from the house last week and hasn't allowed me back in until
now."

"It's more like an excited nervous, you know? It means
we're getting closer to having the rest of it done. Closer to
moving in."

"It finally feels real," Blake agreed with his sister.

It had been a long five months, with one more yet to come. The projected finish date was mid-October. There was still so much to do, and most of the rooms still looked like a disaster zone.

The exterior of the house was complete. After years of neglect, the grand old lady now sported a fresh coat of paint. The pale gray had been the right choice, Madison noted with satisfaction. Traditional yet modern. Excessive amounts of gingerbread trim, painted a few shades off from purest white, added distinction and grace. Cranberry accents provided the pop.

The grounds were groomed and restored to their former glory. Even the cobblestone walkway they traveled upon had received a makeover. All around them, the grass was lush and green, the flowerbeds brimming with color.

Madison knew a moment of panic as she gazed over the massive showpiece. She had never had a lawn this size before. The house stood upon a full city block; how would she ever manage all this?

She thought of the starter home she and Gray bought when they first married, and the time they had devoted to the yard there, cultivating it into a modest but eye-pleasing refuge. She had taken such pride in the flowerbeds and hedges, and in the pear tree out front. In the summertime, the tree's low-hanging limbs offered challenge and adventure for the twins and their neighborhood friends. Each fall, it offered up delicious bounty that she turned into cakes and jam. Madison had loved that tree. When they moved into their grand new house, the one they could little afford but that Gray and his mother insisted they must buy, she had missed the tree almost as much as she missed the house itself.

Their house in the new up-and-coming neighborhood came with a much larger lawn and a much grander presence. It also came with a gardener, so her efforts at gardening were no longer needed, nor welcomed. Despite the fancy neighborhood and the fancy yard, there was nothing about the house that Madison missed. Nothing she mourned. Not like she mourned her beloved pear tree.

The consolation was that now Madison had plenty of trees. Giant, old, mature trees, the kind with billowing arms and thick, massive trunks. The kind not found in fancy new subdivisions, no matter how up-and-coming they might be. These trees had roots. The kind Madison craved for her and her children.

"Look, there's my sign," Madison pointed. "It will direct clients to the side porch for *In a Pinch.*"

Blake offered his arm to his mother and mimicked a bow. "Shall we, my ladies?" he asked in a formal voice.

"I think we shall." Madison's nervous reply floated out as a giggle.

Nick waited for them by the French doors.

"Are you ready for this?" he smiled in welcome.

"Yes. Absolutely."

He went through a spiel that none of them heard. He talked about the age and condition of the house when he first saw it, spoke to some of the improvements made, mentioned the generosity of their fine sponsors. And finally, he swung open the doors.

Amanda had coached them on the proper response. Try to look genuinely shocked, she encouraged. Thrilled. Speechless with delight.

Madison promptly forgot the guidelines. Her speechless delight was genuine.

"Oh my," she breathed. "Oh my."

Kiki swept toward them, wearing her signature flowing dress and three-inch heels. "Is that a good 'oh my?'" She asked it as a question, but her smile was confident.

Madison's eyes traveled the room. To preserve the integrity of the home's history, the extensive woodwork in the room remained the same. With its many built-in bookshelves and cabinetry, heavy crown molding, and exquisite burled-walnut paneling, the room could have felt dark and drab.

Yet the room felt anything but drab. Where possible, the walls were painted white to offset the massive amounts of wood, which now glowed with new vitality. It was amazing what a good cleaning, satin polish, and plenty of light could do to century-old wood, even when the grain had darkened with age. Subtle track lighting was integrated into the bookcases. Original brass sconces glowed against the dark panels. Lamps lit multiple surfaces, chandeliers twinkled overhead, and natural light streamed in through gauzy white curtains.

Madison's desk was the highlight of the room. Built by master carpenters in Europe, Juliet Randolph had the fine mahogany creation custom built to her own specifications. Through the years, the patina of the wood became more beautiful than ever. A tufted executive chair, done in luxurious cream-colored leather, complemented the beauty of the desk and kept it feeling fresh and timeless.

And somehow Nick, a master craftsman in his own right, had duplicated a smaller version of the desk for Derron. It sat close to the French doors, welcoming visitors as they arrived.

Madison's throat thickened with emotion. "That is a wonderful 'oh my.'"

As they toured the space, Nick and Kiki took turns pointing out the room's many features.

"Aren't these seating vignettes scrumptious?" Kiki gushed. "Can't you imagine sinking into these wonderful chairs, curling up with a delightful book that whisks you away to another place and time? And look, this grouping has an ottoman and these divine afghans. Feel these. They are part of the signature collection from *Deep Water Weavers*."

The cream-colored chairs clustered around the fireplace and within the cozy nook of the turret.

"Or for confidential conversations," Madison murmured, thinking of her would-be clients. No more public café booths. "I like how the rugs pull the room together. Cream and dusky blue."

"They have a deep, decadent pile. The finest wool, also by *Deep Water*."

Accessories and artwork throughout the room were light and airy, a tasteful blend of shabby chic and timeless elegance. Bethani and Blake wandered about the room, delighted to see their own faces in several of the photographs.

"You can keep your files in here," Nick told her, indicating the built-in file cabinets with their intricate trim. "And this cabinet opens to reveal your new state-of-the-art computer center, compliments of *Tramar Electronics*."

"This is... amazing." There was no other word for it. Madison was overwhelmed.

Nick pointed out more surprises. "I know how important security is to you and your family. *Balford Security* has stepped forward to provide your home and grounds with the latest in security. From this panel, you will be able to monitor and control all alarms. There are additional panels in the kitchen and master bedroom."

"You didn't take out the secret passage, did you?" Blake fretted.

"No, Blake, we didn't. But if we reveal it on national television, it won't be a secret, now will it?" Nick smiled.

"Why don't we see what your friends and other family members think about your new office and library?" Kiki suggested with a bright smile.

Someone ushered Granny Bert and Genesis into the room. Derron, Megan, and Brash were close behind. It was a special surprise to have Brash here to share this day with her. One look at her grandmother's face, and she knew who to thank for the pleasure.

After the appropriate oohs and ahhs from the group and Derron's very pronounced squeals of delight, Nick called for everyone's attention.

He stood at the doorway leading into the small sitting room off the library. Steeped in all that was proper and fitting, Miss Juliet insisted on multiple rooms in her magnificent home, all with a distinct purpose. The sitting room beyond had been more casual than the others, consistent with a den or family room in modern-day homes.

"We have one more surprise for you today," he said. "We know you all have busy lives. Sometimes you just need to unwind and spend a little quality time together, even if it's only to watch movies. *Tramar Electronics* wanted to do more for you. Something special. Along with *Today Furnishings, Deep Water Weavers*, and the very talented hands of our own Kiki Paretta, *Tramar* would like to welcome you to your new family media room."

Nick opened the door and presented them with a tasteful yet casually decorated room, fit for the cover of any home magazine. Being an interior room—snuggled behind the grand stairway and between the formal library and the newly expanded laundry—it had no windows, making it the perfect choice for a media room. With pale walls, white woodwork, and a large beige wraparound sectional, the color scheme kept the room light and airy. With a flick of the remote, the lights dimmed, a huge flat-screen television appeared on the wall, and the room vibrated with soft music from the surround-sound speakers.

"Did you know about this?" Madison asked Brash. He had materialized at her side the moment the lights dimmed.

"Not at all."

"This is magnificent! Truly, truly magnificent." She hugged Brash's arm to her side as she wiped away happy tears.

"This is so super awesome!" Blake beamed as he bounced from one electronic wonder to the next. Nick showed him the control panel and all the multimedia features. "Sweet!" he kept repeating.

"Look as this sofa! Feel how soft it is!" Bethani and Megan curled up on the modular unit, delighting in the many features it offered. One button provided a heated seat, another helped them to recline. Built-in headphones, cup holders, and charging ports were only a few of their discoveries.

"And is that a popcorn machine?" Blake spotted the snack center right away, complete with refrigerator and sink. "Sweet!"

"At least there's a bathroom right here," Granny Bert noted, opening another door. "Might come in handy during a long movie."

"Sweetheart?" Brash murmured, bending to speak in Madison's ear. "Are you all right?"

Madison knew cameras were rolling. She knew the world was watching. She was too overwhelmed, and too happy, to care. She slipped her arms around Brash's waist and squeezed.

"I am very all right," she assured him.

"This calls for a celebration," Genny decided. "Everyone over to *New Beginnings*. I'm buying."

"I guess it is lunchtime," Madison said, glancing at her watch. "Okay, you kids can eat before you go back to school."

"Ah, Mom, do we have to?" Blake protested.

"School just started and you're already missing half a day. Yes, you have to."

Hearing the finality in his mother's voice, he gave up arguing. "Okay. But can I drive to the restaurant?"

Maddy rolled her eyes. The twins were taking Driver's Ed so they could apply for driver's permits when they turned sixteen. Like an ostrich with its head stuck in the sand, Madison refused to acknowledge how quickly that day was coming up. She had trouble assimilating the fact that her babies—her precious, adorable babies—would soon be sixteen. Her method of management, so far, was to ignore the fact.

Seeing them behind the wheel of a car was a nasty reminder of how her babies would soon be adults. Already, their cries of "I call shotgun!" had morphed into "I'm driving!" Soon it would be "See you next semester" and "I'm getting married."

Before she could sink into depression, Madison snapped herself out of it. Today was about celebrating. Realizing Blake still waited for an answer, she fished inside her pocket for the keys.

She turned toward Brash. "You'll join us at the restaurant, right?"

He consulted his wristwatch before agreeing.

The small convoy converged upon *New Beginnings* and flowed inside. Genny called ahead and a large table awaited them. With the stars from the show joining them, they caused a stir as they hustled around the table and found their seats. Seated across from Kiki, the teenage girls were more than delighted to be in her shadow. Blake claimed a spot next to Brash so they could discuss football and fishing. Madison snuggled between him and her grandmother. Nick and Amanda claimed the end by Kiki, Derron made a point to sit by Nick, and Genny settled in one of the empty chairs across from Maddy.

"Oh, look, Cutter just came in," Maddy noticed. "Let's ask him to join us." She waved to get his attention.

He looked hot and tired after a morning of work. He still wore his welding cap, its bright color at odds with the faded blue jeans and denim shirt that he wore. Tiny holes scattered up the arms of his shirt and splattered onto the front, their edges singed from hot sparks. Genny heard Megan and Bethani giggle beside her. They were obviously impressed with the blue-collar look of a working man.

Ambling their way, he greeted them with, "Howdy."

"Have a seat," Brash invited.

"Ah, that's okay, I'm meeting my grandfather for lunch."

"Oh, is he still in town?" Genny asked, somewhat surprised. Hearing the way everyone talked, she didn't think Sticker Pierce was the kind to stay in one place for very long.

"Sure is."

"We have plenty of room. There's two chairs right there. Please, sit down and eat with us," Madison insisted.

He looked uncertain. "Are you sure?"

"Of course. You're practically family. In fact, we should have invited you to the reveal."

"Yeah, man, it was so cool!" Blake gushed.

The teenager proceeded to tell all about the media room and its many electronic wonders. Bethani and Megan broke in with their own favorite features, and Madison squeezed in a review of the library-turned-office. Cutter was bombarded with details from every side. Even Kiki and Nick joined the discussion. Granny Bert was the only one who did not actively join in.

Madison noticed her grandmother's uncharacteristic silence. Dipping her head toward her, she asked, "Are you okay? Is your stomach bothering you again?"

"No, no, it's fine. Hungry, but fine."

"You're being awfully quiet. You sure nothing's wrong?"

Her smile seemed forced. "I'm fine as a frog's hair."

"If you're sure..."

"I am. Stop worrying over me, child. This is your day. A day to celebrate. It won't be long now, and your house will be done."

A thought occurred to Madison. "You know, Granny, there's plenty of room at the Big House. A bedroom on the first floor, three more empty ones upstairs. We would be thrilled to have you live there with us."

Her grandmother patted her hand. "Thank you, Maddy dear, but I don't want to leave my home until I'm forced to. That old house is where I raised my boys. Where Joe and I built our life together. You don't just walk away from roots like that." Memories made her eyes turn dewy. "I told you, I loved that man with my whole heart. Remember that."

It was an odd statement to make. Madison wondered about her grandmother's strange mood, even as she nodded. "Yes, Granny, I remember."

"Good. Now tell Cutter about that new alarm system you have, and all those monitor screens. It's almost like we're at the White House."

She had been dismissed. Recognizing the signs, Madison turned back to the other diners and left her grandmother to wallow in her funk.

Minutes later, the bell jingled above the door and a new-comer stepped inside the café. Considering that two television personalities sat at the long table, the man's arrival caused quite a stir. A surprised murmur rippled through the crowd. Most of the diners recognized the man by sight. The others recognized their recognition, and knew he must be someone important.

"Hey, that's the rodeo guy," Megan said.

"Who?" Bethani was clueless.

"He's like a five-time world champion bull rider. Royalty in the rodeo world. And in the western-wear world, too." Megan grinned, jutting out her latest pair of dress boots. Turquoise shafts with crosses and bling, brown vamps with coordinated turquoise insets. And sure enough, stamped right along the collar next to the pull strap, was a sprawling signature that said 'Sticker Pierce.'

"Sticker," Cutter called, waving his hand. "Over here." He stood to greet his grandfather.

"I hope you don't mind. My friends asked us to join them. Let me introduce you. Everyone, this is my grandfather, Sticker Pierce. You already know Genny. Beside her are Megan, Bethani, and Derron." He proceeded around the table, past the *Home Again* team, Blake, Brash and Maddy. He concluded the introductions when he reached the end of the table and Granny Bert.

Sticker dipped his head with each introduction, smiling in polite greeting. But the smile slipped from his face when his eyes traveled to the end of the line. His animated face grew still. One side of his white mustache twitched.

His voice came out strangled. "Bertha Hamilton."

Granny Bert hitched her head up a notch and corrected him. "Bertha Cessna."

"That's right," he recalled. "Joe Cessna." He looked around in a conspicuous manner.

"My Joe's been gone for eight years," she supplied. "Longest eight years of my life."

"Better than sixty." He uttered the cryptic words as he took the chair at the head of the table, capped on either side by Granny Bert and Cutter.

"So you two know one another?" Madison asked. The vibes radiating from the two of them were hard to miss. Madison guessed they had been adversaries, back in the day.

"Oh, Bertha and I go way back," Sticker said. His eyes settled on her grandmother. "So how have you been, Belle?"

"Belle?" Madison echoed, her face skewed.

Neither paid any attention to Madison's confusion. Their eyes were riveted on the other.

"I've been fine, Sticker. I've had a fine life. This is my granddaughter. Did you know that? One of eight. Well, five granddaughters, three grandsons. Eight in all. Joe and I were blessed with four sons."

Madison slid a suspicious eye at her grandmother. Was she rambling? She seemed nervous, if the two bright spots of color in her hollow cheeks were any indication. Cheeks that had been unusually pale, just minutes ago.

"Well, she's as pretty as her grandmother," Sticker said, but his eyes lingered on the older woman. He finally slid his gaze to Maddy and smiled. The gesture took years off his wrinkled, weathered face. And she noted that it was every bit as charming and attractive as Cutter's. Even close to eighty, the old cowboy was still quite handsome.

"That's why I always called her Belle," he explained, his eyes traveling back to her grandmother. "She was much too pretty to be hampered with a name like Bertha. To me, your grandmother has always been as pretty and pure as a bell."

Madison noticed the way her grandmother gulped down a sudden surge of pleasure. She pretended not to be affected by the flattery, but her face softened. Her tense shoulders relaxed. Something flickered in her eyes. Strangely enough, it looked a lot like guilt.

Beneath the table, Madison nudged Brash, so that he could watch the interaction between the two older people.

"Some things never change," Sticker continued quietly.

"I see you still have a silver tongue."

"You know what they say. Silver tongue, lead heart." The last words held the slightest of accusations.

"So, Mr. Pierce, what brings you to town?" Brash broke into the awkward silence at the end of the table.

"Call me Sticker. I'm here celebrating my daughter's birthday. Mary Alice Montgomery, Cutter's mom."

Brash nodded. "I know Mary Alice well. I just didn't realize you were her father. I guess Henry Pierce was her stepfather?"

The old cowboy nodded his head. There was absolutely no bitterness in his voice as he explained, "My first cousin stepped up and became a fine father to my little girl. And a better husband to her ma than I could have ever been."

Brash understood. He felt much the same about his oldest and best friend, Matthew Aikman. He could not think of a better man to co-parent with. And Matt and Shannon were suited to one another, so much more than he and Shannon had ever been. He supposed it had been the same with Sticker and Henry Pierce.

"So how long will you be in town?"

Sticker slid a sidelong glance to Granny Bert. She pretended disinterest, fiddling with her utensils, but Madison felt her shoulders tense once again. She was waiting to hear his answer.

"Well, now, I reckon that all depends on the weather. Depends on whether I feel a cold front coming on, or," he turned his head to look straight at the woman he called Belle, "a warming trend."

"It's a hundred and one outside, you old fool," Granny Bert blustered. "Is that not warm enough for you?"

"I don't know, Belle. You tell me."

Granny Bert chose to ignore his words and the intensity of his gaze. "Genesis, what is wrong with your help today? We've been waiting on our meal for ages. I'm an old woman. I might expire, right here in this chair, before I get to enjoy my last meal."

Genny giggled at the old woman's discomposure. It wasn't often she saw her surrogate grandmother so flustered. She hopped from her chair, but the plates were coming out as she turned. "Oh, good," she said with an impish smile. "You won't expire hungry. Here's our lunch."

18

Madison returned to the Big House after lunch. With the cameras off and the crew gone, she had the room to herself.

"Knock, knock."

She looked up from her task of unloading a box and smiled at her best friend. "Hey, Gen. I didn't expect to see you here again today."

"I thought you and Derron might be able to use some help. Where is he, by the way? He left the café early."

"When he saw the playback tape and realized how sallow that yellow shirt made him appear on television, he took the afternoon off to go shopping," Madison informed her. "*Macy's* is having a sale. We won't see him for the rest of the evening."

"That man is a hoot," Genny said affectionately.

"And the best darn secretary-slash-receptionist I'll ever hope to have, so I'm willing to indulge him," her friend admitted. "So it's just me and the boxes."

"And me. Don't forget me."

"As always, you are a lifesaver, my friend. You can start with that box. Most of that will go in Derron's desk."

"I'm sure he'll rearrange to suit his own needs, but I can at least unload it."

"I'm trying to get my files in order. Not that I have all that many, but I can always dream big." Madison fanned her arm Vanna White style to indicate the elaborate built-in filing cabinets.

"Too bad Kiki didn't organize those, as well."

"I'm not sure I want her to see how pathetically slim my case files are," Madison admitted. "And how few there are."

"We can talk freely in here, right?" Genny questioned, glancing around for cameras.

Madison nodded vigorously. "That is one thing I refused to back down on. Amanda can film and record just about everything else that is said and done in the house, but my office is officially off limits. I'll use my handy little bug detector every day if I have to, but this room is mic-free. I want my clients to be free to discuss their cases in confidence, without fear of having it broadcast to the entire nation."

Genny flashed her dimples when she grinned. "We're going to miss your business meetings at the back booth."

"No disrespect, but *I won't*," Madison said emphatically.

Genny dusted her hands and announced, "I'm through with this box. You want me to start on this next one? It has your binoculars and spy gadgets in it. Where do you want them?"

"How about those cabinets over there?"

Genny fished the first item from her box and examined it with curiosity. "What the heck is this thing?"

"Surveillance equipment," Madison announced proudly. "Compliments of Murray Archer."

Genny eyed it with suspicion. "Go figure."

Madison merely chuckled. "Just pile it up in that cabinet. I'll sort through it later. When we get the boxes unloaded, I want you to help me look over my files on Gloria Jeffers. I feel like I'm missing something. Some link that ties everything all together with the fires."

Genny's dimples flashed. "Aw, I'll get to play like a real PI, with an office and everything! And spy gadgets, to boot!"

Madison wagged her finger and spoke as if to a six-year-old.

"Okay, but no playtime until you're done with your work."

"Yes, mother dear."

As Genny tackled another box, she asked, "So what was all that at lunch, between Cutter's grandfather and your grandmother?"

"Good question. She's not saying a word, but unless I'm sadly mistaken, I do believe Sticker Pierce is the mystery man from my grandmother's past."

"What mystery man?"

"I know, right? See how well she's kept him hidden? But she recently dropped a little bombshell that Grandpa Joe was not her first love. Her first love was a man younger, and shorter, than she was."

"Hmm. Sticker is a bit shorter than I expected. Of course, it's hard to know how tall he would be if his legs weren't bowed so much."

"He's still a handsome man."

"I know. It's like looking at an age progression of Cutter, and what he'll look like in another forty or so years."

"Which is how we came across the subject in the first place. I was supposed to tell you not to let the age difference between you and Cutter stand in the way of your happiness. Granny says you'll live to regret it. She did."

"But she and Grandpa Joe were so happy together!"

"They were. She says she loved him with her heart and soul and never once regretted her life with him. But I think a part of her always wondered what might have been, had she chosen her first love."

Genny paused in her task of filling a bookshelf with Madison's collections. "He broke her heart, huh? Cutter says he's never been known to stick around for long. Apparently he's been married several times."

"No, it was the other way around. Granny broke *his* heart and he left town." She did some quick calculations in her head. "Of course, I'm guessing he bounced back pretty quickly. There couldn't have been too much time between him leaving town and Mary Alice's arrival into the world."

"Or maybe he never really recovered, at all. Maybe he's loved her all these years. Maybe that's why he could never settle down with another woman." Genny swept her arms across her heart, finishing on a dramatic note. "Maybe she was his one true love and his heart still belongs to his Belle."

"Or maybe you are an incurable romantic. And maybe, just maybe," Madison said, wagging her finger in her direction, "you should take Granny's advice. What if Cutter is your one true love and you let a little thing like numbers stand in your way of happiness?"

"What is it with everyone's preoccupation about me and Cutter? Now even his family thinks we're an item! We are just friends."

"Humph. *Friends* don't look at each other the way you and Cutter look at one another."

"I have no idea what you're talking about," Genny said breezily, but her face colored. "So where did you want this box?"

"Smooth transition," Madison noted dryly, "but I'll let it slide this time. You're cheap labor."

"Wine," Genny reminded her. "I work for wine."

Two hours, half a pizza, and an empty bottle of wine later, they were still studying the papers strewn across Madison's desk.

"I think you're stalling," Genesis accused. "Things are no clearer now than they were an hour ago. You just like the look of having those files laid on your desk, looking all official and important-like."

Madison nibbled a slice of pizza. "You might have a point," she conceded. "But I keep thinking if I stare at it long enough, something will pop out at me."

"So let's look at what we have."

Madison grabbed yet another sheet of paper and started over with new notes. She indicated each party by their initials.

"We know there was a connection between the fire suppression equipment in use at three of the five fires. *A+ Fire Systems* installed and serviced the exhaust system at *Montelongo's*. They partnered with *Allied Industries* to design the system used on Ray Sam's motor home and Carson Elliot's new home. All three were faulty."

"And all three tie into the Libenthal brothers," Genny agreed. She wiggled her finger like a pen, prompting the correct notations on paper.

"We know that Slim, at least, is on the take and willing to sway an investigation whichever way pays the most money. But that's only three of the five. What about the other two?"

Arrows and lines circled the paper, leaving those two fires noticeably unmarked.

"Well," Genny offered, "both Jerry Don Peavey and William Shanks had insurance with Omega, parent company of Magnus. Put a squiggly line between them. And Magnus ties back to Slim and Tiny, so add another squiggly there. Plus, *Montelongo's* had insurance through Magnus." She air-painted another squiggle with her finger. She peered over her wineglass to the paper. "Is it looking any better?"

"Full of lines and arrows and squiggles, but no complete circles. No one single thing that ties all of these together."

"There is one thing," Genny pointed out. "*Lone Star Law.* Maybe Gloria discovered her boss was crooked."

Madison shook her head. "I tried that scenario, too, but it didn't make sense. What would he have to gain? He lost half the cases."

"So we're back to equipment failure."

"But what equipment could there be to prevent Jerry Don Peavey's pasture fire?"

"So we're back to insurance fraud."

"They didn't all have the same carrier."

"So we're back to square one."

Madison blew out a weary sigh. "Bingo." She drew a big square onto the paper and stabbed it with her pen.

"Granny mentioned someone else. What was the story on him?"

"Newly somebody or another. He had a repair service where the taxidermy store is."

"You mean Cash Montgomery's store? Cutter's brother?"

"Yes. Apparently this Newly fellow didn't have insurance and couldn't afford to rebuild."

Genny nibbled her bottom lip before admitting, "I overheard Cutter and Brash talking the other day. Did you know they suspect that last week's fire out at Bob Peterson's might have been intentionally set?"

"Really?"

"Looks that way."

"Do you know if he had insurance?"

"Yes, but not enough. He lost his tractor, his barn, his winter hay, and several acres of grazing pasture. Cutter overheard him saying he may have to sell out."

"So it's doubtful that he set the fire himself," Madison reasoned.

"They were trying to think of who else could benefit from the fire."

"You mean like the insurance company or something?"

Genny shrugged. "I guess."

"So maybe this has been an insurance scam all along. And maybe Miss Gloria got lucky and uncovered a real conspiracy this time."

"You know, when we were at her house, we were looking for evidence that she was a drinker. We really didn't look for any notes she might have left lying around."

Madison nodded thoughtfully. "So maybe we should go back."

19

They let themselves into the house and turned on the lights.

"You look here in the living room, I'll look in the bedroom," Madison suggested. "Look for notes she made, ideas she scribbled down."

"You can take the bathroom, too," Genny offered sweetly.

"Gee, thanks. Although it's doubtful she took many notes while sitting on the throne."

"I don't know about that. Judging from all those bottles under the table, I'd say she spent more than her fair share of time in that room. You never know where inspiration may have struck."

Madison gave her friend a playful shove. "Just start looking. The sooner we get this over with, the better. There's something about searching through a dead woman's house after dark that gives me the willies."

"Especially when that dead woman may have been killed for the very information we're searching for."

"Did you have to bring that up?" Madison grumbled, shuffling her way to the back bedroom. "I'm trying to forget that very fact."

After searching their respective rooms, they met back in the dining area.

"I found an old Christmas gift list and three reading lists, but no notes on a potential arsonist," Genny reported.

"Same here. I found her so-called 'research' into the meat conspiracy theory, a to-do list dated a few years ago, and experimental recipes for herbal remedies, but nothing that relates to the fires."

Genny wandered into the kitchen. "Do you think we had it wrong? Maybe she didn't suspect a scam, after all."

"What are you doing, making all that noise in there?"

"Getting a glass of water. I'm thirsty."

"I don't think you should be doing that."

"Why not?" Genny pulled a glass from a cabinet and filled it with tap water. "I'll clean up after myself."

Madison rolled her eyes as she joined her friend. "Next thing I know, you'll be brewing a cup of coffee."

"No, she only drank decaf, remember? But this tea looks rather interesting." Genny took the clear glass canister from the counter and held it up for closer inspection. "It has all kinds of leaves and herbs and spices in it. I wonder if Miss Gloria mixed it herself." She took the lid off and took a whiff. "Smells good."

"Put that back!" Madison chided. "You can't seriously be considering drinking her tea. The poor woman's dead, for heaven's sake!"

Genny's dimples appeared. "So my guess is she'll never say a word."

"Genesis!"

"Okay, okay, don't have a cow. I'm putting it back." Sulking, her friend slid the canister back in place. She washed and dried her water glass and returned it to the cabinet while Madison supervised with a scowl upon her face.

"Satisfied?" Genny asked with a too-sweet smile.

"Yes, thanks."

"So now what?"

"We keep looking. We need to see if we find anything here in the dining area and kitchen."

"I saw a bunch of papers stuffed over there in that cabinet. I'll start there."

Once again, they came up empty handed. "Carson was right. The woman loved to read. I found more reading lists. Titles of books and authors she wanted to read. Favorite passages from some of them, notated pages to read or re-read. She was obsessed."

Madison agreed with her friend's assessment. "I agree."

"This is a tiny house, and I've counted three bookcases already, all crammed with—" Genny stopped mid-sentence and cocked her head. "What was that?"

"What was what?"

"That noise. I heard something." Her voice dropped to a whisper and she pointed toward the window. "I think it came from outside."

Madison moved closer to the wall, keeping out of the line of sight from the window. She inched her way to the curtain and pulled one corner back, peering into the darkness.

"Too dark to see anything," she reported in a low tone.

Or had that shadow just moved? She studied the night, trying to distinguish one black image from another.

While Madison stood vigil at the window, Genny moved quickly about the room, turning out the lights. She groped her way back to join Madison at the window.

"I hear something else. What is that?" she whispered.

"It sounds like something popping. And what is that smell?"

"It smells like fingernail polish."

They both sniffed the air. "Not fingernail polish," Madison disagreed. "It's more like—"

Her friend finished her sentence for her. "Gasoline!"

Madison clutched Genny's arm in a frantic gesture. "That's the popping noise. Genny, the house is on fire!"

"We've got to get out of here!"

They tried the kitchen door.

"Jammed! I can't open it!"

"Neither can I. Let's try the front door."

Already flames crawled up the side of the house, glowing eerily through the window they had vacated moments before. They raced past the window, to the living room.

They tugged and pulled, but the door refused to budge. "Genny," Madison said, fighting back hysteria. Her voice was low and paced. "There's a screw through the door. Someone screwed the door shut."

"Call 911," Genny yelled, attempting to kick the door down. She succeeded only in jamming her foot and exhausting herself. The door remained steadfast, even with Madison's combined force.

"Try the windows."

"Screwed shut!"

"Break the window."

"Panes are too small to crawl through."

"The bedroom."

Together, they ran through the old frame house. Smoke curled up from the floorboards. Flames flickered from the eaves. Constructed completely of old, dried lumber, it would not take much for the house to ignite, even without the gasoline.

"It's getting harder to breathe," Madison gasped. "And the windows back here are painted shut!"

"Can you hear sirens?"

"Not yet. Where are you going?"

"Wet towels. We need wet towels."

"We go together."

Inside the bathroom, Genny jerked the faucets on full blast as Maddy threw every towel she could find into the old claw-foot tub. The bathroom air was relatively clear of smoke. Genny slammed the door shut and stuffed the narrow space beneath it with wet towels, hoping to buy them more time.

The rest of the house quickly filled with thick, choking curls of smoke.

"What's taking so long?" Madison cried. "The fire department should be here by now!"

"They'll be here," Genny insisted with a confidence she did not feel. "Cutter will come."

The air inside the bathroom thickened. Around them the old house popped and sizzled. A crash in the kitchen caused them both to jump.

"We've got to get out of here," Madison said.

Genny nodded. "Damned if I'm dying in this same bathroom as Miss Gloria."

Madison peered at the window above the tub. "That window is awfully small."

"All that matters is that my hips fit through. Just in case, you go first. Here, I'll boost you up."

They climbed into the tub, oblivious to the cold water that swirled to their knees. Genny grabbed soaking towels and wrapped one around each of their necks. With every few breaths, they sunk their noses into the refreshing wetness.

They made a comical sight, two women inside a bathtub, trying frantically to crawl out a tiny portal filled with glass. Genny made a stirrup with her hands and dropped Madison the first two times she tried to hoist her up. The third time was a charm, but Madison had trouble with the window's latch. By the time she worked the lock free and the glass open, the fire was feeding on the added oxygen of an open window. Another crash came from the living room as part of the ceiling caved in.

Madison made it out the window and reached back to drag Genesis to freedom.

"I—I don't think I can make it," Genny said, her breathing shallow and her face pale. Smoke whirled thick in the air. Fire glowed on the other side of the bathroom door, making the wooden door appear almost translucent. "Go. Save yourself."

"Not without you!" Madison bellowed. She hung halfway into the bathroom, jerking violently on her friend's arm. "Stand on the side of the tub. Come on, Genny, work with me!"

Coughing, Genny tried to make her legs obey her mind's commands, but her feet tangled in the heavy towels.

"Come on, Genny, we have to go! Now!"

Madison gave a powerful pull, just as flames crawled through the door. A bright flash from the area of the bathroom table illuminated the haze as Genny flew through the window.

Both women landed in an undignified heap in the fresh night air. Their arms and legs were tangled and askew, but they were out of the house. Sirens and lights blended with the sounds of people shouting and a house crashing behind them.

Huddled together, watching the house literally disappear into a horrific plume of flame, their skin hot and scorched by their proximity to the blaze, neither had the energy to crawl away.

20

"**M**addy! Maddy, Genny!"

Genny heard their names being called, but it was too much of an effort to answer. If she could just rest her eyes for a moment longer... Her eyes were so dry and blistered, just like her throat. She should have drunk more water earlier when she had the chance...

"Maddy! Where are you?" The voices grew stronger, closer.

"Brash," Maddy mumbled, pushing the name from her parched throat. "I hear Brash." She shook her best friend, whose head had fallen forward onto her chest. "Genny? Genny, wake up!"

When her companion did not respond, Madison became frantic. "Genny, wake up." She shook her again. Trying to gather enough saliva to swallow, Madison tried calling out. "Brash!" Her voice was but a croak. She tried again. "Brash, back here! Cutter! Someone help us!"

Brash and Officer Schimanski came at a run.

"Maddy, are you all right? Talk to me! Where's Genny?"

"She's here. She's not responding, Brash! Hurry. Help her."

Brash took only enough time to squeeze Maddy in a tight hug and brush his face against her smoky, tangled hair. He released her as quickly as he swept her against him, turning his immediate attention to the blond woman still crumpled upon the ground.

"Get the paramedics back here!" he barked to his officer. He carefully stretched Genny out on the grass, making sure her airways were unobstructed and nothing was broken or burned.

"How long has she been unconscious?" he asked over his shoulder, his hands still moving over her prone body.

"N—not long... watched the... fall... awake then." The words scraped past her scorched throat, only some of them strong enough to make their way through the arid dessert that had swallowed her whole and left her parched and withered.

"Shh, sweetheart. Don't try to talk anymore. I'm sorry I asked."

"'Kay," she managed.

His eyes flickered over her, hungry and worried, even as he attended her friend. "Are you all right? Just nod your head if you are."

She bobbed her head up and down, and then signaled for him to turn his full attention back to Genny.

The paramedics came with a gurney and whisked her friend away. A second set came right behind her and insisted that Madison go with them.

"It's okay, sweetheart. I'll be right here with you." Before she could struggle with the words and ask, he read her mind and assured her, "I'll have Granny Bert and the twins meet us at the hospital. You and Genny will both be fine, sweetheart.

Now be a good girl and go with the medics. I'll be there when the doors open."

As promised, his was the first face she saw when the ambulance doors opened and they pulled her from the box. Floating in and out of awareness, she had only a glimpse of him before the attendants wheeled her away amid a flurry of white coats, tubes, and wires, but it was enough to ease her heart.

A smile ghosted her lips as she floated into oblivion. Brash deCordova was a man of his word. He said he would be there, and he was.

And he said Genny would be all right. Drifting out of consciousness again, she had to trust that he was right about that, as well.

A small crowd huddled in the waiting area, eager for word on their loved ones. Granny Bert looked old and ragged as she sat between Sybille and Derron on the crowded bench. Bethani and Megan huddled together in a single chair, while Blake stood beside them protectively, as if his towering height could somehow shield them from bad news. Brash alternated between pacing the corridor and staring through the tiny window on the swinging doors, hoping for a glimpse into the ER beyond. Cutter consistently paced the small confines of the room, still wearing the lower half of his bunker gear, raking both hands through his ravaged hair. Shannon and Momma Matt passed out hot coffee and cold drinks to anyone who would take it. Various friends, co-workers, and clergymen drifted in and out of the waiting room throughout the long hours of the night.

As daylight peeked through the vinyl blinds and streaked the floor with weak rays of hope, Brash made a decision. While most of the others had either gone home or found a way to catch a few winks in various odd and cramped positions, Bethani and Blake were still too frightened to sleep. Worried they might miss the doctor should he come back out, they slumped together on a loveseat. Even Megan had stretched out on the floor and fallen asleep a few hours ago.

Squaring his shoulders, Brash pushed away from the wall he supported and ambled his way toward the pale-faced twins. His knees popped as he walked, protesting a night with no rest.

"How y'all doing?" he asked quietly, taking the empty chair beside them.

Bethani sniffled and shrugged. Blake rubbed his weary eyes. "Okay, I guess," he mumbled. "I just wish they would come back out and give us another update. It's been three hours since we heard anything."

"Both their vitals were improving the last two times they updated us. I'm sure things are still going good, or else they'd be out to say." Brash offered the weak rally speech. "No news is good news."

"That's a stupid saying," Bethani grumbled. "No news is just that. No news."

"She's going to be okay, Beth." This time, Brash's voice was deep and reassuring, and full of a confidence that he did not fully feel. But he couldn't tell Maddy's kids that.

There was something he could tell them, though. And it was time that he did.

"Bethani, Blake, I want to talk to you two about something." He kept his voice low and intimate. This was not a conversation for other ears to hear.

Bethani bristled. Crossing her arms across her chest, she stonewalled him. "Don't," she said coldly. "Don't give us the 'if anything happens to your mom' speech. I won't let you." Her words were brave, but her chin trembled with emotion.

His smile was indulgent. The girl had spunk, he would give her that. "I wouldn't dream of it," he said, his voice warming along with his smile. "This is the 'when your mom wakes up' speech."

Bethani did not say anything, but he knew she listened. Blake's expression was more inviting, so Brash continued.

"You two and Granny will go in first, of course. But when you're ready to share her for just a minute, I'd like to see her. I promise not to stay long."

Blake looked over at his sister, who struggled to keep up her aloof facade. "Yeah, I guess that would be all right."

Brash cleared his throat and spoke clearly, so that there was no doubt to his intentions. "You need to know that when I see her, I'm going to tell her that I love her. Because I do."

Bethani's head shot up and her startled blue eyes met his. Again Brash smiled. He looked both twins straight in the eye as he told them, "I've loved your mom for quite some time now. And I have reason to believe that she loves me, too. But out of respect for the two of you, and the fact that you're still grieving your father's death, neither of us have acknowledged our feelings."

He blew out a deep breath, realizing how nervous he had been to bare his soul to Maddy's children. His weak chuckle was humorless, revealing his vulnerability. "The fact is, I'm saying the words to you before I've even said them to her. But tonight reminded me of how precious life is, and how none of us have a guarantee for tomorrow. I could never forgive myself if I let another day go by without telling your mom how I feel about her. So I just wanted you to know what I plan to do." He faltered over the next words. "I would be honored to have your blessings, but I know I can't really expect them, not yet. Unless you want to give them. Then I'd be honored."

Brash knew he was babbling. To his amazement, Blake grinned and stuck out his hand. "Relax, son," the teen said, using his most mature voice. Pumping Brash's hand with gusto, he turned the tables on the lawman as he played at being the elder. "Her grandmother and I approve."

With a sidelong glance down at his sister, Blake spoke out of the side of his mouth and added, "I can't speak for her, but I think she'll come around."

Laughing at the boy's antics, Brash slapped him on the shoulder before giving in to the urge to hug him. "Thanks, Blake. That means the world to me."

"You're pretty cool, even being an old lawman, and all."

When the girl between them still made no comment, Brash dared to look at her. Tears brimmed in her eyes.

"I know this is hard for you, Beth," he said softly. "And I don't mean to hurt you. But I love her."

Bethani sniffed. "I—I guess she has a right to know," she whispered, her tone still somewhat sullen.

It was more than he had hoped for. He settled a large hand onto her shoulder and squeezed. "Thanks, sweetie."

"Mr. de?" Her voice was small, her eyes large. "Do you—Do you think you could hug me, like you did earlier tonight?"

Brash gathered the girl into his arms and cradled her as she cried. He realized then that it had been much too long since she had felt a father's arms around her. Putting a hand onto Blake's shoulder to include him in the embrace, Brash settled back in the seat and gave what comfort he could to Maddy's children. Soon Bethani was asleep against his chest and Blake's head lolled back against his arm. With a tender smile and a humble heart, Brash gave in to his own exhaustion and closed his eyes.

They all enjoyed a solid thirty minutes of sleep before the doctor came into the waiting room, wearing a smile.

"I am pleased to say that both ladies are going to be fine." He smiled at the twins. "Your mom will be released in a few hours. She needs to get plenty of rest and fluids, but other than having a bad case of a sore throat, she should be fine in a day or so."

"And Genny?" Cutter asked. "How is she?"

"She'll be fine, too, but it may take a few days longer. She inhaled more smoke than her friend. Her lungs are a bit hazy and her body bruised, but with plenty of fluids and bed rest, I see no reason why she won't be good as new within a week or so."

"When can she go home?"

"I'd like to keep her for a couple of days, just to be on the safe side."

"But you say they'll both be fine?" Granny Bert wanted to hear the words again, just to be certain.

"Absolutely. They are both strong, determined women with a will to thrive."

"When can we see them?" Brash asked.

"You can only stay for a few minutes, but you can go back now, one at a time." The doctor saw the frustration on Bethani and Blake's faces. "Okay, in your case, both of you can go," he relented. He spoke to their backs when he called, "But don't stay long."

Cutter claimed first visitation with Genny. The nurse frowned at his filthy attire, but she led the way back to the cubicle.

"She's heavily sedated," she warned. "She may not even know you're here. Don't stay longer than five minutes."

Cutter stepped into the stall, hating how small and pale she looked against the white sheets. Her hair was streaked with soot and filth, much as his own. A red mark stretched across her forehead, peeking from beneath the white bandage that circled her head. A bruise darkened her pale cheek and there was a scrape under her chin. Cutter immediately missed the warmth of her twinkling blue eyes and her easy smile.

He slipped his hand over hers, not wanting to disturb her. He just needed to see for himself that she was all right.

He had let her down tonight. He had been on another call across town. A small, unexplained fire that broke out alongside the highway. They had the blaze out in a matter of minutes, but it cost him precious time when the call came in for a structure fire. Details were sketchy, but occupants might still be inside.

When he reached the house, he knew it should be empty. He had attended the homeowner's death just over a month ago. And then he had seen her car, and he knew Genny was inside. Fear like he had never known before raced through his body, leaving him momentarily useless. The wail of the ambulance's siren snapped him out of his trance and into action.

Unbeknownst to him, Genny was already out of the house and on her way to the hospital before he ever reached the scene. And for that fact, Cutter could never forgive himself. He had failed her.

Lost in self-loathing, he did not register the slight pressure of her fingers the first time she squeezed his hand. Genny stirred slightly, her red, pain-filled eyes fluttering open before shutting again. Her fingers tightened on his, ever so slightly.

"Cutter." Her hoarse words were rusty and weak. Smoky.

"How are you, Genny darlin'?" he asked, his own voice shaky.

She attempted a smile, but only one side of her parched lips lifted. "I knew you'd come," she breathed.

With a satisfied sigh, she drifted back out.

Brash waited his turn. Only after the twins and Granny Bert went in did he take his turn at Madison's side.

She was asleep when he walked in, still groggy from the medication and trauma of the night. Other than the grunge of smoke and soot that clung to her like a second skin, she looked largely unscathed. One long cut on her forearm, the two stitches that held it together, and an IV drip were the only indications of recent troubles.

His heart contracted painfully as he watched her sleep. Tonight could have turned out so differently. The very thought stole his breath and gnawed a hole through his gut.

Brash stepped forward silently and pressed a kiss onto her forehead. Her eyes slowly opened and a lazy smile spread across her face.

"Hey," Madison croaked hoarsely.

"Shh. Don't talk, sweetheart. I don't want you overdoing it."

She nodded in agreement as she reached for his hand. Brash rubbed her fingers and watched as she struggled to keep her eyes open.

"It's okay, sweetheart. Go back to sleep." His words were low and soothing. "I just had to see for myself that you were okay."

She managed another groggy nod.

"And I had to tell you something." His voice was still steady and low, the same reassuring murmur that had encouraged her to sleep. She might not even be awake. She might not hear him. But he had to say the words. "I love you, sweetheart."

A smile curled her lips, even though her eyelids were too heavy to lift. "Love you, too," she rasped in a whisper, just before sleep claimed her once again.

21

There was never any question as to where Genny would convalesce. Granny Bert had her room ready before the doctor released her.

With Maddy in her own room and Genny stationed in Blake's, they found the easiest way to communicate was through text messages. Madison was granted full release within two days, but Genny was ordered to stay in bed for a full five.

"Obviously, you cannot count," Madison said when she saw her friend standing in the doorway of the kitchen just three days later.

"Three. Five. Close enough," Genny croaked.

Granny Bert clicked her tongue. "Your voice is still all scratchy and haggly. You should be in bed."

"My voice has nothing to do with my legs."

"Come, on, Gen," Madison said, "let us pamper you for another couple of days. You deserve it."

Her dimples had come through the ordeal unscathed. She flashed them now. "True."

Granny Bert pulled out a chair. "At least sit down. I will grant you chair privileges if you promise to go back to bed in one hour."

Genny wiggled two fingers in the air.

"Okay, two. But you have to stay in that chair."

Genny crinkled her nose but took what she could get. She joined her friend at the table, where an array of papers was scattered. She recognized the chart she and Madison drew up at her office.

"Still no circles?"

"More like arcs, with huge gaping holes." Madison's voice was filled with frustration. "We must be getting close. Why else would someone have tried to kill us? Brash confirmed that the doors and windows were screwed shut. Cutter confirmed the fire was started with gasoline. Someone knew we were inside and deliberately set that fire. Obviously, they are afraid we would uncover whatever it was Miss Gloria found."

Genny studied the paper. "Try adding another field," she suggested. "Who could have benefited from the fires?"

"Well, let's see." Madison picked up her pen. "On the Montelongo fire, Bernie Havlicek was the biggest winner. Carson Elliot came out on the winning end of his fire, even though he lost his lot in the process. We don't know much about Ray Sams, other than his insurance paid to keep him quiet, so I suppose he benefited the most. And even though the Shanks and Mr. Peavey eventually won their claims, neither was reimbursed the full amount of their loss."

"Just like Bob Peterson," Genny put in.

Stirring something on the stove, Granny Bert added, "Don't forget Newly McArdle's fire. Who benefited from it?"

Madison shrugged. "I guess the real winner was Cash Montgomery. He eventually bought the lot and built a taxidermy store on a prime piece of property in downtown Naomi."

"Prime being a relative term," Maddy remarked dryly. Even a prime location in a small town did not always translate into foot traffic. There were only two thousand residents in both towns, combined.

"At least it sounds like Newly got a little something for his loss," Granny Bert said. "He left town soon after the fire, so I never knew for sure."

"Not really," Genny denied. "Cutter said the bank repossessed. They were the ones to sell the lot to his brother."

A shadow crossed Maddy's face. "That's a bit odd, don't you think? That's almost the same thing that happened to Carson. The bank repossessed his lot, too."

"Do we know which banks they used?"

While Madison looked through her papers, Granny Bert brought Genny a plate of scrambled eggs and grits. She pushed aside a stack of papers to accommodate the plate. "These ought to slide easy down your throat."

"Where's Maddy's plate?"

"She's already eaten. And my guess would be Naomi State Bank on most or all of those. I know they were the ones who financed Wanda and gave her such a hard time about getting her money. Same thing with Jerry Don."

"That sounds like Barry Redmond," Genny mumbled in her scratchy voice.

"That was the bank Carson used, too," Madison confirmed, seeing the notes she had jotted down.

"So how would that work?" Granny Bert squinted down at the messy chart. "They may have repossessed two of the properties, but what about the others? It doesn't add up. All they got from Cheap Willie were the payments he already owed them."

"I admit I don't have all the answers. But it definitely raises some questions. And it might explain why Barry keeps harassing me and making cheap threats. I thought he was referring to his divorce and custody of his daughter, but maybe he knew I was getting close to discovering his secret."

Her grandmother looked less than impressed. "You'll have to figure it out without me. I ran out of slippery elm. I'm going over to Myrna Lewis' to pick up a fresh batch so I can make you both more of that tea. It seems to have helped with the soreness, don't you think?"

"Actually, I think it has," Madison said, putting her hand onto the slender column of her throat. "That and the honey."

"Genny, what about you?"

She made a facial expression of semi agreement.

"It hasn't helped?" Granny asked in surprise.

"It has," Genny admitted in her raspy voice. Her face colored. "But… now I have Miss Gloria's problem."

Madison looked confused at first, then amused. "Oh, I see. What was all that talk about bran and fiber and not needing any help?" she teased.

She shifted uncomfortably in the hard chair.

"Well, it's no wonder," Granny Bert said. "Both teas I've been feeding you are made of binding herbs. Slippery elm, peppermint, cayenne, marshmallow root, just to name a few. No wonder you're bound up, girl! You need to be taking something with the opposite effect, like prune juice pumped up with rhubarb or licorice. Here, I'm make you a tonic right now. We'll have you right as rain in no time."

With a frantic look in her eyes, Genny grabbed for the older woman's arm to stop her. In her haste, she sent the same stack of papers off the edge of the table. A book tumbled with them, landing on top.

"I've got it," Maddy insisted, bending to retrieve the mess. She turned the book over in her hands. "What is this?"

"It's Blake's. He said it was for a science report," Granny acknowledged. "Second week of school, and already he has a report due."

"What sort of report is it? Look at this title. *Strangest Deaths in History.*"

Her curiosity piqued, Madison abandoned her chart and flipped through the pages of the book. "Some of these are pretty wild. Like this one. While playing golf, a thirty-year-old man had an extreme allergic reaction to something they used to keep the golf course green. He had a habit of carrying his golf tee in his teeth and unknowingly ingested the chemical." She flipped a page. "And this one. A middle-aged health food nut in England died after drinking ten gallons of carrot juice in ten days. He OD'd on Vitamin A and died from severe liver damage."

"Folks think just because things are natural means they're safer, but it's not always the case," Granny Bert nodded sagely. "Arsenic is natural, but it will kill you deader than a doorknob."

"And listen to this one. A man here in Texas died of alcohol intoxication after his wife gave him an enema of two large bottles of Sherry wine."

"You laugh, but I've heard of such," Granny Bert acknowledged. "I had a friend in Grimes County who was a nurse. There was an alcoholic in the hospital that was going through withdrawal. The cramping was so bad that his wife sneaked into the room and put liquor directly into the enema bag so he could get his fix." Her grandmother hooted as she remembered the tale. "The doctors came in and he was sitting up there in bed, plastered out of his mind. Turns out you absorb alcohol much faster when administered rectally than orally. Only took a few minutes to get that man higher than a kite!"

While Granny Bert continued to snicker, Madison and Genny exchanged sharp looks.

"Granny," Madison said slowly. "That tea you've been making for us... What would happen if someone drank tea every day, made from those ingredients you mentioned?"

"I would imagine they would be pretty miserable. Much worse than Genny here."

Madison grabbed her phone and scrolled through her photos, looking for the ones she had taken at Miss Gloria's. "What if that included things like White Oak and Raspberry Leaf? Agrimony and Comfrey?"

"You'd never take those things, particularly all combined, unless you followed it with a large dose of castor oil."

"Or perhaps with an enema?"

Genny pushed her plate away. "That's it! The herbs!" she croaked.

Madison nodded vigorously. "Those are the exact herbs we found at Gloria's. And I'll bet they were in that tea she drank, too."

"Why would a woman with her troubles take these particular herbs? It would be like colon suicide," her grandmother fretted.

"Maybe someone misinformed her. Maybe they told her these would produce the results she needed."

"What fool would do a thing like that? And why?"

Madison thought about all those pre-filled enemas, lined up neatly on the bathroom shelf. Darker in color than ones purchased over the counter, they obviously held a special solution.

A solution that burst into a bright blaze when exposed to the flames...

"Wait. Are you thinking what I think you're thinking? That someone deliberately gave Gloria Jeffers binding herbs over and over, so that she would get dependent on enemas? And that someone filled her enemas with alcohol? Are you thinking that's how a teetotaler would die of alcohol poisoning?"

"That's exactly what we're thinking."

"But who would do such a thing to that poor woman?"

"There's only one woman I know of that's mean enough and hateful enough to do something like this," Madison said, her face settling into hard lines.

Genny nodded in agreement. "Myrna Lewis."

22

"You are not coming with me, Genny. You are supposed to be in bed."

Genesis glared at her friend and stood her ground. Shoving her feet into the first pair of shoes she found—a pair of Blake's cowboy boots that were too large for her—she grabbed the car keys before Madison did.

"We don't have time to argue about this," Madison said emphatically. "We need to confront Myrna Lewis before she figures out we're on to her."

"You two can argue about it on the way," Granny Bert said. "Come on."

"There would be no reason to argue if Genny was already in the car," Madison pointed out.

"Exactly. So come on. And I'm driving, by the way."

Resenting her grandmother's takeover, Madison grumbled a complaint. "Who said you could even come along? Both of you should stay home and let me and Brash handle this."

"Both of you are still recovering. I called Myrna earlier, so she's already expecting me. And let me do the talking. I'm not necessarily a fan of hers, but I'm not sure you have it right about Myrna."

"When I zoomed in on these photos, I see there's a label on one of the jars. *Myrna's Majesties*. So Miss Gloria was definitely getting her herbs from Myrna Lewis."

"Doesn't mean she killed her. But I'll steer the conversation around to what herbs are used for what. We can't just rush in, accusing her first thing. We'll ease our way in."

Madison glared at her grandmother from the passenger seat. "After all, *Subtle* is your middle name," she said with sarcasm.

Granny Bert's smile was smug. "Darn tootin'."

"But why *would* Myrna want to kill Miss Gloria?" Genny asked worriedly. "And why would she want to set the fires? The bank seemed a more likely suspect."

"Maybe it was an insurance scam, after all. Maybe Barry and Myrna were in on it together."

She recalled a past conversation. *I think you are forgetting a certain business arrangement we have, one that your husband knows nothing about...*

"Where is her shop?" Madison asked. "I'll send a text to Brash and tell him to meet us there."

"She has a hothouse in her backyard."

Madison composed a brief text to Brash and marked it urgent. With the Lewis house only blocks away, they were pulling up by the time she pushed 'Send.'

"We'll go around back. With Genny still in her pajamas, Myrna will never suspect we're here to accuse her of murder." Granny Bert leered at Genny's outfit, a cute little leopard ensemble that declared her 'Purr-fection in Pink.'

The older woman led the way around the manicured path. Myrna's backyard was abloom with color, despite the hot and dry summer. Even with its various elements of a redwood deck, gazebo, and now a large greenhouse, the yard was large and spacious.

"Yoo-hoo, Myrna! It's Bertha Cessna. I came for my herbs."

"Back here."

They followed the sound of her voice and found her clipping a flowering plant at the back of the building.

"Oh. You brought someone with you." She swept Madison and Genny with a less-than-welcoming glance.

"Yes, the girls wanted to learn more about herbs. I told them if there is anyone who can teach them about the useful benefits of herbs and plants, it would be you. Isn't that right, girls?"

"That's what she said," Madison said, smiling through her teeth. Genny bobbed her head up and down with an enthusiastic nod.

Myrna eyed the latter with scorn. "I see you were so eager to learn that you didn't even bother to dress."

"Haven't you heard?" Granny Bert gasped. "My girls here were in an accident. A fire. We almost lost them both when Gloria Jeffers' house went up in flames."

They awaited her reaction to mention of the fire. Her total lack of concern surprised them all. "I heard about that. What were you two doing there?"

Madison came up with a quick excuse. "Uhm, *In a Pinch* was hired to clean it out."

"Better hope you don't get sued for burning it down."

Sore throat or not, Genny could not help but retort, "Gee, your concern is underwhelming."

"What happened to your voice? You sound awful."

"That's why we're here," Granny Bert said. "We need something to soothe her throat."

"You need Slippery Elm."

Granny Bert nodded smartly. "See, girls, how she said that right off the top of her head? I told you she knows her stuff."

Pretending to be impressed, Madison asked several questions about other herbs and their uses. She was sure to include the ones she had seen at Gloria's.

Satisfied that the answers supported her theory, Madison hoped her voice came out conversational as she said, "I know Miss Gloria was one of your biggest supporters, too."

Myrna looked up in surprise. "She was?"

"Why, yes, of course. She had a ton of your herbs and teas."

"That's odd. I don't recall ever selling her anything."

So certain they were on the right trail this time, Madison and Genny exchanged a confused look. It was Granny Bert that said, "Maybe your helper sold them to her."

"Lisa?" Myrna's voice was filled with surprise. She shrugged her compact shoulders. "Actually, she *has* developed a few loyal followers of her own, as surprising as that is."

The woman's inflated ego was legendary, but Madison pretended not to notice. "Why is that so surprising?"

"I've tried to teach her, but Lisa Redmond is a slow learner. And such a timid little mouse." Her voice ranged from disdain to superiority. "Why would someone prefer *her* over *me*, considering my vast experience and knowledge?"

"Lisa Redmond is your helper?" Surprise hiked Madison's voice.

"That's right. Business has been so good I needed help."

Lisa Redmond. Plain, solemn, meek Lisa. Barry's fourth and most recently discarded wife. The one who hired *In a Pinch* to get the lowdown on her cheating husband. The one who hadn't seemed quite so plain and meek when Madison saw her at the lawyer's office.

"Lisa Redmond works here," Madison reconfirmed, still trying to fit the pieces all together in her mind.

"Did the smoke damage your hearing? Yes, Lisa Redmond works here."

"Oh. Uhm, well, I, uh, I was hoping to get the recipe for an herbal tea Miss Gloria made." Madison was surprised how easily the lie slipped from her mouth. Her mind was working overtime. "I understood she got the recipe from here."

"Lisa might have given it to her. She's all the time mixing up herbal recipes." Not bothering to turn her head, she bellowed, "Lisa!" Her loud voice startled the women standing only a few feet in front of her.

There was rustling from the front of the hothouse. "Yes ma'am, Mrs. Lewis?"

"There's someone here to see you."

Lisa came around the corner, shoulders slumped and hair stringy once again. She looked more like the down-trodden woman Madison had first met.

"These women want a recipe you mixed up for that woman who drank herself to death."

Madison winced at the crass way Myrna referred to Gloria's death. Poor Lisa. It was bad enough to lose one of her first few customers while still establishing her meager following. Worse, having her client die in such a sudden and unexpected way. And worse, yet, to have the death referred to so carelessly.

Madison caught Lisa's eye, trying to convey her apologies. Instead of sadness, Lisa's eyes flashed with the strangest expression of panic. Then they glazed over with a cold, hard glare and her entire countenance changed. She squared her shoulders and stiffened her slight body.

And suddenly Madison knew.

Gloria's death had not been unexpected. Not to Lisa.

Granny Bert noticed the change in Lisa's demeanor and took an involuntary step backward. Genny edged closer and whispered, "We were wrong. It was her."

"I know." Madison took comfort in knowing she had already sent her text. Under her breath, she assured her friend, "Brash is on his way."

"No he's not," Genny hissed from the side of her mouth. "You sent the message to me by mistake."

Lisa sauntered down the narrow rows brimming with potted plants. "My, my, who do we have here?"

Oblivious to the pending danger, Myrna reprimanded her employee. "Lisa, that is no way to speak to customers. Even these two."

Granny Bert took offense, momentarily forgetting the woman looming ever closer. She whirled toward Myrna and said, "Hey, watch it, sister. These are my girls you're talking about."

"Not now, Granny," Madison hissed.

"Barry always did talk about how spoiled you were," Lisa jeered. "Looks like your old granny still fights your battles for you."

Granny Bert bristled. "Who are you calling old?"

Madison stepped forward, deliberately putting herself between Lisa and her grandmother. She tried easing away from Genny, but her friend stuck by her side, step for step. Leave it to Genny to have her back.

"So what was in it for Barry?" Madison asked.

"What else is there? Money."

"Was it some sort of insurance fraud?" With a sinking feeling of disappointment, Madison had to know. "Was Dean involved?" She wouldn't put it past his wife, but she thought Dean Lewis was above such depths of deceit.

"Dean?" Myrna chirped. "My Dean? What are you talking about? And Lisa, what is wrong with you? I've never seen you look so... agitated."

"What is wrong is that I have had it up to here..." she slashed her hand across her forehead "...with your snide, sniveling, caustic attitude. Get your fat butt up here with the rest of them so I can see you."

Myrna was outraged that anyone, particularly an employee, would speak to her in such a manner. Fire flared in her eyes and spittle flew from her mouth as the squat woman roared, "How dare you speak to me like that!"

When Madison first met Lisa, she thought her weak, both physically and emotionally. A timid wife seeking the truth about her husband's affair. The day Madison handed over the findings of her covert investigation, she wondered if she had misjudged the woman. She detected a glint in her eyes. A calculated expression of manipulation. Madison remembered worrying that day, afraid she may have unwittingly helped to further Lisa Redmond's greedy and selfish agenda.

She had definitely misjudged the woman, Madison realized now. Lisa was stronger and more toned than Madison suspected. Up close, with her tanned arms exposed by a sleeveless tank top, Madison could see how fit she was. Lisa Redmond worked out.

"I dare," Lisa informed her boss coldly, "because I quit. More accurately, *you* are about to quit." She reached behind her back and pulled a gun from her waistband. She pointed the barrel straight at Myrna's chest. Her voice was cold. "Breathing, that is."

The boom of the gun exploded in their ears, echoing within the tight walls of the hothouse. Myrna shrieked as she fell to the ground. Madison was relieved to hear the string of obscenities and rage that flowed from the fallen woman's mouth. At least the shot was not fatal.

"Shut up or I'll do it again," Lisa threatened.

Myrna's shrieks dwindled down to a pathetic gruel, punctuated by an occasional whimper.

The other three moved together to form a united front. Madison remained front and center. She crossed her arms over her chest and tried to look tougher than she felt. Genny huddled close at her side, pretending to cower as she kept one arm tucked behind her friend. Madison suspected she had her phone in her hidden hand, but she did not dare turn to look.

"You were explaining about the insurance fraud?" Madison asked coolly.

"There was no insurance fraud, you fool. It was flat out money, plain and simple."

Some of Madison's bravado mingled with her confusion and stalled. It was her grandmother who demanded, "Then what about Tiny and his brother? How did they work into this?"

"My uncles? They did anything I told them to do."

"Tiny is your *uncle*?"

"On my mother's side. I know, no resemblance. Thank God." She rolled her eyes for emphasis.

"So how did it work?" Madison asked. "If not for insurance purposes, why did you need them to tamper with the results?"

"Again, *money*." She said the word louder, as if volume alone would make her meaning clearer.

Granny Bert propped her hands onto her hips. "You're going to have to be more precise than that, girlie. There were several fires, every one of them different. So what was your angle?"

Lisa eyed the old woman, her eyes glittering. "I like you," she said. "You have gumption. Not that it's going to do you any good in the end, but you have gumption."

With a slightly bored expression, Lisa went on to explain. "Of course they were all different. I had to be creative, else someone might notice the similarities and investigate."

"Obviously someone did," Madison pointed out. "Gloria Jeffers."

"Yes, well, we'll get around to her in a minute. I was having a conversation with your grandmother. Try not to interrupt again."

She flounced her stringy hair toward the older woman. "As I was saying, I had to be creative. That's where my uncles came in. A little loose wire here, and *oops!* A restaurant almost burns down. Another one there, and a poor overpriced motor home just goes up in smoke. Poof! You really have to appreciate the power of electricity."

"This woman is a nut," Genny muttered under her breath.

"Watch it, blondie!" Lisa snapped, swinging her attention to Genesis. "You're supposed to be dead, anyway. You and your princess friend."

Her attention riveted back to Granny Bert. "Barry isn't always the brightest of businessmen. He doesn't always see things as clearly as he should. He's made a few bad business decisions through the years. As his wife—and the one who

will be inheriting most of his money when he has an unfortunate heart attack—it was my responsibility to set those bad decisions right. He had no business loaning that kind of money
for a motor home."

"Just between us, how much did Ray Sams pay for that
baby?" Granny Bert wanted to know.

"Granny!"

"What?" she asked innocently. "He did it to one-up me. I
just want to know how much it set him back."

"He got his money back, just like the bank did," Lisa said.
"And at a far faster rate than we would have if he had paid it
out, one long year after another. That fool husband of mine
financed him for fifteen years!"

"Hmm. Maybe I should have done business with him,"
Granny Bert murmured.

"Back up a minute," Genny said in her hoarse voice. "How
did you profit from the restaurant fire?"

"Well, until you came to town, it was the biggest and best restaurant in town. Unfortunately, the Montelongos owned it free
and clear. With no mortgage to hold over their head, we had no
leverage." She cocked her head and smiled sweetly. "Now we do."

"What about my friends the Shanks?" Granny Bert asked.
"Granted, William is no longer my friend, that sorry no-good-
for-nothing weasel. But Wanda is one of my nearest and dearest. What did you gain from their fire?"

"That sorry no-good, as you so aptly call him, had fall-
en behind on payments to the bank. The house itself wasn't
worth repossessing. But a nice, fat insurance pay-off would get
their payments up to date. Uncle Slim made sure the insurance claim was settled to our satisfaction, even if your friends
got short changed."

"Jerry Don Peavey?" Madison asked, her voice almost weary. Listening to the extent of the woman's greed and evil spirit was mentally and emotionally draining.

"Again, behind on payments because my foolish husband loaned him too much money. I did him a favor, really. We got his payments down to a much more manageable price range and he found he could make do with a barn half the size of his old one." She beamed proudly, as if she truly had done a good deed.

"Carson Elliot?" Genny rasped. Her throat was getting worse from so much talking.

"Ah, yes, what a charming and delightful man! But he was building on prime property. The bank could make so much more money, selling that particular lot as commercial property. His house simply had to go."

"The same thing happened to Newly McArdle," Granny Bert noted.

"If you mean that dirty little mechanic with grease under his fingernails, then, yes. I much prefer doing business with one of the handsome Montgomery men." She slid a sly look at Genny. "I'm sure you agree, don't you, kitten?"

Understanding the reference to her pajamas, Genny answered, "*Purr*-fectly."

When the effort caused her to cough, Genny curled her body inward with exaggeration, taking the opportunity to glance at her phone. She scrolled to Cutter's number and hit speaker. She ignored the possibility that she may have selected the number directly above his, *Cuts of Prime*, a meat market over in Riverton. The important thing was that was no matter which number she dialed, the person on the other end could hear, and Lisa would never be the wiser.

"So, what?" Madison asked, trying to redirect Lisa's attention from her friend. "You just set fire to all of these places?"

"Basically, yes."

"How did you know what to do? Setting the fires, I mean."

"I've always been fascinated with fire. On the one hand, it can mean the difference between life and death. Freezing to death, that is. And on the other, it can mean sheer and total destruction." She let her eyes trail over the arch of the building and down the curved sides. "And, again, death."

In that instant, Madison knew what Lisa planned to do. She planned to lock them in and set the greenhouse on fire.

Determined to stall, Madison kept talking. Help would be here soon, she had to believe that.

"I wouldn't know the first thing about setting fires. Not without getting caught." She hoped her voice sounded a bit awed by Lisa's prowess.

Flattery was always helpful in situations like this. Like a true maniac, Lisa glowed with what she considered a compliment. "It's amazing what you can learn on the internet," she confided. She smiled broadly. "It walked me through the process, step by step."

"What about the latest fire, the one at Bob Peterson's?"

Her smile was cunning. "No, the latest fire was at Gloria Jeffers'. But since you asked so politely and did not interrupt this time, then, yes, I also had a hand in the Peterson fire. I already have a buyer for the property," she added, as if that explained everything.

"Which brings us back to Gloria."

"Ah, yes, Gloria. Sweet, gullible, mystery-loving Gloria."

She came forward, waving her gun in the air as if it were a wand. She glanced to the back of the room to where Myrna

BECKI WILLIS

moaned with renewed vigor. "Keep it down back there, boss
lady. I hate interruptions. I'll get to you soon enough."

Myrna quieted and Lisa continued. "Gloria imagined
herself some sort of amateur detective. I found her folder
at the law office by accident, filled with half the fires I had
instigated."

"Half?"

Lisa smirked at Genny's question. "Oh, honey, you two
don't know as much as you think you do. Of course there were
others. Your little boyfriend is lucky I've never shown off my
full potential as a fire artiste." She twirled her hand with dramatic flair, immolating a flame.

"How did Gloria figure it out?" Madison asked.

"She was cursed with a suspicious mind. She noticed that
in each of the cases handled by the law firm, the bank was the
mortgage holder. When insurance was involved, the money
had to travel through the bank before it reached the client.
Of course, she had the specifics all wrong. She thought it was
Barry behind the fires. She even came to me to warn me of my
husband's mean and vicious streak."

"Why didn't she go on to the authorities?"

"I begged her to wait. I needed time to protect myself
and provide for my dear, sweet stepdaughter." With huge,
sad-looking eyes, the crazed woman managed to look both
vulnerable and sincere. "We would discuss my dire situation over tea. I made a special blend, just for my friend.
And when she became irregular, I had a special formula
for that, too." She flashed a smile that was pure evil. "After
a particularly nasty bout of constipation, she was desperate
for relief. She was more than happy to triple the special
formula I concocted for her."

"With friends like you, who needs enemies," Madison grumbled beneath her breath.

"Watch it, your highness."

The highness reference reminded Madison of Barry. He often called her that in mocking terms. "So what about Barry?"

"What about him?"

"I think you mentioned an upcoming heart attack?"

"Yes. Poor thing has been having trouble with his blood pressure lately. He's become highly agitated."

"I've noticed."

"It can't be good on his heart," Lisa predicted. She glanced at an imaginary watch. "I would say in about... oh, a day or two at most, his old ticker will just give out. I'll be distraught, of course. I'll play the grieving widow, right up until the part where I cash in all the insurance policies and empty out the checking accounts. I'll offer to sell my part of the bank to his sisters and I'll leave town. Too many sad memories here, you know."

"I thought you were divorcing him."

"Didn't you hear?" Lisa looked appropriately wide-eyed. "I had a change of heart. My lawyer thinks we took his advice and went to marriage counseling. Even though he lost the divorce fee, he offered to help update our wills. Wasn't that generous of him?"

"Oh, yes."

Lisa rambled on, haplessly waving her dangerous would-be wand through the air. "We were most concerned about poor little Miley. Shawn helped with the precise wording, making certain I retained custody of her, should something unthinkable happen to Barry. I explained that the child's birth mother was a drug addict and not to be trusted with all of Miley's money. Between her trust fund and what she stands to inherit from her father, the brat is filthy rich. She needs someone steady to help manage her finances. Someone to look out for her best interests."

"I'm guessing someone like you?" Maddy asked, her tone as dry as her throat.

"Of course."

"And Barry agreed?"

"According to his signature, he did."

"Forged, I'm sure."

"They'll have to prove it first. After eight years of marriage, I have it down to the dotted 'i.'"

No one bothered pointing out that there were no 'i's in her husband's name. Her demented brain could not be bothered with such minor details.

"And I'm sure they'll discover that it was Barry who instigated the fires, should anyone think to look," Madison noted.

"With you three out of the way, I doubt anyone will bother looking. But yes, if they do, all evidence will point to my dear, deceased husband. All the more reason for me to leave town. I won't be able to live with the shame."

"So how do you plan to get rid of us?" Genny ventured to ask.

"Why, by fire, of course. It's a funny thing about these greenhouses. There are gasses inside that few people are aware of. And once a flame gets started, it's hard to extinguish."

Granny Bert made an odd noise. Madison looked over her shoulder and saw that her grandmother was unusually pale.

"Granny? Are you okay?" she asked in alarm.

"Just a bit—a bit weak," her grandmother said. Her voice came out faint as she staggered to one side.

"Granny, what's wrong?"

"Does it really matter?" Lisa asked cold-heartedly. "Very soon, you'll all be dead."

"You know how weak my heart is. Don't—Don't mind me. Save yourself," Granny Bert insisted weakly, just before crashing into a shelf laden with pot plants.

Her grandmother had gone to the doctor just last week. Madison knew she came back with a glowing report of just how strong and healthy her heart was. Madison recognized the coded message, even before the elderly woman started to 'fall.' In the process of going down, she gave the shelf a mighty shove, cramming it against the outer wall of the greenhouse. The heavy film bulged.

"You imbecile!" Lisa shrieked. "What are you doing? You'll rip the plastic and ruin the gas effect!"

When Lisa would have rushed forward, Genny tripped her. The unsuspecting woman went down and landed hard upon her back. The gun skittered out of her grasp, sliding beneath the plants that littered the floor after Granny Bert's exaggerated fall. Madison immediately pounced atop the younger woman and held her down. Genny added her weight to Lisa's legs as Granny Bert came back up, clutching a handful of purplish-blue flowers in her gnarled fingers.

There was a hard-fought struggle that involved flailing arms, elbows, and muttered curses, some of them Lisa's. Amid it all, Granny Bert managed to stuff the crazy woman's mouth with colorful blooms and forced her to swallow. Lisa sputtered and coughed, trying to spit the bitter plant from her mouth.

"Won't do any good, girl," Granny Bert advised on winded breath. "That was wolfs bane."

"Wolfs bane?" she shrieked. "That will kill me!"

"Only if we're lucky."

Granny Bert struggled to stand. She hoisted her hands upon her hips and glared down at the neutralized menace. "Can you feel it?" she goaded. "The burning, tingling sensation in your mouth and face? Vomiting and diarrhea will set in soon. Your organs will fail after that."

"Serves you right," Maddy added. "Gloria suffered a cruel, undignified death. So will you."

"You're insane! You both are!" Lisa squealed. She turned wide, frightened eyes to Genny, who still sat on her legs. "Help me! They'll kill me! Get this out of my mouth."

Genesis knew that neither Madison nor her grandmother would deliberately kill another soul, no matter how deserved that death might be. Their nonchalant attitude was a dead giveaway to their ruse, but Lisa was too frantic to notice. The woman was close to hysteria.

With a casual shrug of her own, Genny raised her palms in a helpless gesture. "The damage has been done. Granny Bert says you'll be dead in a few hours."

The power of suggestion was a dynamic thing. Within moments, Lisa began coughing. "I—I can feel it!" Her eyes grew frantic. "My mouth is going numb. My throat is closing up!" Tears streamed down her face. "H—Help me! I'm choking to death!"

"What did you give Barry?"

She wheezed out the answer.

"Is there an antidote?" Unsympathetic to her gagging, Granny Bert pressed, "Might as well tell me. You won't live to see the results."

It was not until Lisa managed to choke out a reply that her captives showed her mercy. By then, the wail of a siren rent the morning air, growing ever closer. Help was on its way.

"Myrna was right. You are a slow learner," Granny Bert chided. "That wasn't wolfs bane, girl. Do you take me for a fool? Now stop your twitching and straighten up. Might as well settle down and get your arrest over with. There's no way out for you, not with four witnesses."

Having all but forgotten the fourth witness, Madison glanced over her shoulder. "Myrna?" she called. "Are you still okay back there?"

"Okay? Okay! No, I'm not okay, you imbecile! I've been shot!"

Madison rolled her eyes, ignoring the rest of her rant. "Jeez, I'm sorry I asked."

Lisa bucked her legs in an attempt to throw Genny off. Genny responded with a raspy growl. "Lisa, my throat hurts. My body hurts. Stick your bony knee in my butt one more time, and I swear I'll stuff that cactus over there down your throat. Then you'll wish you *had* been poisoned."

The sirens came closer, drowning out even Myrna's tirade. Brash all but ripped the door from its hinges. He barged down the aisle with his firearm drawn and reinforcements behind him. He looked dark and dangerous, and more handsome than Madison could ever remember seeing him.

"Back here, Brash. We've got Lisa, but Myrna needs help. She's been shot."

"You're okay?"

Granny Bert was the one to answer, her wrinkled face split with a lively grin. "It's the three of us against one little pip-squeak. Of course we're okay!"

"I knew you'd come," Maddy beamed. She and Genny still held Lisa to the ground, but she lifted her face to accept his quick kiss.

"I swear, woman, you are going to be the death of me. We got a call from a butcher over in Riverton. Said he had a strange phone call from Genny's number, something about an older woman, two younger ones, and a nutcase." He shook his head wearily. "I knew it had to be you."

23

The fire department wasn't far behind. Once Cutter was certain all three women were safe and the danger was past, he teetered between amusement and aggravation.

"I thought the doctor said to take it easy," he scowled. "And Genny, what are you doing out of bed? The doctor said five days."

Madison answered for her friend. "She obviously can't count."

"Obviously." His frown slowly turned into a smirk as he read Genny's pajama top. "I guess that's a purr-fectly good explanation for why you're out here, instead of recuperating like the doctor told you."

Genny crossed her arms over the thin top and lifted her chin. "I guess so."

He merely shook his head as he pushed past the women and made his way into the backyard. The ambulance was already on scene, loading an injured Myrna Lewis onto the gurney. They had called the fire department for lift assist.

Brash had Lisa Redmond cuffed and seated in the back of the police cruiser. She kept glaring at the three women who waited impatiently in the front yard. Brash had given them instructions not to leave, not until he had taken their statements.

"What is keeping that man?" Granny Bert grumbled.

"I'm sure Myrna is ranting about something. Too bad the paramedics didn't give her something to calm her down," Madison said.

"Aka, to shut her up," Genny added with a grin. "Look, here they come now. And listen to her. Still cussing and carrying on."

"They should drop her, just for good measure," Granny Bert suggested. "I don't care if she was the one to get shot; we're the ones who have suffered the most, having to listen to her mouth."

Brash broke away from the group as they headed toward the ambulance. He came toward the trio with a weary smile.

"Sorry to keep you waiting. I'll try to make this brief."

"Can't we do this at home, Brash? Genny's not even supposed to be out of bed."

"I know, sweetheart. But the fact is, she is out of bed, and right smack in the middle of a crime scene. But I promise, I'll just take preliminary statements now and finish the rest at the house. Who wants to go first?"

Granny Bert gave her rendition first. As expected, it came with a few embellishments and personal opinions. Maddy added more details and tried to keep to the facts. By the time it was Genny's turn to talk, her throat was bothering her a great deal. She kept her version to the minimum.

"What they said. Lisa Redmond is a nut, she shot Myrna, and tried to kill us all. Again."

Brash gave her a stern look. "You could offer a few more details."

Cutter had joined them by now and spoke up in Genny's defense. "Come on, Brash, give her a break. Her throat hurts and she should be in bed. Can't the details wait until this afternoon?"

"Oh, all right," Brash decided with a sigh, snapping his little notebook shut. "Go home, all of you go to bed, and I'll be by in a few hours."

"Thanks, Brash," Madison smiled.

"Come on, Genny. I'll walk you to the car. Granny Bert, need any help?" Cutter offered.

"Are you kidding me, boy? That little episode in there did me good. Got the ole' heart pumping and the blood zipping through my veins. I feel twenty years younger already."

The firefighter laughed as he put a supportive arm around Genny's waist and pulled her along toward the car. "That's good to know. By the way, I have a message for you from Sticker."

"Is that old coot still in town? I plumb forgot he was in for a visit," she lied.

"He said to tell you he wants a weather report, whatever that means."

Granny Bert paused in her step, staring thoughtfully over at the handsome young man. He looked so much like his grandfather. The grandfather she had once loved but had been too foolish to acknowledge. Her face clouded and her eyes flickered with distant memories.

"You tell the old coot if he has a question, he should ask it in person," she replied gruffly.

Madison listened to the exchange from where she stood beside Brash. She wanted a moment alone with him before his duties whisked him away.

"Thanks, Brash, for coming so quickly."

He groaned, putting a hand behind her neck as he stepped closer. "God, Maddy, you've got to stop doing this to me. I don't know how many more times my heart can take it, knowing you're in danger."

"Oddly enough, my life in Dallas was quite dull. Nothing like this ever happened to me there," she murmured, fingering the badge on his shirt.

"What are you saying? Are you thinking of going back?"

"Of course not." She looked at her best friend and grandmother, crawling into the Buick with the help of the attentive fireman. Thank God they were all safe. "My life is here now. With them." She raised bright hazel eyes back to his. Her hand slipped from the badge and pressed against his chest. "With you."

Brash pressed his forehead against hers. "Maddy, I know this is hardly the time or place. And I don't know if you even heard me that night at the hospital, the first time I said it. It's been too crazy since then to discuss it, but there's something I've got to say to you, sweetheart."

He pulled back, so that he could look her directly in the eyes. An ambulance sat behind them, its strobe lights throwing stripes of weak color across the lawn. Emergency personnel and policemen passed by them as they trekked back and forth from the crime scene and their vehicles, heedless to Myrna Lewis' prized lawn. Nosy neighbors lined the sidewalk and leaned over the hedges Myrna was so proud of, trying to get a closer look. Her grandmother and best friend waited on her. Lisa sat just feet away in the cruiser, complaining about being hot and thirsty and the abuse she had suffered at the hands of Maddy and her 'gang.' And just before the paramedic slammed the door on the box, Myrna's angry tirade floated from the depths, punctuated by words that could make a sailor blush.

None of that mattered. He had to tell her.

"I love you, Madison Reynolds."

She was a grown woman. A widow. A mother. A professional. Still, a goofy smile lit her face and her knees turned wobbly. "I thought I had imagined it before," she whispered. "I thought I was dreaming."

"No, sweetheart. I told you that night. And I'm telling you again. I love you."

"That's good. Because I just happen to love you, too, Brash deCordova."

Instead of a long, lingering kiss, they were interrupted by an irate Lisa Redmond. "What is this?" she squawked. "Misconduct! Misconduct unbecoming an officer of the law. I want my lawyer!" She drummed her feet against the floor of the cruiser, making as much noise as she could muster, given her restraints. "Let me out of here! I could have been poisoned by that witch, and you're over there kissing her!"

Brash's sigh was heavy as he pulled away and leaned his forehead against Maddy's once more. "Duty calls."

"I know. Come by when you can. Love you."

"Love you, too, sweetheart." He gave her one last peck and stepped away.

He was already speaking to Lisa as he walked to the cruiser, his knee protesting with a pop. "You can and will be charged with destruction of public property if you do any damage, Mrs. Redmond. Just so you know."

"Just so you know, I want my lawyer."

"You can call him from the jailhouse."

An officer was dispatched to Naomi State Bank, where he escorted Barry Redmond to the emergency room. The doctors believed that with the right antidote and a few days' rest, the banker would suffer no lasting effects from the poison his wife had administered.

Madison personally delivered the news of Lisa's cruel and twisted mind to Carson Elliot. Despite Brash's admonishment to go home and rest, she thought Carson deserved to know that while his friend had, in fact, died of alcohol poisoning, it was not of her own doing.

When he wrote her a bonus check for four thousand dollars as promised, she balked and tried to return it.

"I don't feel right accepting this, Carson."

"I promised you a bonus if you proved her innocence."

"Yes, but…"

"Madison, my dear, I had no idea that what I asked of you could be so dangerous. You and Genesis could have been killed. Twice. This check is the least I can do for putting your lives in danger."

"None of us had any way of knowing the outcome of this case."

"Still, I insist. Take the money."

"But…"

"Take it." He deftly changed the subject and effectively squelched her protests. "And tell me. Where is your delightful friend? I had hoped she would come with you."

"She is still confined to bed rest, even though she broke the rules and went with me to Myrna's. But don't worry. When I left, Cutter was standing guard at the door. He says she's not getting out again."

A frown puckered the older gentleman's forehead. "I have heard you mention this Cutter before. Is this Genesis'... brother?" he asked hopefully.

"No, not brother. A friend."

"Close friend?"

She understood what he was asking. With a kind smile, she dashed the gentleman's hopes as gently as possible. "I think so. Perhaps closer than either of them is ready to admit just yet, but, yes. A close friend."

There was a grain of sincerity as he half-jested, "And what about you, Madison? Do you have a close friend?"

This time, her smile was unabashedly wide. "As a matter of fact, I do. A boyfriend, in fact." She hadn't said those words in twenty years, since before she and Grayson married. A lifetime ago. She tried them again for good measure. "I have a boyfriend."

"Well, good for you, Madison dear. You deserve to be happy."

Madison cocked her head to one side as the words in his pleasant voice registered. "I do deserve to be happy, don't I?" she murmured.

"And you deserve that check. So please, take it with my blessing." He stood, signifying that their meeting was over. His silver-frosted hair was down today, flowing behind him in the breeze. Madison knew it was not a word normally used to refer to his gender, but there was no denying this man's beauty.

"And please, remember me if you should ever wish to brush up on your dancing skills. For an upcoming wedding, perhaps?" He lifted his brows in speculation.

"I don't know about that," Maddy laughed, "but I will definitely keep you in mind." She thrust out her hand for a firm handshake. "Carson, it has been a pleasure. Thank you."

"It is I who is thankful. You have eased my mind and cleared my dear friend's name and reputation. You have added a bit of dignity back to her tragic death. Goodbye, my new friend."

24

B ack at the house, Cutter settled in on Granny Bert's sofa. Genny was resting, Maddy was out on an errand, and the twins were still in school. With any luck, they hadn't heard about the day's events yet, but he wouldn't count on it. The grapevine that connected The Sisters was a powerful and prolific thing.

Even Granny Bert had disappeared into the kitchen, Sticker close on her heels. This left just him and the television.

He flipped through the channels, knowing the polite thing to do was ignore the conversation taking place in the kitchen. But knowing and doing was not always the same thing.

With a grin, Cutter turned down the volume.

"You look good, Belle. Damn good for a woman your age."

Sticker took an uninvited seat at the kitchen table and grinned up at the woman towering over him.

"Who invited you to come here, Sticker Montgomery?" she demanded, hands upon her hips.

"Why, you did, Belle. You told my grandson I should ask my questions in person. So here I am. In person."

With a huff, she turned away to make coffee. He watched her move about the task with sure, quick moves. Even at eighty, she moved with grace and efficiency. It was more than he could say about his own battered body.

When the coffee was done, and not until then, Granny Bert joined him at the table. She pushed a cup his way.

"Might as well speak what's on your mind," she said.

"I just want to visit with you, Belle. Get to know you again. It's been a long time, you know."

"I know."

He blew on the dark brew to cool it down. "You broke my heart, Belle," he finally acknowledged.

Her snort was less than graceful. "Seems to me you got over it mighty quick. You were married within the year."

"You made it clear there was no future here with you. And back then, marrying the girl was the proper thing to do."

She arched a judgmental brow and sipped her coffee.

"And you're wrong, Belle. I never did get over you."

"I say you have five kids that would beg to differ."

"Loving my kids and loving their mommas are two different things, Bertha Hamilton. Two different things altogether."

"Tell me about your kids, Sticker." It seemed a safer topic at the moment, safer than all this nonsense he spouted.

"Well, you know Mary Alice. Don't tell the others, but she's the prettiest one of the lot. And the sweetest. Yes ma'am, Margie and Henry did a fine job raising up my daughter. And she married right, too. Tug Montgomery is a good man. A good provider. And they've made me right proud with all those young 'ns they had." He sat back with a pleased expression upon his face. "Yes ma'am, my little Mary Alice did all right for herself."

"The others?"

"Her sister Loretta, now she's a different story. Margie and I had already split by the time she was born, so she never thought of me as her daddy. Truth is, I often wondered if I was. She's the only one with dark hair and a sour attitude. But still, I sent just as much money for her as I did for Mary Alice. Even when Henry married their momma, I paid my share. But for Loretta, it was never enough. Especially when I made it to the big time. She's always spouting off about back pay, wanting me to give her a part of the business. Truth is, she married herself a lazy no-good for a husband. It's easier to ask me for my money than it is to ask him to get a job."

"I met her husband a time or two," Granny Bert acknowledged. She agreed with his assessment of the man.

After a few sips of coffee, he continued.

"I had a few wild years," Sticker acknowledged. "I was riding high on the standings. Didn't seem to be a bull I couldn't ride. And the ladies do love a cowboy," he chuckled. "Those buckle bunnies were in every town, always eager to make me feel welcome. And I was running from a broken heart after you rejected me. I was just fool enough to try and drown the memories in a bottle of Jack Daniels and my ego. That's how Jack came about. Truth is, I hardly remembered his momma at all. But the boy never held it against me. He came out on the circuit when he got old enough, trying to live up to his daddy's name. When I started sliding in the standings and he still hadn't made his way up them, he convinced me there was more money in raising stock than raising hell. Together, we started the Blazing

P Brand. Now he manages the ranches in Colorado and Montana, and is president of the company."

"Sounds like a smart man."

"He is, he is. Must have got that from his momma." He gave a wicked wink and added, "Whoever she was."

"Sticker Pierce, you should be ashamed of yourself!"

He had the grace to hang his head. "I am, Belle. I didn't always do the right thing. I wasn't as good a man as Joe Cessna. I remember Joe, you know. He was a good bit older than me, but I always looked up to him. He was a good and decent guy, a real leader, even when we were kids. But I can tell you one thing, Belle. I loved you every bit as much as he did."

She fluttered her hand in the air. "You were telling me about your last two children."

"Wynona came along in Wyoming. Seemed a right fitting name. I tried to be a husband to her momma, but as it turns out, she was a bigger hellcat than I was. We parted after a few years. But Wynona, now she's a smart one, too. She heads up the western wear line."

Granny Bert got up to freshen their coffee.

"And the baby?"

Sticker gave her his signature charming smile. "Truly a baby. I have grandchildren older than Roper."

"This mother must have been quite a bit younger." She was surprised to hear the dismay that seeped into her own voice.

"That she was," Sticker agreed. "After a couple more wives in a couple more states, I found me a pretty little thing in Oklahoma. Just as sweet as she could be, too. Before I knew it, she agreed to marry me and we had a baby on the way. I thought that marriage might last, but I reckon she finally grew up and realized I didn't hang the stars, after all. She's the only wife I still keep in touch with. I drop by to visit her and her new husband, every time I'm in Oklahoma. In fact, he and Roper manage my ranch there. So it all worked out for the best."

Something spiteful inside made Granny Bert speak out. "Except for the fact that, even with all those wives and all those kids, you still ended up alone."

He nodded without remorse. "Except for that."

A long silence settled between them, before he asked in a low, sad voice, "Why, Belle?"

He didn't have to say anything more. She knew what he was asking.

"I was young and foolish, Sticker. I used a yardstick and a calendar to decide my future."

"Bull feathers, Belle. The girl I knew was strong enough not to pay attention to those things."

"Maybe I wasn't as strong as you remember."

He studied her with cunning eyes, absently twirling the ends of his handlebar mustache. "I don't think so. I kept up with you through the years, you know. You were mayor here for years. An elected county official. A daredevil. A role setter. You never backed down from a challenge. Except from one. Me."

"You are full of yourself, old man," she snorted.

"Maybe. But I'm also right. You didn't even give us a chance, Belle."

"And what if I had?" she challenged. "You still would have left. I knew it then, and I know it now. You were never the sort to stay in one place for very long."

"So before I could say goodbye, you said it first." His voice was heavy with sadness.

She lifted a shoulder but made no denial.

"We wasted all those years, Belle."

Granny Bert turned her head to look around her kitchen. The room had stood the test of time. Weathered family arguments and teething babies. Witnessed the laughter and cries of four rowdy boys. Seen a marriage through good times and bad. Fed her family with love and support, even when times were lean. Welcomed her home, even after her soulmate was gone.

"It wasn't a waste, Sticker," she assured him, her voice clear and strong. "I loved my Joe. Loved the life we had together. I don't regret it for one moment."

"I envy you that, Belle. Because that was something I never had, not even with all those wives."

"I'm sorry, Sticker. I wish you had been as happy as I have been these past sixty-something years."

"It's not too late, Belle. We could still be happy. Together."

She looked at him sharply. "What are you saying, old man?"

"You know what I'm saying. I'm tired of living on the road. Tired of seeing one town after another through the windshield."

"Funny thing is, I've discovered I like to travel. I've racked up quite a few miles on my motor home out there. I leave again next week for Colorado."

His hazel eyes lit up. "I could go with you. Be your guide. I have a ranch there, you know. A huge spread with a big house. You could meet my son. He'd get a kick out of you." Sticker reached out to cover her hand with his. "What do you say, Belle? Take me along with you?"

"What are you doing?" Genny's voice hissed out raspy and deep, sounding more accusatory than she intended.

Cutter jumped, not realizing she was behind him. He had abandoned the couch in favor of the kitchen door when the voices on the other side dropped to conversational tones. "Uh, listening," he stammered.

She propped her hands upon her hips. "You mean eavesdropping."

He shrugged, not bothering to quibble over words.

"Who are you eavesdropping on?"

"No one, with you jabbering so much," he said in disgust.

"But before?"

"Granny Bert and Sticker."

"Ooh, let me hear!" she said, sidling up beside him. She pressed her ear to the door. "I don't hear anything," she complained.

A crash sounded from the other side of the door.

"I heard that!" she squealed. She beat Cutter back to the couch, but not by much. And just seconds before the door swung open and Sticker stormed through, followed by an angry Granny Bert.

"Get out!" she yelled. "Get out of my kitchen! I don't know what kind of trollops you've been associated with over the last sixty years, but I am not one of them, Sticker Pierce! How dare you suggest a thing such as that!"

"You damn fool woman," Sticker grumbled. "Throwing a coffee cup at me, and it still full of hot coffee!" He wiped at his shirt in disgust. A dark stain was already spreading down the front of it.

"Quit your bellyaching. You own a whole factory of shirts. Just go get yourself another one. Make sure it has those fancy initials on the pocket, so you can remind all your *buckle bunnies* just who you are!" Granny Bert sneered.

"I don't know what bee got in your bonnet, woman. I just offered to be your guide."

"I haven't seen you in over sixty years, you old coot. No way am I going away with you, cooped up in my motor home for two weeks. You have lost your ever-loving mind."

Sticker looked down at his grandson. He and Genny were sitting on the couch, their eyes and their mouths hinged open in amazement.

"Boy, are you done with your courting? I think the weather in here just got a might chilly."

Cutter did not bother to correct his grandfather on the status of their relationship. He scrambled to his feet. "Genny, I gotta go. Try to stay in bed." He glanced over his shoulder at Granny Bert. She stood in the doorway like an ancient Amazon warrior. Her sides heaved in anger and fire flashed from her eyes. "And try to do something with her," he suggested. "I'll call you later."

"Text me," she suggested, hand going to her aching throat.

Cutter tugged on his grandfather's arm. "Come on, Sticker, I think we should go. See you later, Granny Bert."

He didn't wait for an answer, just pulled his grandfather along.

When they got to the other side of the door, Sticker wrenched his arm free and began laughing. He laughed so hard he became winded and had to bend over to catch his breath. He came up with bright eyes.

"Cutter, my boy, you see those two women in there?" He hitched a thumb over his shoulder.

"Yes, sir," Cutter said slowly, seriously questioning his grandfather's state of mind. "What about them?"

"I do believe you and me are just going to have to marry those two."

25

With Madison and Genny fully recuperated, Granny Bert and Wanda Shanks left for Colorado as planned. Sticker Pierce did not travel with them, but he did meet Granny Bert in the Rockies. He did give her the grand tour of his ranch. He did introduce her to his son. And he did follow her back to Texas.

How long he would stay was anyone's guess.

As always, the end of summer was a long, drawn-out process. There was little autumn to speak of in this part of the South. Temperatures were known to go from the seventies to the thirties, often in the same day. A favorite saying among locals was, "Fall? I think it was yesterday."

While the heat often lingered until Thanksgiving, winter could be barren and cold. The days between then and spring could bring sunshine, could bring snow. But for now, before the rollercoaster rise and fall of the Texas thermometer set in, the weather was nice. Warm, sunny days and cool, pleasant nights.

With the project deadline looming closer, work at the Big House picked up pace. A tropical system brewing in the Gulf brought much-needed rain to the area, but the daily downpours hampered progress on the remodel. When the skies cleared and the sun came back out, crews worked overtime to make up for the loss. After Madison made a handful of final decisions and selections, she was promptly banned from the house. The next time she and her family were allowed inside the house, it would be for the final reveal.

The thought was oddly terrifying. After months of having the house overrun with carpenters, designers, and crew members, after wading through the media, the curious sightseers, and all the hoopla that came with filming a television reality show, Maddy and the twins would have the house to themselves. Just the three of them.

"You're not crazy, Maddy. Of course you're nervous about it," Genny reassured her best friend.

"The house is so huge," she said, sipping on a cup of freshly brewed coffee. "I don't think I ever stopped to think about just the three of us, rattling around in all those rooms. And can you imagine what my electric bill is going to be?"

"Yes, but you have the energy-efficient version of everything. It probably won't be as bad as you think."

Madison turned to stare out the café window, but her hazel eyes were blind to the cars gathered out front. "It's just that it's all coming down to the wire now, and they won't even let me in to see it," she grumbled. "Plus, there's so much else going on. We've seen a surge in clients—thanks for letting me borrow my old booth, by the way—Murray Archer has me working on this new case, the Centennial Celebration is just around the corner, and, in between it all, my babies turn sixteen." Emotion pricked at her eyes and her voice turned melancholy. "I can't believe it, Gen. Where did the time go?"

Genny's voice was firm and upbeat. "We agreed. No more of that. This is a happy, exciting time, for all of you. And this party is going to be great."

"Thanks to you. You're the one doing all the heavy lifting."

"Pfft." Genny made light of all her hard work. "It's a few hay bales and a few strings of light. How hard is it to throw together a bonfire and weenie roast for a bunch of kids? With Carson loaning us his portable dance floor, all we have to do is add music and kids. Voilà. A starlight ballroom."

Maddy laughed at her friend's downplay of the upcoming event. "You make it sound like nothing, but I know you, my friend. You will transform it into magic, just like you do with everything you touch. To be honest, I am still in shock that my daughter has agreed to this. I knew Blake would love it, but last year, we had their party at the country club. This year, we're just having it at the country." She shook her head in amazement. Their lives had changed drastically in the past twelve months.

Genesis gave her a sassy smile. "I may have pointed out how her new crush, Drew Baines, is into this sort of thing. How all her friends will be jealous that Cutter Montgomery is coming to her birthday party out at the ranch. And how she'll be known as a trend setter, having a pasture party with a twist."

"All I know is, Brash loved the idea of having it at the ranch and being a part of the celebration."

"Now let's cross our fingers and pray it doesn't rain."

The weather cooperated and the party was a huge success. Dozens of people, teenagers and adults, alike, streamed out to the deCordova ranch to celebrate Blake and Bethani's sixteenth birthday. There was no time for Madison to be sad. The evening was full of friends, family, and food.

As the party wound down, only a handful of people remained. The kids mysteriously disappeared as clean-up began, wandering off to the far side of the pond. The few remaining adults had the food and trash put away quickly and stole a few moments of quiet time for themselves. Brash pulled out singles of wine for the women and bottles of beer for the men.

The twinkling lights faded as the generator powered down. The only illumination now came from the fireflies and the starlight, and the fire's dying embers. Darkness descended, punctuated by peaceful silence.

"This is the life," Brash mused thoughtfully, taking a long draw on his beer and staring into the fire. "Good food, good friends, good beer."

Madison begged to differ. "Good wine, you mean."

"You tell him, sister." Beside her, Shannon lifted her bottle to clink against Madison's and grinned.

There was no trace of leftover hostility between the two women. Not even a trace of old hostility between Brash and his former wife. Through the passage of time and through the mutual love for their children, all had overcome the bitterness of the past.

That thought occurred to Madison now. "Who would have ever thought, all those long years ago, that we would ever become friends?"

Shannon Aikman's laughter was tinged with guilt. "All because of jealousy. You liked Brash, he liked me, I liked Matt, he liked you." She reached for her husband's hand and squeezed it. "A mad cycle of teenage rivalry. And poor Genny got sucked into the cycle, just because she was your best friend."

"What's that old saying?" Madison murmured. "All's well that ends well?"

Brash heard the conversation and broke in with a protest. "End? What end? This is just the beginning for us, Maddy sweetheart." He reached out to take her hand. He literally pulled her and her chair through the sand, so that her chair butted up against his. "That's more like it," he said with satisfaction.

Maddy curled her arms around his in a snuggle. Shannon and Matt sat in much the same fashion, their murmurs turned low and intimate. Cutter and Genny sat at the far end of the firelight, slightly apart from the others, lazily tracing the patterns of the overhead stars with their transfixed gaze.

"There goes a shooting star," Cutter said, pointing out the streak of light. He leaned in her direction to track its path.

"Look! Another. And another!" Fascinated, they counted at least three more.

"It must be some sort of meteor shower," Genny guessed.

"Hmm. Maybe so." Cutter settled deeper into his chair and studied the starry heavens. After a few moments, his eyes grew heavy. Without the shooting stars, the peaceful night sky lulled him into a trance.

He looked so content, Genny decided to try it for herself. The night air was perfect, with the barest hint of a breeze. The sky was a velvet canvas, painted with sparkling diamonds. A smile curled her lips as her eyelids drooped. It had been a long time since she slept beneath the stars.

The peaceful chirp of crickets and frogs blended with the pop and sizzle of the fire, creating a beautiful lullaby. Nature's music. *Sounds you could never hear in a city*, she mused groggily, *drown out by so much traffic and noise.* It had been the right decision to come home last year. This was where she belonged.

"Look at those two," Brash said quietly, keeping his voice low.

"Which two? All four of them are asleep," Maddy whispered.

"So they are." His quiet chuckle vibrated her cheek as she lay against his arm.

"Thank you for tonight, Brash. It was a huge success. The kids had so much fun."

Every so often, they could hear a shout of laughter, or the squeal of happy voices. The sounds floated across the pond, carried on the breeze.

Brash smiled and squeezed her leg where his hand rested. "My pleasure," he assured her.

"I think Bethani is warming up to you. To us."

"I hope so, because I plan to be in your life for a very long time."

"Brash?" she murmured after a few moments of silence. "What you said earlier, about this being just the beginning?"

"Yeah?"

"For the first time in a very long time, I feel like I'm at the beginning of a new chapter in my life. A wonderful, exciting chapter. The one where all my dreams come true. Maybe it's having the house almost done. Maybe it's finally being able to admit we're in love. Maybe it's having a strong, supportive man in my life, one who wants to grow a life *with* me, not *for* me." She ran her hand along the strong column of his arm.

"But I truly feel like I'm starting over. That I have a home again, not just a house. I feel like I'm where I belong."

"You are where you belong, sweetheart. And you do have a home, here in The Sisters. Here with me." He brushed a kiss into her hair.

Maddy hugged his arm again. "Here's to starting over," she whispered.

So much better than clinking two glasses together, they made their toast by clinking their souls together.

"To starting over," Brash murmured. "Together."

Watch for *Genny's Ballad*, coming Spring 2017.

AUTHOR'S NOTE

I hope you have enjoyed spending time with the characters of The Sisters, Texas.

If you liked my story, please consider leaving a review on Amazon here: . I hate asking for this favor, but it has such a huge impact on placement, visibility, and sales. It is one of those dreaded evils on the business side of my otherwise delightful career.

Please feel free to contact me personally at beckiwillis. ccp@gmail.com or connect with us via Facebook or www. beckiwillis.com. I love visiting with readers and I promise to write you back.

I hope you'll join us in the spring, when Genny gets her own story.

ABOUT THE AUTHOR

Becki Willis has been writing since grade school, though her earliest works are best left unpublished. Since November of 2013, Becki has released nine books, been awarded first place awards for Best Mystery Series and Best Suspense Fiction from the Association of Texas Authors, and is living out her dream as an author.

Becki likes to create believable characters in believable situations. Her stories have a healthy dose of romance, but if you're looking for graphic sex scenes, you won't find them here. Like the magic of a good book, Becki believes some things are best left to the imagination. When she's not writing, Becki enjoys spending time with her family. Other addictions include reading, junking, unraveling a good mystery, and coffee. She loves to travel, but believes coming home to her Texas ranch is the best part of any trip. Becki is a member of the Association of Texas Authors, the National Association of Professional Women, and the Brazos Writers organization.

You can connect with her at www.beckiwillis.com. Better yet, email her at beckiwillis.ccp@gmail.com. She loves to hear from readers and encourages feedback!